WHITE ROSE BLACK FOREST

ALSO BY EOIN DEMPSEY

Finding Rebecca

The Bogside Boys

WHITE ROSE BLACK FOREST

EOIN DEMPSEY

This is a work of fiction. Names, characters, organizations, places, events, and incidents are either products of the author's imagination or are used fictitiously.

Published by Lake Union Publishing, Seattle

www.apub.com

ISBN-13: 9781503954052 (paperback)
ISBN-10: 1503954056 (paperback)
ISBN-13: 9781503954069 (hardcover)
ISBN-10: 1503954064 (hardcover)

Cover design by Shasti O'Leary Soudant

Printed in the United States of America

First Edition

This book is for my son Robbie

AUTHOR'S NOTE

White Rose, Black Forest is inspired by true events. However, certain factual elements and the timing of events have been altered for the sake of the narrative.

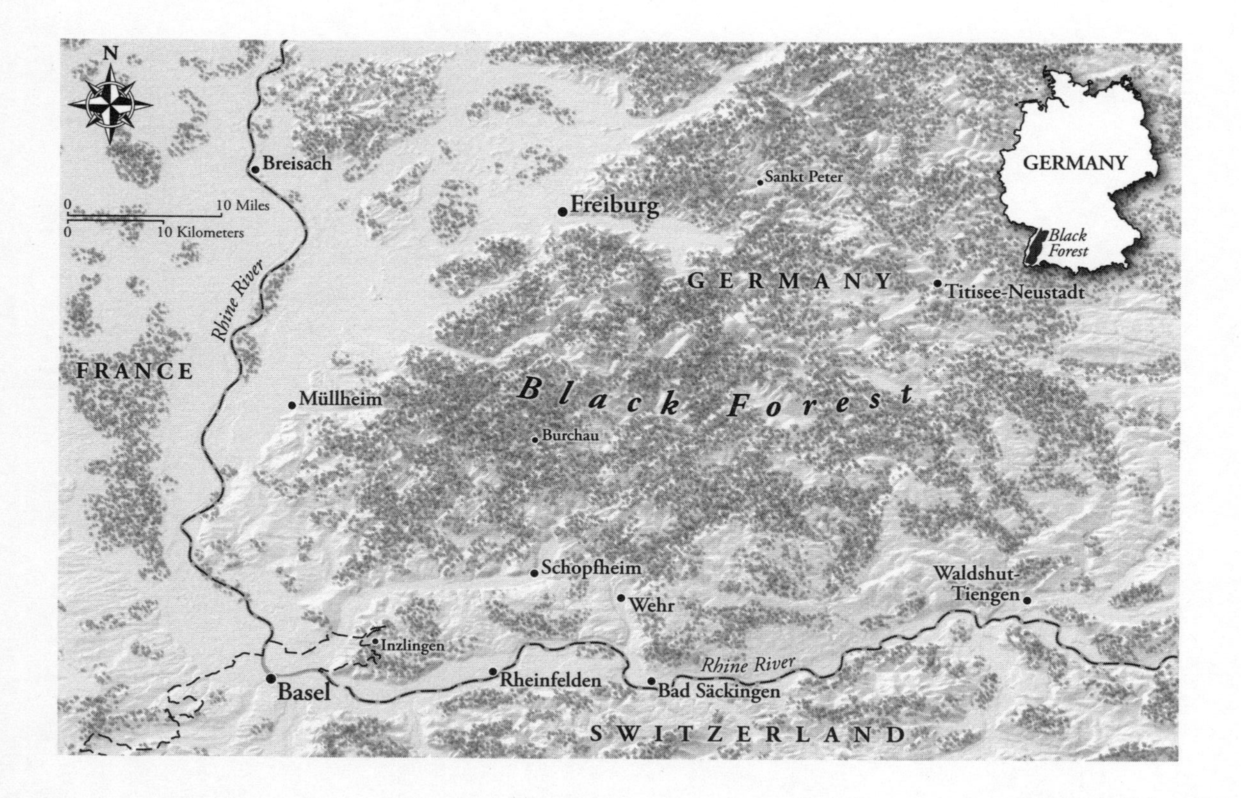
N
Breisach
0
10 Miles
0
10 Kilometers
Rhine River
FRANCE
Müllheim
Freiburg
Sankt Peter
GERMANY
Black Forest
GERMANY
Black Forest
Titisee-Neustadt
Burchau
Schopfheim
Wehr
Waldshut-Tiengen
Inzlingen
Basel
Rheinfelden
Bad Säckingen
Rhine River
SWITZERLAND

Chapter 1

The Black Forest Mountains, southwest Germany, December 1943

This seemed a fitting place to die. A place where she had once known every field and tree, every valley, where the rocks had names, where meeting places were described in clandestine languages adults could never understand. A place of gushing mountain streams shining like burnished steel in the summer sun. This was where she'd felt safe. Now even this place felt poisoned, ruined, all beauty and purity choked to death.

The quilt of snow was thick on the ground, unrelenting as far as she could see in any direction. She closed her eyes, pausing for a few seconds. The haunted howling of the wind, a rustle in the branches of snow-laden trees, the rushing of her breath, and the beating of her heart. The night sky loomed above. She kept on, the crunching sound of her footsteps resuming. Where was the right place to do such a thing? Who would find her? The thought of some children out playing in the snow coming across her body was too much to bear. Perhaps it would be better to turn back, to relent for one more day at least. A tear formed in the corner of her eye and slid down the numbed skin of her face. She walked on.

The falling snow began to thicken, and she adjusted her scarf to cover her face. Perhaps the elements would take her. That would be a most fitting end—a return to the nature she'd loved so much. Why was she even still walking? What was there to gain from wandering through the snow like this? Surely the time had come to just be done with it, to end the agony. She reached into her pocket and felt the smooth metal of her father's old revolver through her gloves.

No, not yet. She continued forward. She'd never see the cabin again. Or anything or anyone for that matter. She would never know how the war would turn out, or see the National Socialists fall or that madman stand trial for his crimes. She thought of Hans, his beautiful face, the truth in his eyes, and the unimaginable courage in his heart. She hadn't even had a chance to hold him one last time, to tell him that he was the reason that she believed that love could still exist in this grotesque world. They'd cut his head off, tossed it into the casket alongside his body, and laid him down beside his sister and his best friend.

The snow was still coming down, but she kept on, the trees of the forest on her left as she crested a hill. Her eyes had adjusted to the darkness, and something ahead caught her attention, a mound in the snow about two hundred yards away. A body, crumpled like a bunch of rags in the pristine white. No footprints leading to it. It wasn't moving, but the still-attached parachute ruffled in the wind, licking at the snow like a thirsty animal. She instinctively swiveled her head, even though she hadn't seen a living soul in days. She moved forward with caution, the paranoia ingrained in her making her perceive every shadow and every breath of wind as a deadly threat. But there was nothing and no one.

The snow was gathering on his unmoving body, much of him almost invisible against the film of white. His eyes were closed. She brushed snow off his face and reached for his pulse. The patter of his heartbeat came through the skin in his neck. Icy-white breaths plumed out from between his lips, but his eyes remained closed. She drew back, looking around in a desperate search for some kind of help. She was utterly alone. The nearest house was hers—the cabin her father had left her—but that was almost two miles. The closest village was five miles or more—an impossible distance in these conditions even if he were conscious. She brushed the snow off his chest to reveal a Luftwaffe uniform with the insignia of a captain. Of course he was one of them—one of the monsters who had destroyed this country and taken away everyone she had ever loved. Who would know if she left him to die? She should just leave him like this. Soon they would both be dead, and no one would ever know. It would merely amount to two more bodies in the snow to join the deluge. She trudged a few paces away. Her legs stopped moving, and then, before she realized she'd made the decision, she was bent over him once more.

She tapped him on the cheek, calling out. She pulled up his eyelids but elicited no response other than a gentle groan. The Luftwaffe captain was propped up by the backpack he wore, his head lolling back, his arms spread on either side. He was tall, probably six feet or more, and might have weighed almost double what she did. A claw of anxiety dug into her as she thought about the impossibility of carrying him back to the cabin. There was no way. Still, she tried to lift him and managed only a few inches before her legs gave way and she slipped, dropping him back onto the snow. His backpack must have weighed at least fifty pounds and the parachute another ten. The parachute could stay on for now, but the backpack had to come off. After a few seconds of trial and error, she undid the straps on his backpack and pulled it out from under him, causing his body to collapse back onto the snow with a gentle thud.

She put the pack to the side and glanced at the sky. The snow was coming heavier. They didn't have long. She checked his pulse again. It was still strong, but for how much longer? An impulse drove her to plunge a hand into his jacket pocket. She took out his identification papers. His name was Werner Graf. He was from Berlin. And in his wallet was a picture of a woman she assumed was his wife, posing with two smiling daughters around three and five. He was twenty-nine—three years older than she. A deep breath billowed out of her lungs as she stood to stare at Werner Graf. She had trained and worked to help other people. That was who she had been—and who she could be again, if only for a few hours. She placed the papers back into his pocket before moving around behind him again. She put her arms under his armpits and heaved with every sinew of strength she had. His upper body moved, but his legs caught in the snow, and he let out a loud yelp of pain as they came free. His eyes were still closed. She placed him back down and moved around to examine his legs. His pants were ripped, and she almost recoiled as she felt broken bones pressing against his skin. Both legs were broken below the knee. It was possibly the fibulae but certainly the tibiae that were affected. They would heal in time if set properly, but walking was going to be impossible for now.

Perhaps it would be better to let him pass gently in his sleep and die here in the snow. She went to his backpack and opened it to find several changes of clothes, and more papers, which she placed at the side. At the bottom, she found matches, food, water, a sleeping bag, and two pistols. She wondered why on earth a Luftwaffe pilot would be carrying such things. Two guns? Perhaps he was dropping behind enemy lines in Italy, but that was hundreds of miles from here. There was little time. Wasting time on questions would cost Werner Graf his life. She thought of his wife and daughters, innocent of the crimes he might have committed on behalf of the Reich.

She wasn't carrying much herself—just the loaded revolver. It was all she thought she'd need tonight.

Memories of the snowbound winters of her youth came to her, the times she'd spent in this very field. The tree line she'd been skirting was only a few hundred yards away, and that distance had proved the gap between life and death for Werner Graf. She would never have found him if he'd landed in there—even if he had survived the landing. She took the sleeping bag out of his backpack, opened it up, and spread it across him before leaning down in front of his face.

"You'd better be worth saving," she whispered. "I'm doing this for your wife and daughters."

The field they were in was on a plateau, with the trees leading down a hill to a valley below. The conifers were covered in snow that drifted to ten feet deep or more. It took a minute or two to get over to where the trees were. She crouched and burrowed into the snow. The powder was soft, and she was able to make quick progress. No one else was coming. This snow cave would be their only chance of making it through the night. Thoughts of ending her own life could wait until she saved his.

She went to check on him. He was still alive. A tiny light flickered within her, like a distant candle in a dark hollow. She made her way back over to the hole, not thinking about how she was going to get him there, just focusing on digging, one handful at a time. Another twenty minutes and the snow cave was big enough. She climbed down inside, using her own body to smooth out the snow. She made a shelf with her hands before poking out an airhole in the top with a long stick she'd taken from outside.

She made her way back over to where Werner lay, took the backpack and the sleeping bag, and brought them across to the snow cave. It was just long enough for him to lie down, with enough space to sit up. It would do. She made her way back across to him. It must have been after midnight. The relative safety of the morning seemed years away. There would be no way to move him farther than the cave until the blizzard subsided. She took the nylon of the parachute, still attached to the straps across his shoulders, and heaved. An ugly grimace of pain came over his face as his body slid along the snow. She grasped the parachute again, pulling as hard as she could. Her legs gave way, but she'd dragged him six more feet. This was possible. Hope ignited within her, sending streams of adrenaline through her beleaguered body. She heaved again, and again. It took twenty minutes. She was wet with sweat under her thick scarf and coat, but they reached the edge of the snow cave. It was the first time she'd felt anything like triumph in what seemed like a lifetime. Perhaps since the first leaflets of the White Rose, when the excitement of standing up for what was right had overtaken them, when the promise of a better future for the German people had seemed like a reality for the first time in a generation.

Werner Graf was still unconscious. Nothing was going to wake him. Not that night. The goal of him opening his eyes again drove her forward. It didn't matter who he was anymore, just that he was a human being and that he was still alive. She took a few seconds to rest before pushing him down the slope she'd constructed into the cave. He moaned again, the bones in his legs giving a sickening crack as she pushed him down.

The snow was still drifting down from the dark sky above, and the wind howled like a voracious wolf. The cave lit up as she struck a match she'd taken from his backpack. She hadn't really looked at him before. He'd only been a stricken body, not a man. He was handsome, unshaven, with short brown hair. She extinguished the match and reached around to pull the sleeping bag around him. She lay down next to him, able to hear the pitch of his shallow breaths and the dull thudding of his heartbeat within his chest. They were going to need each other's body heat to make it through this night. She put an arm around him. She hadn't touched a man like this since before Hans died, ten months earlier. Overcome with exhaustion, she spiraled into a deep sleep.

The sound of screaming jarred her, yanked her from the escape of sleep. It took her a few seconds to realize where she was, what was going on. The dark of the cave dulled her senses until she peered up at the opening above her head. The light of the moon was visible now. His head flipped to one side. His body was still warm. He was dreaming. She settled back down beside him, using his arm as a pillow. Her eyes were just closing when he screamed out again.

"No, please, no! Please, stop!"

Her blood froze. What he said was unmistakable—it was English.

Chapter 2

She lay motionless, paralyzed by shock. No more words escaped his lips. His eyes were still clamped shut. It was still night. She was still lying beside this man, whoever he was. His chest expanded in time with his breath, more solid now. She had already saved him, but to what fate? She tried to reason that he was indeed Werner Graf. But how could he be? What Luftwaffe officer would call out in English in their sleep? She wasn't fluent by any means, but she knew the smooth rhythm of English words. It wasn't hard to recognize. Who was this man, and what would happen to him if she turned him over to the local police? It would be tantamount to giving him to the Gestapo. He was dressed in a Luftwaffe uniform. If he was British or American, there was no question that he would be treated, and shot, as a spy. She would die before she'd help the local Gestapo extend its reign of terror. So what was she to do?

She raised herself off his body and shimmied out of the snow cave. The icy air bit at her exposed face and felt almost liquid as she pulled it into her lungs. The snow had stopped. The clouds had been cleared aside like a soiled tablecloth and revealed the stars burning against the ink black of the sky. The winds had calmed to a gentle tickle on the tree branches. All else was unmoving. What would happen if she left him? Would he ever emerge from his sleep? Would he even be able to raise himself out of the cave once he came to? The field she'd dragged him across was smoothed over, beautiful now. Anyone could have wandered past them and never known that they were there. But the morning was coming. They were isolated up here. People were rare but far from unheard of. She estimated that she had at least three hours until the low winter sun limped over the horizon to illuminate the forest—only three hours before they might be spotted. A cross-country skier could happen upon them as they were struggling back through the snow, and then any decision-making would be taken out of her hands. This man would succumb to the Gestapo by the consensus of strangers. It was always easier to side with the Gestapo—a citizen would be rewarded for doing so, thrown in jail for not. It required supernatural strength not to do the Gestapo's bidding. That was the genius of their system—it took fortitude of an almost unimaginable scale to do the right thing. Not reporting your neighbors was as dangerous as the antisocial activities that the Gestapo was so interested in. It meant that they had spies everywhere. It meant that the "German look"—a swift, furtive glance to make sure no one was watching—was a part of everyday life now.

The specter of her previous plans returned. She had expected her body to be found the next day, had wanted it that way. She could have wandered into the middle of the forest, where no one would have found her for months, where her flesh would have faded from her bones, leaving only the white of her skeleton to be uncovered. It seemed she had little choice now but to abandon those plans and help this man instead. If she left him in the hole, he would die. If she turned him over to the authorities, he would die. She would have to live with the knowledge that she had helped further the perverted will of the Gestapo and the regime they represented. If she waited until dawn, she might meet someone else who would force her hand, and he would die, and perhaps she along with him. There didn't seem to be any choice at all.

The snow had smoothed over the footprints she'd made getting here, but she knew these hills and meadows, snow covered or not. She began hiking back to the cabin. It would take more than an hour to get there, and the same to return to him. Was he a spy, or an escaping prisoner of war? But if he was a POW, why would he have jumped out of a plane into Germany? Perhaps his plane had been shot down or had run into some technical trouble and he'd been forced to bail out. Why else would he be here, in the middle of the mountains? Freiburg was only around ten miles away. Maybe he had been blown off course. Yet she'd heard no plane and seen no flak in the sky on the way out here. The bombing raids were coming more frequently. Even here. Thoughts of the bomb dropping brought with them the memory of her father, and the pain that had driven her out here with his pistol in her pocket soon followed, but the remembrance of the man in the snow cave forced her back into the moment, driving her feet forward.

She made her way down the hill she'd found the man on, back the way she came, and soon she could no longer see the snow cave, nor the tree she'd dug it under.

"Try not to worry about things you can't control," she said out loud.

It felt good to hear her own thoughts, felt almost as if there were someone there with her and she wasn't alone in trying to save this man's life.

"What are you doing?" she said. "Why are you getting involved with this man you don't know?" The words had come out as if spoken by someone else.

She was in a state of near exhaustion when the cabin came into view. The door was unlocked, and she pushed it open. She had never expected to come here again, yet she had left it immaculately clean, a gift for the people who would find it. She took off her snowshoes, leaving them at the door as she went inside. She removed her gloves before fumbling with the matches that lay on a nearby table. The room glowed from the candle she lit, and she caught a glimpse of herself in the mirror before jerking her eyes away. She had no desire to confront her own reflection. The embers of last night's fire were dead in the fireplace. The wood was out back. That would be a job for later. She paced down the hall into the living area and found a bottle of brandy she then stuffed in her coat pocket. She put her hands on her head and searched her mind for anything else that might help her on the way back here with him. Her journey alone had been arduous enough. She began to wonder if it was even possible and contemplated sitting down and closing her eyes, just to rest for a while.

She poured herself a cup of water and finished it in seconds. She put the cup back down and placed a kitchen knife in her pocket. The door to the bedroom she'd slept in last night was ajar, the bed stripped, the covers stacked at the end in a neat pile. The bed represented an impossible luxury, everything she could possibly have wanted in that moment. She knew what her resting would mean for the man in the snow. She closed the bedroom door and walked out the back and into the night once more. The firewood she'd gathered the week before sat untouched, speckled with a light coating of snow blown under the awning that protected it. She eyed the sled she'd used to drag the logs back from the forest. It was sturdy, well able to take his weight. She dragged it around the side of the house before going inside again.

The cuckoo clock on the wall struck 5:00 a.m. The two-inch-high figurine of a man emerged and struck the bell five times with a hammer. Fredi, her brother, had loved that clock. The joy that stupid clock gave him had been the only thing that had stopped her from smashing it. Everything he'd loved, anything he'd touched, was pure gold now.

"Fredi," she said as the man disappeared back inside the clock. "You see what I'm doing, don't you? I need you with me. I need to feel you with me. I can't do this without you."

She hadn't said his name aloud in months, hadn't allowed herself to. It had been too much. It was best to forget—to ignore the past in order to control the agony. But she needed him now, needed to feel love again. She tried to remember the love she'd felt, tried to draw it from deep within her like precious water is drawn from a desert well. She balled her hand into a fist, took a heavy breath, and opened the front door.

The wind was gone. The air was as still as death itself. She grasped the cord attached to the front of the sled and set out across the snow. Her footprints were still visible and would remain that way until the next snow came. Anyone would be able to follow her. The blanket of night would hide them for another couple of hours, but after that they'd be visible to anyone out for a morning stroll. How would she explain hauling a prostrate Luftwaffe airman through the snow on a sled? She'd think of those lies if she needed to. For now, the only thing that mattered was putting one foot in front of the other.

The fear that he would be dead haunted her for the entire journey back. What if the Gestapo had been tracking him? What if they'd seen his parachute and hadn't had the chance to capture him during the storm? Surely they'd be on their way up to the field now. Savage memories came to her of interrogations, of jail cells, of the cold gray eyes of the Gestapo man who had questioned her. Relief only came as she sighted the field. The pressing matter of evading detection drowned out her thoughts.

The field was empty, as she'd left it. She listened. No sound. The silence of the night had a story to tell. The trees were still, the snow dense and heavy. She waited two minutes but then realized she was wasting time. No one had seen him, but someone would unless she acted soon. She peered around the tree she was hiding behind and made her way across the field toward the snow cave. Seeing that the entrance was only a few inches wide now, she knelt and cleared it out. The man was still lying on the sleeping bag she'd taken from his backpack, his chest still moving with his breathing. He was still unconscious.

"Hello?" she said. "Are you awake, sir? Can you hear me?"

Her voice seemed to echo through the vacuum of night. The man didn't stir. She reached down and poked his shoulder—still nothing. The sun would be up soon. It had to happen now. She took the nylon strands of the parachute and pulled until they were taut against his weight, then dug her feet into the snow and heaved. The man's body inched up the ramp and out of the snow cave. She collapsed, gasping beside him, her heart pounding. He was out. Now all she had to do was get him onto the sled and drag him two miles back to the cabin. That was all.

She lay on the snow, staring up at the flickering stars. Exhaustion was taking hold—the desire for sleep was overwhelming. Nothing could have been more wonderful than to close her eyes and succumb to it. Her body ached; her shoulders and arms still burned from dragging the man out of the snow cave. But she had to keep on. Stopping now would mean failure. She wouldn't accept that. The sled was four feet long. He was about six. If it weren't for his broken legs, she would have pulled him behind her, letting his limbs drag on the snow as they went. She could hardly let his head flounder over the end of the sled, could she? She brought the sled alongside his body. It was his only chance. If his legs had to drag, so be it. Perhaps there was a way she could make him more comfortable.

The man's backpack was still in the snow cave, and she went back inside to retrieve it. The rope she'd seen earlier was coiled at the bottom. She drew it out. It was too long, but she had the knife she'd taken from the house. She cut six lengths, each about eighteen inches long. This was going to take a few minutes, so she took the brandy from her pocket and, reaching down, opened the man's lips to pour it into his mouth. He spluttered it back up at first, but she lifted his head and noted with some satisfaction how he swallowed back at least some of it. She took some herself, feeling the heat of it all the way down to her stomach.

It took her about two or three minutes to collect several sturdy branches, each about three or four inches in diameter. She dropped them down next to the airman's body in preparation for what was going to be the hard part. She took off her gloves. The cold seemed to attack her hands, but she ignored the pain, focusing on what she had to do.

She placed one hand on the man's left ankle and pushed her other hand up inside his pants, feeling for the bone. It was broken a couple of inches below the knee. Ideally, she would have set it as soon as she'd found him, but she'd had more pressing matters to deal with at that time. The man grimaced under her touch, but she pressed on, lining the bone up under his skin as she applied a slow, strong pull to the bottom of his leg. The bone moved back into place, and she took two branches and tied one to each side of his leg with the rope she'd cut. The leg was set and immobilized—as long as the rope held. She checked the lengths again. They were tight. It was as good as she could have expected. Now she had to do the same for his right leg. She reached under his pants leg again, feeling for the bone. This break didn't seem as severe. She set the bone in place and tied the branches to each side of his leg.

She stood still for a few seconds. "Who are you?" she whispered.

She waited a moment, as if he was going to sit up and answer her question. But there was no sound from his lips, just the whine of the wind as it began to swirl around them once more. It had to be almost seven. There was no time to waste. She took his backpack on her shoulders and slipped him out of the parachute, its purpose served. She couldn't leave it on him: It could catch on the ground. It was heavy. People had been executed for being caught with less. Even if the Gestapo wasn't looking for him, someone finding a parachute up here would lead to questions that would lead to him. She could risk bringing it, because if they were caught, there would be no explaining him away, with or without the parachute. She folded it up as best as she could, getting it down to a manageable armload of nylon before placing it on top of him. She took the remaining length of rope, around twenty feet, and looped it around the sled, securing him to it, and the parachute to his chest. She pulled the rope tight but allowed the man space to breathe. Then they were ready.

She took the tie at the front of the sled and pulled. The sled moved along the smooth surface of the snow, and they set off. The first few hundred yards were relatively easy as they made their way across the snowy meadow, but the fastest way back to the house involved moving through some trees and across a frozen stream. That wasn't going to be possible while pulling the man behind her. She was going to have to stick to the trails, and that increased her chances of meeting someone. She thought of whom she might meet, and of the deficit of trust the Nazis had created among the German people. The pistol still weighed heavy in her pocket. She had forgotten to take it out of her coat.

For every easy downhill slope, there was another uphill to negotiate, and the steep climb to the cabin at the very end of the journey awaited her. She would be at her absolute weakest then. She kept on, though her muscles were beginning to fail. She could feel the strength leaking from her. Her breaths grew deeper and more pronounced. Sweat began to freeze against her exposed skin. She knew how dangerous that was, how frostbite could follow, but she didn't stop. There could be no stopping. She kept on as the sun peeked over the horizon. There was no joy in its coming, no comfort in the dawn. She was almost a mile from the cabin, and the cloak of night was unraveling by the second.

The sound of footsteps came from in front. It was hard at first to tell quite where from. She stood silent, her pulse racing. Her ears were attuned to the silence, and she could clearly make out the sound of approaching footsteps along the trail. She looked back at the man on the sled. It was hard to tell how much time they had, but she doubted it was more than a minute. The trail curved ahead, which meant that the person approaching would be out of sight until it was too late. She pulled the sled off the trail and down behind a line of trees. She did her best to hide him, covering him with some loose branches. The tracks they'd made along the path itself were still visible. Anyone could have noticed where they'd stopped. She pressed her hand over her mouth to stop the sound of her breathing.

A minute dragged by, the noises getting ever louder. The figure came into view. She recognized the man and almost laughed as she shook her head. It was Herr Berkel, her ex-boyfriend's father. She knew without hesitation that he would report her. Daniel was in the Gestapo. Nothing would have given Herr Berkel more pleasure. He was about sixty feet away now, ambling along the trail, walking stick in hand. It had been years since she'd spoken to him, back when she and Daniel were together. He was a gruff man, lacking any charm or refinement. He lived close by. This was probably his morning routine.

He was a large man, well over sixty years old. Her hand went to the gun in her pocket. What was she prepared to do to protect a man she'd encountered just hours before, one whom she'd never spoken to? She probably didn't even know his real name. Looking at Herr Berkel brought back clear images of the evils that had swallowed her country. She moved her eyes to the man on the sled and felt every bit of hope left within her. He had already saved her life, just as she had saved his.

Berkel stopped on the trail about twenty feet short of where they were hiding. He leaned back, stretching out his lower back, and retrieved a cigarette from his pocket. He placed it between his lips, struck a match, and inhaled the smoke. She could just about make out his face from where she was hiding. His eyes appeared to focus, and he began to walk again, although more slowly this time, while staring down at the trail. He looked right and then left, within a few feet of where they were hiding. He stopped, and her heart almost stopped with him. Her finger was on the trigger. She was ready. She was prepared to draw her gun on a man she'd known for most of her life to protect a man she'd found only a few hours before. Where would she hide the body? She had to make sure it didn't come to that. Herr Berkel shook his head and resumed along the trail. He moved past where they were hiding and kept on, seemingly unaware of their presence.

She waited five minutes until she poked her head out onto the trail. Tears formed in her eyes as tension gripped her. She grasped the rope on the front of the sled and managed to coax her aching arms into dragging the man back up onto the trail. The sun was bright in the crisp blue sky, illuminating the beauty the snows the night before had created. The layer of white was undisturbed except for the trail Herr Berkel had left. She resumed pulling the man along, her thoughts returning to getting him back to the cabin alive.

There were no other walkers out that morning. She removed her hand from the pistol in her pocket and used it to pull the sled. Every thought disappeared from her mind until the only thing she could picture was getting back to the cabin. There was nothing else now. It was all that the world existed for. One painful step followed another until the last hill came into view. She hadn't taken a rest other than the one that Herr Berkel's presence had forced upon her, but she sat now, regaining her breath before the final test. She had come so far. There was just this one hill left, and then the house on top held the promise of food, water, painkillers, and, more importantly, sleep.

She looked over at him. "We're nearly home. It's just a little farther now."

The muscles in her legs almost gave out, but she fought the pain and weakness and stood up straight and tall, grasping the rope tied to the sled. She pulled and heaved and sweated and made it to the house.

She struggled for breath as she put a hand on the front door and pushed it open. She dragged the sled inside, leaving a trail of snow and muck that she'd have to clean up later.

He was here, inside the cabin. It felt like a miracle. She dragged him into the living room and left him in front of the embers of last night's fire. There was just enough wood there to make it up again, and she took a few minutes to light it. Her hat and coat felt like a second skin as she peeled them off. She went to the kitchen and gulped down several cups of water before going to him. She held the cup to his lips, dribbling water into his mouth. He managed to swallow some of it. He was a filthy, stinking mess and had two broken legs, but he was alive, and that was enough for now. She left him there, unconscious but safe, in front of the fire. Then she went to the bedroom, took off her clothes, and was asleep as soon as she felt the pillow against her face.

Chapter 3

The ticking of a clock. The chimes. He blinked his eyes open and found himself lying in a pool of filthy sweat and tied to a length of wood. A stormy haze had settled between his ears, and it took a few seconds to remember where he was, let alone why he was here. The agony in his legs shot up through his torso. He could take pain, but enough was enough, and he looked around the room for an escape. The dying embers of a fire glowed red in the fireplace a few feet away. He was alone. Had he been captured? He could expect no mercy. Where were they? The memory of his family appeared through the clouds of his consciousness. His father, his mother, and his wife—his ex-wife now. The vague remembrance of their divorce was new to him again for a few seconds. Then the letter she'd written him appeared in his mind, and he was back there, hovering above his bunk in basic training, watching himself reading it. Glimpses of his past life appeared and then retreated into the abyss. He tried to recall something about the present, about where he was now. The feeling of hands on his body, of being dragged along—it all came to him more as an essence than a solid memory he could cling to. It was as if he could feel the moment—perhaps even smell and touch it. Picturing it was beyond him. He tried to rouse himself off the wooden platform he was on, whatever it was, but his efforts came to nothing as he fell back onto it again. His eyelids felt like they weighed a thousand tons. He had time just to glance around the room before they shut and he succumbed to the mercy of sleep once more.

The light of the day had dwindled by the time she awoke in the early evening. She sat up in the bed. Her empty stomach growled. The muscles in her arms, shoulders, and back were as stiff as a tortoise shell. She worked her fingers into the grooves where hard muscle met bone and sinew at the top of her shoulders, doing her best to massage away the pain. The living room door was ajar a few inches. She peered out at the man passed out there. She sat still, listening for sounds that weren't there. Nothing was moving other than the wind through the trees outside. She got out from under the covers and stood beside the bed, almost against her own will. She went to the wardrobe and slipped into a simple gray dress. The cold floor stung her feet, and she put on thick woolen socks before sliding into slippers.

She inched out, a stranger in her own house. The first things she saw were his legs and the splints she'd fashioned on either side of each one. He wasn't moving. His eyes were still closed.

"Hallo, sir," she whispered. "Are you awake?"

Nothing.

She took a deep breath, trying to slow down her heart. Sweat was forming on her palms. His short brown hair was thick with muck and still wet from the snow. His unshaven face was scratched and caked with filth. He didn't seem to have moved. She reached down to check for a pulse. His heartbeat was steady and even. He would survive this. She went to the kitchen and came back with a cupful of water and dribbled some in between his lips. Once again he seemed to swallow some of it between coughing and spluttering away the rest.

She knelt beside him and reached under the sled to untie the rope that held him in place. She thought about slicing the rope but decided against that. She might need it again if he proved unwilling to cooperate. The rope fell beneath the sled, and she moved the parachute aside. She reached for the straps on his shoulders, which had held the parachute in place, and had little difficulty slipping them off. The problem of what to do with the parachute remained. Hiding a parachute was the kind of subversive act that could land a citizen in jail, or worse. Burning it would produce toxic fumes. For the time being, she dumped it in a pile near the back door.

He was going to need bed rest. The sled, even though it had left a trail of dirt when she pushed him into the house earlier, was still the best way of moving him around. She got down on her knees and turned the sled around, angling it toward the spare room where she and Fredi had slept on summer nights as children. It had been empty for years. The man lay immobile as she pushed the sled into the bedroom. The door was already open, the bed made, and the room immaculately clean. She tried to remember who had slept there last. It must have been her, or maybe even Fredi. She could recall her father taking Fredi up here, but that was years before the war—before Fredi had become too much for their father to take care of alone. Before she'd deserted them. She wiped the memories away like grime off a windshield and endeavored to focus on the problems at hand. She went back into the living room for his backpack. Clean civilian clothes lay folded at the bottom, but there was nothing he could sleep in, and she certainly wasn't going to have him lying around the house in his underwear. Some of her father's old clothes would fit him. Within a few minutes she'd found a pair of his old pajamas and a wine-colored bathrobe. She went back in and threw the pajamas on the bed but held on to the bathrobe for a few seconds, feeling the smoothness of the material between her fingers. The past was everywhere here. There was no escaping it.

The man was soiled and grimy. The first thing he'd need was a bath, and that would be easier while he was still unconscious. She reached down and ran her fingers along the rough splints she'd made to keep his bones in place. They would need to be replaced. Getting him to a hospital, or even a doctor, didn't seem worth the risk. She couldn't trust anyone.

Could *he* be trusted? She had heard the radio reports about the Allies, and knew better than to trust the Nazis' view of the Americans as uneducated mongrels, and the British as treacherous wretches. Still, she had never met an Allied soldier before. The countless newsreels and stories over the years had reinforced in her mind the Nazis' view of the Allies. It was impossible to dismiss all she'd seen and heard, even with her mistrust of the government and the media it controlled. She had seen what the Allies had done to Germany. They'd bombed cities full of citizens without mercy. It was difficult to see them as saviors, no matter how much she wanted to.

His lips twitched, his eyes rolling like slugs under his closed eyelids. She stood back in fright, expecting them to open. She hadn't even considered what she was going to say or do when he awoke. Fortunately, his face settled back into its previous catatonic state, and the dilemma was postponed.

Franka walked into the kitchen. The house was frigid. Herr Graf, or whoever he was, could wait until she set a fire. She cleared out some of the ashes from the burner, pushing charred logs out of the way with a poker that had been in this house longer than she'd been alive. She struck a match, and the light from the fire enveloped the kitchen. She always took so much pleasure in setting a fire and stood back, watching the logs take to the kindling she'd placed underneath them. Satisfied, she went to the cupboard. There wasn't much food, just some old cans of soup. The provisions she'd brought were almost gone. The roads to town would be cut off for days—her car would be useless. She went to the medicine cabinet and found an old bottle of aspirin with nine pills left—enough to last him about twelve hours. He was going to need more, and stronger medicine than that, especially if she had to set the bones in his legs again. The bottle rattled like a baby's toy as she put it in her pocket.

She took one of the wooden chairs from the old table in the middle of the room. It would do. She raised the chair above her head and brought it crashing down to the floor below. Nothing happened—the chair remained intact. She shook her head, laughing to herself. She went to the sink and got a hammer and several screwdrivers of various sizes. A few minutes later she had the sturdy wood she would need to set his legs until she could do a more permanent job of it.

She went to the bedroom. The man hadn't moved. She had dealt with worse breaks before, but that had been in a hospital. How would his bones heal without casts? The question of getting the plaster and setting it herself didn't worry her so much as the suspicion that purchasing it might bring. If she was careful, she might just be able to get away with buying it, and the food, and the morphine she was going to need. The question of how she was going to get into town remained, but she pushed it away for now.

She untied each of the ropes holding the twig splints in place and set the splints aside as firewood. The next part was going to be difficult for the man, unconscious or not. Those filthy pants and boots had to come off. She began working on the laces, intermittently glancing up at his face, aware of every grimace she was causing him. She opened the laces and applied gentle pressure to the boot as she tried to pull it off. The bone in his leg moved, and he cried out. It was bizarre to see him react. It was like a marionette wailing after being dropped on the floor. She stopped, expecting him to waken, but he didn't. The boot came off, and she moved her hands back up to feel the bone. It had moved, but not much, and she set it back in place, lining it up. The man's right boot dropped onto the thinly carpeted floor with a thud. She took a deep breath and steeled herself for the next leg. She didn't want to cut the laces. Boots were a valuable asset these days. It took another five minutes to get it off. The experience she'd garnered on his other leg lent to a smoother process this time. The socks came off one inch at a time, revealing bruised and swollen feet. Scissors from the living room made short work of the man's pants, and soon he was lying in his underwear, still on the sled.

The pieces of the chair made for adequate splints, and his legs held taut. The Luftwaffe blazer came off next, and she tossed it into the corner of the room. The shirt came off with similar ease, and he was ready to be put on the bed. She made her way around behind him and eased him off the sled. The bed was mercifully low, and she leaned his torso against it. She dragged him up onto the clean covers, aware that he was still covered in dirt. But he was on the bed. She stood back in momentary triumph, marveling at the sight of this unknown man lying on her old bed in her father's summer cabin in the mountains.

It was good that he was going to be unconscious for his bath. It would not be the first one she'd given, but it would be the first she'd given to a sleeping stranger, and not in a hospital. Time was of the essence. The last thing she wanted was for him to wake up while she was rubbing him down. Nothing could have been more improper.

"Bath time, darling," she smiled. "How was your day? You won't believe what happened to me on the way home from the hospital." She made sure not to speak loudly enough that he might wake. No joke would have been worth that. She put a tub of water she'd warmed down beside the bed and took the washcloth in her hand. Dried dirt turned to mud as she sprinkled water from the cloth on his face. She wiped him off with strong hands. "I found a man—yes, a man—lying in the snow. In a Luftwaffe uniform, no less." She hadn't talked to another soul in days. It felt good to be speaking out loud, even if it was to an unconscious stranger. "No, darling, I'm being quite serious. You know it's not the place of a good German wife to make fun of her husband, not with our brave soldiers risking their lives for the future of the glorious Reich on the Russian front as we speak." She placed her hand on his now-clean face. "What's that? You want to hear the radio? Well, it's my duty as a good wife to obey your every whim." She went to the living room and flicked on the battery-powered radio. The usual mess of news and propaganda was soiling the airwaves of the German stations. Radios were issued by the government and were only capable of picking up the government-sanctioned stations. Most people knew how to doctor them to get the foreign channels, however, and she was able to tune in to a Swiss broadcast of a new hit from Tommy Dorsey and his band. The big-band swing drifted through the cabin. The music gave her pause, washcloth still in hand. Somewhere people were still creating music like this, still listening and dancing and living. Suddenly she felt connected once more with a world she'd given up on.

In silence she finished washing down the man and let the music flow through her.

"All clean," she said. She placed the aspirin on the bedside table along with a glass of water. She tucked him under the sheets and stowed hot-water bottles by his feet. Who was he? Why was he here? How on earth was she going to keep his presence here a secret over the six weeks or so it would take those bones to heal? How would he react to her once he woke up?

She stood in the doorway, staring at him for several minutes, the music still floating through the air, before giving into the hunger pangs stabbing at her stomach. "Tomorrow will be the day," she said out loud. "Tomorrow I find out who you are." She took the key from the door and locked it behind her.

Her hunger took precedence over her need for a bath, so she went to the cupboard for a can of soup. Some bread would have been fantastic, but she'd finished the last of it along with the cheese she'd brought the night before. It was to have been her last meal. She sat back at the table, staring into space as the soup heated on the stove and making a mental list of what she was going to need to keep her and the man in the bedroom alive through the winter. Somehow she was going to have to make it to Freiburg to get food, gauze, plaster of paris, aspirin, and morphine—a journey of almost ten miles each way. In ordinary circumstances she would have driven in, but the weather had taken simplicity out of the equation. She got out of the seat and went to the closet near the back door. Her old cross-country skis lay untouched at the back, behind some old winter coats and other pieces of assorted junk that had built up over the years. It had been more than a decade since she'd used them, not since she was a teenager, back when her mother was still alive and they'd come up here every winter. She reached in and felt the weight of the skis in her hands. It seemed she had no other choice. She took the skis under her arm and brought them back to the kitchen. The soup was ready, and she poured it into a bowl, devouring it in seconds. It seemed only to awaken her hunger. She made herself another, promising that she would replace it when she went to Freiburg.

The second can of soup did the job, but the sweat-stained filth clinging to her body remained. The thought of heating on the stove all the water she would need almost seemed too much, but the sheer smell she must have emanated was motivation enough. She put the kettle and two large saucepans of water on the stove and sat, watching as they came to boiling point. The awareness of a strange, albeit immobilized and unconscious, man in the house was with her as she closed the door to change. Emerging in her bathrobe, she paced to the bathroom, shutting the door behind her. The candlelight lent the room an air of relaxation, but the lack of water did not. The wonderful bath she'd been dreaming of ended up being a case of sitting in the tub and scrubbing herself down.

The coldness of the cabin hit her as she emerged, dripping from the bath. She grabbed a towel and rubbed herself as hard as she could, using the friction to warm herself. Once she was dried and in her bathrobe, she went to the mirror. She hadn't looked at herself in days. Her shoulder-length blond hair lay straggly, stuck to her neck. Her blue eyes were bloodshot, and large, darkened circles hung underneath them. She ran a comb through her hair, wincing in pain as the knots came out.

She thought about Herr Berkel and remembered his son, the charming Hitler Youth she'd fallen for during her time in the League of German Girls, the female equivalent of the Hitler Youth. Everyone she knew joined. It became a rite of passage. To not join would have singled out a young boy or girl as a weakling, an upstart, or a malingerer. Perhaps even a pariah.

A wave of paranoia hit her. How did she know Berkel hadn't seen them? Maybe he had seen them and had already reported them to the Gestapo. It seemed unlikely, but there was no room for error when no one could be trusted.

Night had settled, and she lit candles in the kitchen and the bedroom, as well as the oil lamp in the living room. The man was still asleep when she peeked in on him. She went to her bedroom again, and though her body yearned for sleep, she couldn't let herself. Not yet. She got dressed once more. The Gestapo could come at any time. He was exposed. Hiding him in the closet would only prolong by seconds the amount of time it would take to find him, and he was too injured to hide outside in the cold of winter. Running through nightmarish scenarios in her mind—each of them realistic—she went back into the bedroom where he lay asleep. They weren't safe, even up here, particularly if she had to go into town. The Luftwaffe uniform was still bundled up in the corner where she'd thrown it. If, on the off chance, he was Luftwaffe, she could give it back to him. In the much more likely scenario that he was British or American, it would only serve to have him shot as a spy. It had to be hidden, but where?

She stomped her foot and heard the hollow wooden sound from the floorboards. She got the toolbox from the kitchen, went to the bedroom where he was sleeping, and pulled up a thin rug, exposing the wooden slats below. If she pried up the boards, she could create an effective hiding place. But first she would have to move the bed. She made her way over to the side of the bed and pushed it across the room, the man still asleep on it.

She dug the claw of a hammer into the space at the end of the long floorboard, then angled it back, wrenching it upward. After a few minutes of wrestling with it, the stubborn board gave way. She finished the job with gloved hands and placed the board against the wall, revealing a two-foot space below. It was filthy, and freezing cold, but would do the job nicely with a bit of cleaning and a few blankets. She set to work on the adjoining floorboard, wondering how many she would have to pry up to fit him in the space. The fewer the better—everything had to look as natural as possible.

A cough from the bed jarred her from her concentration, and the hammer fell out of her hand into the hole she'd created. She stood up as the man's eyes flew open. He sat up in the bed, his face contorted into a horrible grimace. He clamped his eyes shut before opening them again and turned to where she, stunned silent, was standing. Pain and confusion clouded his eyes.

"Who are you? Why are you keeping me here?" he said in perfect German.

Chapter 4

His accent was hard to place. She'd known Berliners before, had heard their slender, harsh accents. He had some of the hallmarks of that, but it seemed there was something missing. It was hard to explain, almost like trying to describe a dance to a blind person. He was sitting up on the bed, his eyes imploring. It had been several seconds since he'd asked her, and his words were still hanging like smoke in the air. A thousand thoughts flashed through her mind, but she wasn't quite able to catch hold of any of them. She stepped forward, her arms outstretched, her hands turned upward as if in a gesture of defense.

"I am a friend," she said.

He didn't reply, seemingly wanting more.

"I found you in the snow. You were unconscious. The pain you feel is the fractures you sustained in both of your legs."

The man ran his hands along the splints she'd fashioned from the kitchen chair, and the grimace came again.

"My name is Franka Gerber. I brought you back here. It's just the two of us. The nearest village is several miles away."

"Where are we?"

"We're about ten miles east of Freiburg, in the mountains of the Black Forest."

The man brought a hand to his forehead. He seemed to recover from his confused state and spoke with some clarity now.

"You are with the police?" he asked.

"No, I'm not."

"Do you have any affiliation with the Gestapo, or the security forces?"

"No, I don't. I have no phone. I found you and brought you back here." The words tumbled out of her mouth. Her hands were shaking by her side. She brought them behind her back.

The man narrowed his eyes before speaking again. "My name is Hauptmann Werner Graf of the Luftwaffe."

"I saw your uniform."

"Why did you take me back here?"

"I found you last night. We were too far from anywhere that could have offered us any medical help. I didn't have any other choice."

"Thank you for saving my life, Fräulein Gerber. Are you associated with the armed forces?"

"No, I'm a nurse. Well, I was a nurse."

The man tried to move his legs. His face twisted in agony, and she stepped forward again, right by his bedside now.

"Lie back down, Herr Graf." It felt ridiculous to be using a name she knew wasn't real. "I know you're in great discomfort." She looked around for the aspirin pills. They weren't going to do anything more than temper his pain, but any kind of relief would help him sleep again. They were on the bedside table, which she'd shoved out of the way to reveal the floorboards, and now his eyes went down to the gaping hole she'd created.

"What is going on here? What are you planning on doing?"

"Just some repairs," Franka said. "Nothing to concern yourself with." She took out three pills and offered them to him. He looked at them and then back into her eyes.

"They're just aspirin. They're not much, but they'll help until I can get something stronger." She could see the pain in his eyes, and also the fear and confusion that he was working so hard to hide. He held out his hand, and she dropped the pills into his palm. She gave him water, and he swallowed the aspirin, gulping down the entire glass in seconds.

"Do you want more water?"

"Please."

She hurried into the kitchen, glancing over at his rucksack on the floor of the living room as she passed. The guns were still inside. Her father's gun was in the drawer of the dresser table by the front door. When she returned, he was trying to get out of the bed, his face sweating and distorted in suffering.

"No, please," she said. "Lie back down. You have nothing to worry about. I am a friend." She handed him the water. It was gone in seconds, as before. She took the glass back. He was still upright on the bed. He folded his arms across his chest as she began to speak. He looked as if he was concentrating on each individual word she was saying. "Lie down. We've no way of moving you. The roads are closed, and both your legs are broken. We're stuck here together. We're going to have to trust one another."

"Who are you?" he said, rubbing the nape of his neck.

"I'm from this area. I grew up in Freiburg. This was my family's summer home."

"Are you here alone?"

"Apart from you. What were you doing out there in the snow? I have your parachute."

"I can't talk about it. That's classified information. If I were to fall into Allied hands, it could be damaging to the war effort."

"Well, you're still in the fatherland. You're safe. The Allies are hundreds of miles away."

The man nodded, his eyes dropping to the floor.

"You must be famished. I'll fetch you some food."

"Yes, please."

"My pleasure, Herr Graf."

She retreated to the kitchen. Her hands were shaking as she reached for the last can of soup in the cupboard. It was hard to know how to play it from here. Trying to out him from his charade could be downright dangerous, but she had to let him know that he could trust her.

"Trust takes time," she whispered. "This isn't going to happen tonight." She went back to him as the soup warmed on the stove. He flinched as she walked in.

"Everything all right?"

"Yes, thank you. It's just that the pain in my legs is quite intense."

"I understand. I'm sorry about that. I'm going to try to get more painkillers for you tomorrow." He didn't answer. "I have your boots, but I was forced to cut the pants off your legs. I also have your backpack. I saw that you had clothes in there."

He nodded, seemingly unsure of what to say. "Thank you for taking care of me," he answered after a few seconds. His eyes drifted toward the window and then back to her.

"I set the bones in your legs, but I'm afraid we're going to need plaster casts to make sure they heal correctly."

"Yes, thank you, Fräulein Gerber. Whatever you think is best."

His eyes were glazing over, and he fell back on the bed.

"I'll be right back," she said. The soup was ready, and she poured it into a bowl for him. She returned to the bedroom. He was lying down on the bed, staring at the ceiling. He sat up as she placed the tray in front of him. He devoured the soup even more quickly than she had earlier. She took the tray, wishing she had bread to give him. "You need to rest now."

"I have some more questions for you."

"Questions can wait."

"Have you spoken to anyone else about my being here? Anyone at all?"

"I haven't spoken to another soul in days, not since before I found you. We've no telephone here, as I said. There isn't even a postal service. I'd have to go into town to get any letters if anyone knew I was up here. But they don't. We're alone." She leaned forward. "I brought you back here so you could get better."

"I'm grateful for that, but it's important that I be on my way as soon as possible."

"You're not going anywhere on those legs for several weeks. Once the roads open up again, we can see about bringing you back to town, but until then you're stuck here with me. You need to accept that and also realize that you can trust me. I'm here to make sure you get better."

"I'm thankful, Fräulein." He nodded to her, but there was little joy or true appreciation in his words. It was as if he were reading off a script.

"Think nothing of it. I could hardly leave you out there to freeze to death, now could I? The important thing now is that you rest."

Even her own words were wooden. It was as if they were two bad actors performing a play.

The man nodded and lay back down, the pain evident on his face. Franka reached for the candle on the bedside table and extinguished it between two wetted fingers. She closed the door behind her, drained from the masquerade. She turned the lock once more, aware that he must have heard her do it. The man didn't protest.

The fire in the living room was dying, so she added more wood, standing back once more to watch it blaze up. She felt like she was alone in a cage with a wounded animal and unsure of anything it might do. His broken legs were her only guarantee of safety. As long as he couldn't move from that bed, he couldn't hurt her, especially without his guns. It was paramount that he understood that she meant him no harm, but also that she was in charge. She would not be subject to the whims of any bully, be they a Nazi or an Allied soldier. She would keep him here, safe from the Gestapo. That would be her final act of defiance against them before she joined Hans and the others.

Her entire body ached now, crying out for sleep. She went to her bedroom. Usually she would have left the door open to collect some of the warmth from the living room, but she closed the door behind her.

She went to the window. It was a calm, clear night, and the stars outside shone like light through pinpricks in black velvet. The weather tomorrow would likely be good enough for her to go into town. The trails would be clear. It was the type of trip she might have relished ten years ago. That seemed like a different world. She'd accumulated so many scars since then.

Franka picked a hot-water bottle out of the closet, the memories of her youth coming at the mere sight of it—nights cuddled up under blankets, her eyes drifting shut as her mother sang her to sleep.

She had never meant to stay here this long. There were too many ghosts. But now she had little choice. Leaving the cabin would mean leaving him and giving the Gestapo their victory. She took the hot-water bottle out to the kitchen and poured the water in once it had heated. It felt good in her hands, like it was giving life back to her. She hugged it, feeling the warmth in her chest, before returning to the bedroom. Could he really be German? Why would he have said those English words in his sleep? Perhaps this was all simpler than she'd made out, and she could drop him off at the local hospital when the roads cleared in a few days. Maybe she'd misheard him talking in his sleep. She didn't speak English and had only heard a few words spoken in front of her. Perhaps he hadn't said anything at all. Perhaps he really was Hauptmann Werner Graf of the Luftwaffe. Franka felt her heart drop at the thought that he wasn't who she thought he was, that he was one of them. Was he a Luftwaffe flier? She had seen the propaganda films that showed foreigners coming to join the glorious German Reich. It seemed unlikely. If he was Luftwaffe, she would hand him over to the authorities as soon as he came to, and that would be that.

The bedroom went black as she blew out the oil lamp at her bedside. No. He had said those English words. She had heard them. She still could hear them, could still sound them out on her tongue. He wasn't Hauptmann Werner Graf of the Luftwaffe. Why had he been lying in the snow in the mountains of the Black Forest? He couldn't have been there for more than a few minutes when she'd found him; otherwise she would have come upon a corpse. If he was a spy or a prisoner of war, the penalty for helping him would be death. She could handle that. The National Socialists couldn't take anything more from her now. Not when she had nothing left for them to take.

Franka turned over in the bed, pulling the thick blankets up to her chin so that only her face was exposed. Beneath the bedcovers was the only warm place in the house apart from the fire. The man only had one blanket, and the hole she'd made in the floor would let in a draft. She got out of bed, taking the key to the man's bedroom door. She put on a nightgown, and a coat over that, before tiptoeing away. The house was still. She unlocked the door, put a hand on the door handle, and knocked with her other hand as she opened it.

"Hallo?" she whispered. "Are you awake, Herr Graf?"

He was lying in the bed, but she could see that his eyes were open. For a horrible second she thought he might have been dead, but soon he turned his head to her.

"I am awake, Fräulein."

"Are you warm enough?"

"I'm fine, thank you."

She didn't take his word for it. It was colder in his room than hers, and he didn't have as many blankets. She'd left the curtains open, and the light of the moon was streaming in. The features of his face were visible in the half-light. She took his hand. She hadn't planned on touching him, just wanted to see how cold he was. His eyes came to hers.

"You're freezing," she said. "Why didn't you ask me for another blanket?"

"I don't want to cause you any more trouble."

"Nonsense. There's no use suffering when there are more blankets in the closet." She let go of his hand and opened the closet. She took out a thick blanket and spread it over him. "This will keep you warm." He was staring at her, and she stepped back. "I'm going into town tomorrow. The roads will be closed, but we need food and I can't bear the thought of the pain you must be in." She paused for an answer that didn't come. "It's obvious that I can't bring you in with me, but if you'd like, I can report your presence here to the local Gestapo." It was her turn to stare at him now.

"That won't be necessary, Fräulein. The local police are not of concern to me. As I mentioned previously, I'm handling some sensitive matters on behalf of the war effort right now. Alerting anyone to my presence here wouldn't be prudent at this time."

"So you don't want me to report that you're here to anyone? They could tell the Luftwaffe, your superior officer, whom sent you up in that airplane."

"Really, there's no need. I'll leave you as soon as the roads are clear. Until then, I'll be your grateful guest."

Franka wondered if he knew how long his legs were going to take to heal or if he was being deliberately ignorant. She was certain of one thing, however: he wasn't an English-speaking Luftwaffe pilot.

"As you wish." She turned to leave.

"Fräulein, how did you get me here?"

"I dragged you on a sled."

"You dragged me back here unconscious?" His eyes were wide in the darkness. He held his hands together in front of him as if he were praying. "You are a truly remarkable person. I am forever in your debt."

"You need to sleep now. Is there anything else you need?"

"A chamber pot, perhaps? Just in case."

"Of course," she answered, and went to the kitchen. She found a basin that would do the job and brought it back to him. He accepted it with a smile and thanked her once more. Franka closed the door behind her, turning the key in the lock. She determined not to use the name Werner Graf anymore. Saying it out loud demeaned them both.

Franka awoke with the dawn. The night had brought a deeper sleep than she'd enjoyed for many months. The man's presence in the house had in some way blunted the memories that found her in the dark. The memories were always worse at night, and sleeping alone had become torture. There was comfort to be drawn from his presence here, and she felt it. She had already done so much for him, and he for her. He was the first thing that came to her mind as she opened her eyes. She wondered if he'd slept, and if he was in pain. She wondered if his bones were still set properly with the splints she'd made, and when, if ever, she'd learn the truth about him. The floor felt like ice, and she searched for her slippers, then slid her feet into them before venturing to the window. Pushing back the curtains revealed the winter sun in a cloudless, cobalt-blue sky. The snow was as it had been the night before. Doubts crept in. Did she really have to make this trip into town today? Could she wait? They had little food left, and she couldn't leave him lying in misery until the roads opened back up. Who knew when that would be? The roads up here could be closed for weeks at a time, although that was before the brutal efficiency of the Nazis. It was decided, then: she would go into town today. She would go all the way into Freiburg. She would find the supplies she needed in the city, and no one was looking for her—she had no one to hide from.

Franka went to his room and put her ear against the door. There was no noise from inside, so she drew back and went to the kitchen. The skis were still against the wall where she'd left them the night before. Ten miles was a ridiculous distance to attempt on skis, particularly considering her lack of practice these past few years. It was less than two to the main road into Freiburg, and she was confident in her ability to hitch a ride into town from there. She restocked the fireplaces in both the living room and the kitchen. The fires would be long extinguished by the time she returned but would provide some warmth while she was gone.

It had only been a few days since she'd been in Freiburg, but it seemed like years ago. She was a different person now. Those few days she'd spent in the city the week before were a blur. She closed her eyes, trying to forget.

Franka unlocked the door to the man's room, listening for any noise before pushing it open. The room was dark, the curtains still closed. The hole in the floor remained. The man was lying asleep on the bed. He didn't seem like he'd moved since last night. She wondered if she should wake him but then decided against it. She went to the desk in the living room and took a piece of paper and a pen.

> *I'm going into town for the supplies we spoke about last night. I shouldn't be more than a few hours. Please stay in bed until I get back.*
>
> *Franka Gerber*

She wondered if she should have signed it Fräulein Gerber but didn't want to bother writing the note all over again. He was still asleep when she returned to his room. What if this man was a prisoner of war? What then? Could she keep him up here for the remainder of the war? With the Allied landings in Italy a few months before, and the calamity of Stalingrad, the eventual defeat of the Reich finally seemed possible. But it wasn't close. The National Socialists still maintained an iron grip on most of Europe, not to mention Germany herself. Could she hide him up here for months, or even years?

"One thing at a time, Franka," she whispered. "Get the man some painkillers, and some food to keep you both alive; then worry about what comes next."

She placed the note and a glass of water on the bedside table. The bottle of aspirin was empty, the last of them taken in the night. The full weight of his pain was lying in wait for him as soon as he awoke. She closed her eyes as she took the empty bottle in her hand, letting a breath out through her nostrils. There was nothing more to be done. Franka locked the door behind her.

The bright sunlight through the windows hadn't lulled her into any false hopes of warmth, and she put on her winter coat, hat, and gloves. She slipped her arms into her backpack, took the skis, and stepped out into the morning. Her sunglasses shielded her eyes from the burning sun. She slipped her feet into the skis, which still fit perfectly. Having them on felt like stepping into the past.

The horizon was clear, broken only by the carpet of snow-peaked trees climbing the surrounding hills. The snow was flawless, innocent white and would have lent a beauty to any landscape, let alone one as inherently spectacular as this. When was the last time she'd truly observed it? Had the darkness that had overtaken her obscured all else? She picked up speed, feeling a giddiness she thought she'd lost. The cabin faded into the distance.

The ground hurtled toward him, the rushing of the air rendering all his senses useless. He reached for a parachute that wasn't there. The ground below him stopped, changed into the field behind his parents' house. He was suddenly on the ground, rolling in the softness of the grass, and as he tried to move, the pain struck. He shook awake to the sound of the front door closing. He bit down on his lip, balling his fists together as a tsunami of agony rolled over him. He struggled against it, taking a deep breath in through his nose. He opened his eyes again. Several minutes had passed, and his brow was damp with sweat. He saw the note on the table. Questions came faster than he could process them. His mind was wobbly, charred at the edges by pain. Who was this person? Was this some Gestapo plot to gain his confidence, to get him to reveal the true nature of his mission? The woman had said they were ten miles outside Freiburg. He tried to remember exactly where that was, and how far it was to his target. The Black Forest—he had landed in the Black Forest. They must have seen his parachute. The woman was a Gestapo agent. How could she have gotten him back here by herself? It didn't seem possible. She must have had help. Her story didn't check out. Her face appeared in his mind. She was pretty as a pearl-handled dagger. He checked his torso for wounds. His head ached, but apart from that, and of course his legs, he seemed okay. She must have gone for help. They'd probably be here in minutes.

He reached down to touch the wooden splints along his legs. They seemed flimsy enough to confine him to this bed, but perhaps that was her plan. He was wearing pajamas, his backpack was missing, and his Luftwaffe uniform was thrown into the corner of the room. He propped himself up in the bed, trying to peer out the window through a chink in the curtains. He saw nothing but white. He needed a plan. Step one: get out of here. But how? The bed had been pushed all the way to one side of the bedroom. The window was about eight feet away across the room but might as well have been a mile. He took another sip of water before the hard part. The avalanche of pain that struck him as his legs dipped down the side of the bed was like nothing he'd ever experienced. He had to cover his mouth to stifle his own screams. It was cold in the room, but he could feel slick sweat on his back. He lay back and took a few ragged breaths. The house was quiet.

A cuckoo clock sounded, the bell chiming nine times. The noise brought him back into the moment, and he found the strength to sit up once more. Gently, he continued lowering his legs down the edge of the bed, carrying the weight of his body in his arms and pushing out deep breaths through pursed lips.

"Control the pain," he said in German. He made sure he did. Any slip now would be fatal. *Maintain your cover.* "You can do this." His useless legs dangled off the side of the bed, and he was sitting now, facing the window. He looked down at the missing floorboards that the young woman had pried up. What had she been doing? Was she trying to make it as hard as possible for him to get to the window? He surveyed the room. There was nothing between him and the window, nothing to prop himself up on once he got there. Perhaps crawling to the door might be the better option.

He twisted his body around toward the doorway and let himself drop to the floor. He brought his hand down. Pain burned through him, but he gritted his teeth, taking as much weight as he could on the palm of his hand. He used his arms to pull himself along, dragging his legs behind him as he made it around to the door. He reached up to the handle. It was locked, but then, he'd known that already. It took him two endless minutes to drag his broken body to where she'd tossed his Luftwaffe blazer. He smiled as he reached into the breast pocket for the paper clips he'd put there after his final briefing.

The keyhole was set in a tarnished plate on the wooden door. He tried to peer through but could only make out the glow of the fire burning. Picking locks hadn't been a specific part of his training. It was more of an extracurricular lesson his instructor had taught him. And he had excelled at it. He propped himself up, one hand on the knob, the other pushing the bent pin into the keyhole to turn over the tumbler. He missed it the first time. Seconds later he heard the click as the tumbler came off. With a turn of the knob, the door fell open.

The fire blazed. A stack of wood stood beside it, and above sat a mantelpiece with porcelain trinkets and a radio. A spot of wallpaper was less faded than the rest, signifying a missing picture. As he looked around the room, he realized that several pictures had been taken down. An empty rocking chair lay still beside the fire, with an old threadbare couch alongside it. The entrance to the kitchen was on his left, and the flickering light told of another fire she'd set in there. His backpack was sitting in the corner next to a bookshelf, and he wondered why she hadn't tried to hide it. Maybe there was no reason to hide it if the Gestapo men were probably on their way here right now. The cabin was silent, no sounds at all apart from the popping wood in the fireplace.

He dragged himself over to his backpack on his forearms, reached into it, and pulled out a change of clothes, maps, and a flashlight. Both his pistols were gone, but he didn't waste time wondering where she'd stashed them. Instead, he sat up against the wall and reached back inside. His papers were intact; his Luftwaffe paybook, his leave papers, and his travel orders were all properly rubber-stamped, signed, and countersigned. And in front of him, not thirty feet away, was the front door.

It took Franka thirty glorious minutes to reach the bottom of the valley and the main road into town. It had been cleared enough to let cars through, with the snow piled up at the side of the road on either side.

"National Socialist efficiency," she mumbled to herself.

Five minutes passed before a truck stopped to pick her up. A Wehrmacht soldier waved her to hop on board as he ground to a snowy halt. Franka stiffened but had little choice now. It might look even more suspicious if she didn't take the ride. She tucked her skis under her arm and tramped up toward the door the soldier had left open for her.

"Good day, Fräulein," the soldier said with a smile. "Climb on board. I'm going all the way to Freiburg."

"That would be wonderful, thank you."

She climbed into the passenger seat, doing her best to return the soldier's smile as she closed the door behind her. He was young, no older than twenty-two, even younger than she was.

"What brings you into town on a day like this?"

"A shopping trip. I didn't expect this weather. We're snowed in and running a little low on supplies."

He glanced across at her longer than was comfortable, and the truck veered toward the curb before he righted it.

She decided not to comment on the young soldier's driving skills. "I haven't used these skis in years. I'm glad you picked me up."

"My pleasure, Fräulein."

She did her best to humor him as he talked and talked, all the way into town. She told him nothing about herself, deflecting every question. It was a skill she'd honed over the years. She had it down to a fine art.

The snow-covered hills around the city came into view first, followed by the roofs and spires, coated with white. From a distance Freiburg looked like any medieval town in Europe. However, like everywhere else in Germany, Freiburg had changed under National Socialism. The Allied bombers hadn't rained destruction upon Freiburg like they had upon Hamburg, Kassel, or Cologne. Indeed, there had been only a few minor bombing raids on the city, but somehow that made the loss of her father even more severe. What had been the point of that raid in October? She wondered if the pilot or the bombardier ever thought about who they were killing when they dropped the bomb on her father's apartment block as he slept. Were they even aware that they'd killed civilians? Would they even care? Somehow she doubted it. She felt her body tensing. They would never know the kind, gentle man they'd taken from her.

The news of her father's death came via letter, and the warden had refused her appeal to go to the funeral on the grounds that "traitors to the Reich should not be shown undue compassion." It was only after she was released from prison that she was able to visit his grave, to utter faint, final goodbyes.

The sight of the soldiers manning the checkpoint on the road into town brought everything back into sharp focus. The escape she'd enjoyed in the cabin was not to be found here. The chokehold that the National Socialists had on the citizenry of Germany was plain to see. Free movement or unsanctioned travel were relics of the past. Franka handed over the packet of papers she was required to produce on demand, sometimes several times a day. The sentry examined them as she sat in silence.

"Ahnenpass?" he asked.

Franka nodded and reached into her pocket for her *Ahnenpass*, a certificate of her Aryan ancestry. The sentry took a glance at it and handed it back with a nod. She hid her shame with a smile. The old joke Hans used to tell about the Aryan lies came back to her.

"What is an Aryan?" he would ask the group.

"Blond like Hitler!"—who had dark hair.

"Tall like Goebbels!" someone else would say—Goebbels was five feet five.

"A perfect athletic specimen like Goering!"—who was a disgusting, fat slug. Jokes had landed many people in jail. The Nazis displayed little good humor. Everything derogatory was censured and carried the threat of jail or worse, no matter how funny the joke was.

The sentry motioned the truck onward. Franka deflected the soldier's offer of a drink that night, with the excuse of having a boyfriend on the Russian front. She jumped out in the center of town. Nazi flags rippled in the breeze. Hitler had explained the reasoning behind the various parts of the flag in the book he'd written during his time in jail, which Franka, and all the other kids, had been required to study in school like a religious catechism—a set of rules for life. The red background represented the social idea of the movement, the white circle in the middle spoke of the purity of its nationalistic goals, and the black swastika denoted the racial superiority of the Aryan race. The Aryans were a made-up race of blond supermen, which the Nazis had convinced the German people they belonged to. She was the perfect Aryan specimen herself—tall, athletic, blond, and with piercing blue eyes she had come to be almost ashamed of. The compliments she'd received on her perfect Aryan looks were flattering when she was a teenager. Now she resented them.

A few hundred yards away the Christmas market was bustling in the shade of the Freiburg Minster, the medieval Gothic cathedral that dominated the center of town. The cathedral was one of the few places of Catholic worship left, but only as a symbol of the religious freedoms that Hitler had promised when he first came to power. There was no Mass—the local priest had been sent to a concentration camp years ago. The Protestant churches were still open, but years earlier they had been merged to form the National Reich Church to ensure that worship was controlled, and that the head of the Protestant church in Germany was both a member of the Nazi Party and an Aryan. Church members called themselves German Christians, with "the swastika on their chests and the cross in their hearts." The National Socialists still allowed Christmas, but its future existence was far from assured. Anything that swayed belief from the Nazi cause was a threat.

Franka kept her eyes on the pavement as she shuffled along, her skis under her arm, her rucksack on her back. Several soldiers in uniform brushed past her, laughing and joking. One of them whistled at her, but her eyes didn't waver from the gray-white slush on the cobbled pavement. She wondered if she would meet anyone she knew, and if she did, would they have heard about her? Would they shun her as a traitor? She hoped not to find out.

A bell rang over the pharmacy door as she pushed her way inside. She kept her eyes to the floor as she made her way to the opiates. The tiny bottles of heroin were the first that caught her eye, but she moved on to the morphine. She bought enough for a few days, along with the syringes she would need to administer it. She took aspirin, plaster of paris, gauze, and nylon socks to fit over the man's legs and brought them to the counter. The pharmacist, a middle-aged man with a thick gray mustache, peered at her over his glasses with suspicious eyes. Franka noted the Nazi pin on his white coat.

"My brother," she smiled. "He broke his legs tobogganing last night, and we're snowed in."

"Quite the predicament," the pharmacist said. "Are you going to make up the cast yourself?"

"I'm a nurse. I'm well able to do it."

"He's a lucky boy."

"I don't know if you could call someone with two broken legs 'a lucky boy,' but I suppose you might be right."

The pharmacist smiled and handed her the brown paper bag. Franka bade him goodbye and edged out of the store, trying to look as casual as possible. Inside, she felt like she was about to vomit.

The air was fresh against her clammy skin, and a light snow was beginning. She only had to get the food before leaving. She missed the solitude of the cabin. These streets in this beautiful town had been perverted, twisted by the all-encompassing Nazi ideology that made it impossible to live a rewarding life, particularly for a woman. No woman was allowed to be a doctor, lawyer, civil servant, or judge. Juries were to be made up only of men. Women could not be trusted to make decisions—they were thought too susceptible to being controlled by their emotions. Women weren't allowed to vote either, but what good was a vote anyway? All parties other than the National Socialists had been made illegal. German women were forbidden to wear makeup or to color or perm their hair. Instead, the three *Ks* were drummed into girls from an early age: *Kinder* (children), *Kirche* (church), and *Küche* (kitchen). She could still remember her League of German Girls troop leaders urging them to forget about the ridiculous notion of a self-satisfying career. It was more important to stay home and bear strong sons that could one day serve the Reich. That was the role a woman had to play in modern Germany, and many of the girls she had known in her youth had adapted to it. Some had received the Mother's Cross—a medal the Nazis gave out to mothers who had more than five healthy Aryan children. Hilda Speigel, a girl she had been in the League of German Girls with, had already received the ultimate honor: the gold Mother's Cross, for the eight children she had by the age of twenty-seven.

Remembrances of Franka's old life swarmed like locusts around her head. Every building she walked by conjured a new memory. The site of the apartment her father had lived in for the last five years of his life was only blocks away, and she felt her footsteps slowing as she neared it. She thought of the man in the cabin. He was one of them—one of the Allies who'd perpetrated that crime. She longed for the luxury of oblivion.

She arrived at the general store. The German people were feeling the ravages of the war. The early days of the war had seen almost as much plenty in the stores as before the battles had started, but rationing began in earnest in the spring of 1942, and many commonly used items were now considered a luxury. The smell of fresh bread made her empty stomach rumble. She found a loaf, as well as some cheese, and dried meats. It was uphill most of the way home, so she tried to avoid heavier goods like the canned soups that had kept for so long in the cabin. When she had gotten as much food as her rationing card allowed, she made for the counter to use some of her father's inheritance money to pay. She remembered the lawyer as he'd read her the will. He knew that she'd spent time in jail, and although he didn't say it out loud, she suspected he knew why. The judgment was in his eyes.

Franka made her way out onto the street. It was almost two o'clock now. There was no use trying to make it back to the cabin on an empty stomach. She had kept aside enough of her ration tickets to afford lunch, and she knew a place down the street. The café was bustling with loud chatter as she arrived. Smoke hung in the air. Several soldiers sat in the corner, laughing and drinking beer. Sitting as far away from them as she could, she ordered schnitzel and potatoes and a cup of café au lait. Five minutes later her food arrived. It was heavenly, and she barely stopped to breathe as she wolfed it down. The man at the table next to her got up from his seat, leaving his newspaper—something she could hide behind. She picked it up and held it to her face. It was full of stories glorifying the führer and the brave soldiers fighting for Germany's future in Russia. She stopped reading after a few seconds and just let her eyes rest there. She was thinking about the trip back to the cabin, thinking about the man, when she heard a voice in front of her.

"Franka Gerber?"

She felt her chest contract as she lowered the newspaper. She saw the black uniform of the Gestapo before her eyes made their way up to the face of a man she had hoped she would never have to see again—Daniel Berkel.

The man placed the maps, compass, spare clothes, and his identity papers back into the backpack, just as he'd found them. He was sitting up, by the bookcase. The front door was about thirty feet away, but the back door was even closer. He could make out the white glow of sun on snow seeping underneath the door. He wasn't dressed to go outside, and escape would be impossible with his broken legs. The truth that his stubbornness had tried to fight became all too clear: without his weapons, he was at Franka Gerber's mercy, whoever she happened to be. He was still wearing the pajamas she'd put him in, but what harm would looking out do? Perhaps she was telling the truth and they were in the middle of the mountains. Perhaps not. He dragged himself along the floor. The hallway was gritty, and he could feel the particles of dirt under his palms as he crawled along. With his right hand he reached up for the door handle, pushing up on his left elbow. He moved his body out of the way as he wrenched the door open. An ocean of white burned his eyes. The cold draft cut at his exposed chest, and he felt the pain in his legs like knives into his flesh. The door opened out onto an area for firewood. Snow-covered trees began just a few feet beyond. *Nothing to see. Damn.* He closed the door.

He took a few seconds to regain his breath before crawling back into the living room. The fire was warm, and he lost a minute or two lying in front of it. What the hell was he going to do, even if they were close to the city? How was he going to get there with two broken legs? If he did make it there alive, which seemed so ridiculous as to be almost impossible, anyone who picked him up would bring him to the local hospital immediately. That would be the end, for him and the mission. More likely he would die in the snow, as he undoubtedly would have if the woman hadn't brought him back here. Perhaps she was who she said she was. Perhaps she was a friend. What were the chances of being found by someone friendly in this country of fanatics? He had seen the newsreels of enormous crowds cheering Hitler's every word, waving flags, beating on drums. The entire nation had seemingly been brainwashed into following the Nazi cause like a new religion. Why else would they do the things they did in the occupied territories? How else could they justify an organization as savage as the Gestapo? He remembered his instructor's words: "Trust no one." He'd said that the only good German was a dead one. The recruits had laughed, but there was no doubting the veracity of his words. They all believed it, just as he himself did.

The view behind the back door had told him nothing. He had to be sure. He began crawling toward the front. The cuckoo clock in the hallway by the front door struck ten o'clock. He kept on, one arm and then another, ignoring the pain in his legs. He reached the door and turned the handle, opening it an inch before moving his body out of the way to open it fully. The glare of white came again, and he saw a Volkswagen covered in snow. He pitched himself up on his palms, as high as he could. There was nothing but snow and trees as far as the eye could see. Not even a road. There was no sound. No other sign of life. It was true: they were alone up here.

He closed the front door and started making his way back to the living area. He wanted to be in bed when she got back, didn't want her to suspect that he'd been up and snooping around the house. He stopped at a hall table beneath the cuckoo clock. More out of a whim than anything else, he reached up to open the small table drawer. It opened, and he recognized the sound of sliding metal immediately. He reached in and pulled out a pistol. He would be ready, and if they did come, he was taking some of them with him.

"It's wonderful to see you. You look better than ever. How long has it been, Franka?" Berkel said.

Franka was staring at the death's-head skull on his hat. He took the cap off and put it under his arm.

"Thank you. It's been years, Herr Berkel. Four years?"

"I haven't seen you since you moved to Munich. Do you mind if I sit down for just a moment?" He pulled out the chair opposite her.

"Of course not." She had no choice in the matter.

"Please, call me Daniel. We shouldn't need to be so formal just because of my position. We're old friends, catching up, and that's all I want to do—catch up. Do you mind if I smoke?" He offered her a cigarette. She hadn't smoked for several years but took one anyway. He lit her cigarette first, then his own. Puffs of white smoke filled the air between them. She sat back, hoping it might calm her nerves. "What brings you back to Freiburg?" he continued.

"I came back to visit my father's grave, and for the reading of his will."

"Yes, of course, I saw his name on the list of dead from the last Allied bombing raid. I am sorry for your loss. Those animals don't care how many of our citizens they massacre. I long for the day when we might avenge the deaths of your father and the hundreds of thousands of German citizens murdered by the Allies."

Franka could feel her whole body shaking. "As do I, Daniel." Berkel seemed convinced.

"And I also wanted to express how sorry I was to hear about you." He took a drag from the cigarette. Franka didn't know what to say, how to answer. "I heard about what happened in Munich." She wanted to ask how but knew that he probably knew everything about everyone from Freiburg. "It's a tragedy that you were brought under the influence of those despicable traitors to the Reich."

Her heart hardened. Hans was a hundred times the man Daniel or any of his Nazi cronies would ever be. She sat still, focusing on controlling the terror below her calm surface.

"Thank you, Daniel."

"I'm so glad that the judge recognized the fact that, as a woman, you needed to be protected. Your good nature left you more susceptible to the horrific lies and propaganda that scum were spreading. I'm sorry that you went through that." He took a drag on his cigarette before continuing. "It must have been a horrible experience. I know it might be hard to recognize sometimes, but the National Socialists do want what's best for the German people."

Franka didn't react. She could tell by the earnest look on his face that he meant every word. "I was lucky. That much is certain."

"Yes. I was glad to see that you didn't end up going to the guillotine, as those other traitors did. You still have a future ahead of you as a wife and mother, and one day you'll produce sons to serve the Reich."

Daniel finished his cigarette and stubbed it out in the ashtray on the table between them. Franka had taken about three drags from hers. He leaned forward. "I know you've learned your lesson."

"Of course. I was foolish, led astray. I should have reported those swine, but I was frightened." She took a deep breath in a vain attempt to douse the pain that saying those words brought.

An elderly woman approached the table. Berkel stood up to greet her.

"Herr Berkel, it's so good to see you," she said.

"And you, Frau Goetsch. You look wonderful."

"I'm so thankful to you."

"Think nothing of it. It was my pleasure."

The old woman lifted up a bag. "I have something for you and your family."

"Oh no, I couldn't possibly accept."

"Take it, for your boys. It's for them—for all you've done for my family."

Berkel took the bag. "Thank you. I'll be sure and let the boys know you were thinking of them this Christmas."

"Bless you, Herr Berkel," she said, backing away. "Heil Hitler."

"Heil Hitler," Berkel said, and sat back down.

"Excuse me," he said.

"Who was that woman?"

"An old friend of the family who was in need. I was happy to help. I wish you'd let me help *you*, that you had come to me when those traitors tried to manipulate you."

"Perhaps if you had been there, I might have been more comfortable going to you."

"It's so good to hear you say that. I know now the judge made the right decision. It's time to get on with your life. Have you thought about how you might give back to the Reich? Nurses are always in demand, especially with our brave troops on the front getting wounded every day in Russia."

"I had that thought. I only got out of jail three weeks ago, however. I need a little time. Perhaps when Christmas is over."

"I understand. Where will you be spending Christmas?"

"Munich. That's where my life is now. I'm only back for a few days."

"Yet you have your skis with you?" he said as he glanced at the floor beside the table.

Suddenly she became aware of the morphine in her backpack, the gauze and the plaster of paris. If he searched it, this would all end.

"My father's apartment was destroyed in the bombing raid. I'm staying in our old summerhouse in the mountains. I can't say I expected to get snowed in, however."

"Yes, this weather has been quite something. But you say that you intend to make your way back to Munich for Christmas? That's just nine days away."

"That's my plan. I don't want to spend Christmas alone in that old cabin. I want to get back to Munich as soon as I can."

"I remember that cabin. We had some good times there."

Franka tried not to shudder as she remembered weekends spent in her father's cabin with him. Those college days when he was the dashing local Hitler Youth leader seemed like eons ago. Most of the other girls had been jealous. They could have him now. She noticed a wedding ring on his finger.

"So you're married?"

"Yes, for four years now. You remember Helga Dagover?"

"Of course."

"We have two sons, Bastian and Jürgen."

"Many congratulations."

"Yes, they are fine Aryan boys, just what this country needs. Of course, by the time they're grown this war will be over, and they'll be able to reap the benefits of what we're trying to sow."

Franka didn't answer. The desire to run, to escape, was almost beyond her control, and it took every fragment of strength within her to sit still.

"Would you like to see a picture of them?"

"Of course."

Berkel reached into his pocket and removed his wallet. A proud smile cracked across his face as he drew out the photograph, and his eyes lit up in a way she hadn't thought possible.

"Are they not the most beautiful boys in the world?"

"Yes."

"I do love them so. The worst part of my job is that I'm away from them so much, but they're always in my heart."

He returned the photo to his wallet. He reached into his pocket and pulled out a silver-plated cigarette case. Franka noticed the initials on it weren't his. He offered one to her once more, but she refused. It had been years since she had smoked, and the previous cigarette had added to the nausea spreading through her like scum across a stagnant pond. Berkel lit the cigarette and sat back. The man in the cabin emerged in her mind.

"You never married, Franka."

"No. I never did."

"What age are you now, twenty-six? You have so much to offer. You don't want to end up an old maid, do you? Your childbearing days are slipping by. You won't see the flower of your youth again once it's gone, you know."

"I'm aware of my age, Daniel."

"I don't mean it like that. I didn't mean to cause any offense. You're more beautiful now than ever."

"That's quite all right, Daniel, and thank you again," she said, unable to keep eye contact for more than a few seconds.

"You were quite the catch in your teenage years." He sat back in his wooden chair and clasped his hands behind his head. "Oh, yes, I remember well. All the other boys were jealous of me. I had the most beautiful girl in all of Freiburg. I felt like the luckiest boy alive. What happened to us? You never explained. You just dropped me."

I saw who you really were. I realized whom they'd turned you into. She wondered whether he was being deliberately ignorant, if this was some ploy to test her loyalties, or if he truly didn't know. Had he not figured it out by now? They had broken up in 1936, when she was nineteen. He had tried to get back with her after that, and while she was adamant about not being his girlfriend, she was careful not to push him too far away. She was fearful of his growing power and influence as a member of the local Gestapo.

On Kristallnacht in 1938, he had joined with the mobs, when the streets of Freiburg and every other town and city in Germany glistened with broken glass from the windows and storefronts of Jewish-owned businesses, when the night sky burned red from the flames of burning synagogues. Thousands died in a state-sponsored, nationwide riot against Jewish Germans, and Daniel Berkel was one of the leaders of the marauding pack of dogs dragging Jewish business owners onto the streets to be kicked and beaten. That night opened her eyes to what the Nazis were really trying to achieve in Germany. She felt changed. Much of the reason she left Freiburg was to get away from him. She abandoned Fredi to get away from him.

"That's ancient history now. Why mire ourselves in the past when the German people have such a sparkling future to look forward to?"

He smiled, but his eyes darkened. He took another drag on the cigarette before speaking again. "You've something to hide? Why not tell, so we can put the past behind us and go on as friends from here? If you're going to be living in Freiburg—"

"I'm not going to be in Freiburg. I'm moving back to Munich in the next few days, as soon as the roads clear."

Berkel took another drag from the cigarette just as the waitress came over. He ordered a beer, and Franka felt her insides tighten.

"So you found someone else?"

"It wasn't that. We grew apart. We were just children then."

"Many of the men I work with—good, loyal men, dedicated to the betterment of this country and the protection of the Reich—were married by that age. Some had children earlier than that."

"That wasn't to be for us."

The waitress came back with his beer and told him it was on the house, as it always was for the Gestapo. He didn't thank her, just leaned forward to stare at Franka again.

"So I read that you were involved with the head of those traitors in Munich. Was he to be the father of your children?"

Hans's name felt sullied by Berkel mentioning it. She brought her hands under the table, balling them into fists so tight she almost drew blood.

"That part of my life is over now." She fought back the tears. She wasn't going to cry in front of him. She'd rather die than cry in front of him.

"You were lucky. You should thank the Gestapo agents that caught him and the others. You should thank the executioner too. They did you the greatest favor the government could ever do for a person. They set you free. They set you free from the madness of the ideas those criminals were preaching, and they even had the mercy and the magnanimity to spare your life."

Each word hurt. Was she meant to be grateful to that judge for sparing her life? She'd wished so many times since for the opposite.

"It sickens me to think that such people exist." He said the word "people" as if it were a curse word. "But it's heartening to know that they received the swift justice they deserved, and that further innocents were protected from their vile influence."

"They did what they thought was best for the German people," she said. Her voice was so low that she barely heard herself.

He shook his head and took a generous mouthful of beer. "Naïve fools. Were they trying to take us back to the days of mass unemployment and social disorder in the streets? Democracy was the biggest calamity ever casted upon this country. The führer rescued us from the curse of Versailles, delivered us from the November criminals, and has cemented our place among the greatest nations in the world again."

Franka wanted to ask why he wasn't fighting on the front if he was so committed to the cause. The Gestapo didn't operate under any rule of law. He could bring her downtown to Gestapo headquarters right now, and she might never be seen again. No one would ask questions. She'd be one more disappeared enemy of the state. Her life depended entirely on the whim of this man whose heart she'd once broken.

"You're right—I was misled. I'm grateful I was spared. The leaders pressured me into attending meetings. They made it seem like it was the patriotic thing to do."

"When it was the opposite. I'm glad to see that you never fell completely under their spell. It's heartening to know that you have a second chance to make up for your mistakes."

"It was a pleasure catching up with you, Daniel, but I really should be going. I have to get back to the cabin before nightfall."

He stared across the table at her for a few seconds before he answered. "Of course. It would be a most hazardous journey in the dark of night. I wouldn't want to be responsible for holding you up."

"Quite, Daniel. If you'll excuse me," she said as she stood up.

He didn't move, just glared at her from his seat. "But wait, the roads up there are snowbound, are they not? That's why you have your skis with you."

"Yes, so I really should get going . . ."

"How did you intend to get back? You can hardly ski ten miles back up there."

"I have that all taken care of."

"How? You can't have a car with you. It must be stuck up in the snow, at the cabin."

"It is, but—"

"So how were you planning to get back?"

"I have someone waiting to give me a ride."

"Who? You don't know anyone here anymore, and after your time in jail, you can't have the best reputation."

"Well, I was going to—"

"Hitch a ride? Nonsense, I will take you."

Franka felt her heart jump. "No, I couldn't possibly inconvenience you. That would take more than an hour away from your busy schedule."

"I'm on my lunch. I can make up the time later." His eyes were boring a hole through her. She went to answer, but it was no good. He stood up. "All right, then; it's settled. I have a car outside. Are you ready to go now?"

"I just need to pay the bill."

"Leave the money on the table."

Franka threw down a few crumpled notes. Berkel didn't say another word as he led her out of the café. A black Mercedes sat outside, and he opened the back door for her to squeeze her skis and poles in. She kept the backpack with her, putting it at her feet as she sat in the passenger seat.

Just keep your mouth shut. Agree with whatever he says.

They spoke about people they'd known and old times as they drove through the city. Franka wondered whether he was investigating her, or genuinely under some illusion that they were old friends. Perhaps it was neither. Perhaps it was both, or perhaps it was something else. Franka still had to present her papers to the guard at the checkpoint. Berkel greeted him with a lazy salute, underscoring the fact that he was a superior officer. She waited until they were out of the city, and on the highway, to ask her question.

"What are your boys like?"

"Wonderful, just wonderful. They're the most beautiful things I've ever seen. They're strong young Aryans too. We're proud of them. Jürgen is just three, and he can already sing 'Deutschland Über Alles.'"

Franka went silent as Berkel told her about his sons. It gave her pause, but soon he was back preaching about the greatness of the Reich and the genius of Hitler. The minutes dragged out agonizingly. The place where he needed to drop her off came and looked like an oasis.

"I'd appreciate it if you let me out here, Daniel. You've been so kind. Lesser men would have held what I did against me forever. I've made mistakes, but I'm determined to live the best life I can from here."

Berkel pulled the car over to the side of the road and turned to her. "It is my job to be suspicious at all times, Franka, and I remain so. It was fantastic to see you, but you are not just an old friend to me. You are a convicted enemy of the state, and while I think that almost every Aryan deserves a second chance, you will need to prove your loyalty to the Reich and to our beloved führer. I hope that we will never meet in an official capacity, but know that I am watching you."

"As I said, I'm moving back to Munich within days . . ."

"And if that is the case, I wish you good luck, and I'll say, Heil Hitler."

"Heil Hitler," Franka said. Her voice was weak. She put the backpack on. He got out to help her with her skis and handed them to her.

"I enjoyed seeing you, Franka. I hope you find the peace you're searching for. Be careful who you mix with."

She nodded, and he got back into the car. She stood still as the car left.

She felt violated, reviled, disgusted. The cabin no longer felt safe, or free from the Nazi regime she despised more than ever. With little daylight left, she had not the time to stand at the side of the road analyzing their conversation, and she was glad of that. She slipped on the skis again and started up the trail toward the cabin.

Surely the fact that she'd told him that she was moving back to Munich would prevent any intrusions by the Gestapo. But what if they were looking for the man? Someone could have seen his parachute.

The journey back up the hill, with the provisions on her back weighing her down, was far more difficult than the way down, and she had to stop halfway for a rest. The light of day was shrinking to nothing, the air darkening by the moment as the cabin finally came into view. Flakes of snow meandered down. The bedroom window was unlit. Franka wondered if the man was asleep. Would he finally begin to trust her now that she'd gone all the way into town on his behalf? How much longer was the Werner Graf charade going to last? How could she trust him when she knew he was lying to her about who he was? She took off her skis as she reached the front door, and shook them off before resting them against the house. The door opened with a creak. The light of the fire colored the living room walls orange and yellow, and she wondered how the man had stocked the fireplace with wood. When she saw him, he was sitting in the rocking chair by the fire, her father's pistol in his hand, the barrel pointed at her.

Chapter 5

Franka let the rucksack slip from her shoulder and let it fall to the floor. The man stared at her and had the gun pointed at her chest. His eyes twitched in the half-light, his teeth gritted in pain. She cursed herself for not hiding the gun better. It was hard to imagine how he'd gotten out of bed, let alone made it all the way to the table by the front door.

"How did you get out of your room?"

"I'm asking the questions here."

She saw his finger tense on the trigger.

"I have your painkillers. You must be in terrible discomfort. I have food too, enough for both of us for days."

"I asked you a question. Why am I here? Why did you bring me back to this cabin?"

His ingratitude was vexing her, and she felt her temper, blunt as it usually was, beginning to rise. He was terrified—a stranger in a hostile land. She was thankful he hadn't pulled the trigger as soon as she'd walked through the door. "Simple necessity. It was too far to the nearest hospital, and I had no way of getting you there."

"Have you told anyone else that I'm here?"

"No."

"Why not?"

"Because you asked me not to. You said even the local authorities knowing you were here might compromise your mission."

He stared on, the gun still pointed at her. He didn't seem to know what to say next.

"I told you, my name is Franka Gerber. I'm from Freiburg, and this was my parents' summer cabin. They're both dead now. My father died just a few months ago in a bombing raid on the city. My mother died eight years ago, of cancer." She thought to tell him about Fredi but realized that she wouldn't be able to without breaking down—she was close enough to that already. "I brought you back here because you needed help. You would have died out there. It is an absolute miracle I found you. There is no one else around here for miles."

"Why are you keeping me here?" His voice quivered as he spoke, perhaps from the pain he was in, perhaps from something else.

She stared at the barrel of the gun. "Because I have no other choice. The roads are closed. I can't get you down to the main road. It's just not possible with your broken legs." She pointed at the bag. "I have plaster of paris, gauze, and everything else I need to set them in casts. I can do this for you if you let me, but I need you to trust me."

"How do I know you're not an Allied agent, keeping me here to win over my trust?"

"I'm not an Allied agent. I'm just a nurse, from Freiburg."

The man let the gun drop a few inches before raising it up again.

"I'm going to take off my hat and gloves now," Franka said.

He nodded, and she did as she said, letting them fall to the ground. She inched toward him with her hands out, as if approaching a frightened dog.

"You have nothing to fear. I'm not working for anyone. I don't have an agenda."

"What are you planning to do with me?"

"I want to see you walk out of here. I don't want you to tell me about your mission. You don't have to talk. I just need you to trust me and know that I don't mean you any harm."

Franka tried to hide it, but her voice was shaking. She motioned toward the chair beside her. He didn't refuse, so she sat down.

"Who are you going to turn me over to?"

He raised his hand to cough, never letting the gun waver from her.

"I'm not planning on turning you over to anyone—not unless you want me to."

"There's no phone here? No one for miles around?"

"We're alone. You can shoot me now, but you'd be killing yourself too. It's snowing again. We could be here for weeks. You won't be able to travel, and you'll die here. You need to trust me. I don't mean you any harm."

"Can you take me into the city?"

"No. You'd never make it. I barely made it myself, and I know these trails. I've been coming up here my whole life. You need to realize that we're stuck with each other for a while. We need to trust one another. I must say I'm finding it difficult to trust you with that gun pointed at me."

"You had no right to take my guns from me in the first place."

"It was a precaution, nothing more. You had no need for them."

"How do I know that?"

"Because if I wanted you dead I'd have left you out in the snow. You were hours from death when I found you."

She could see his eyes yielding, perhaps to logic, or perhaps to necessity.

The man lowered the gun a few inches and closed his eyes for a second. "How do I know you're telling me the truth, about any of this?"

"If I were some kind of Allied agent, how on earth would I have known you were going to land in the snow, in the middle of nowhere, in Germany? Why would I be here, in the mountains, waiting for you to drop out of the sky? Your theory is someone found you when you were unconscious and deposited you here to be snared by a woman?"

He closed his eyes but didn't speak.

"Who else is here other than the Gestapo? The Gestapo doesn't deal in subtlety and nuance. They don't try to coax information out of their victims. If I were Gestapo, I'd be torturing you right now."

"Why on earth would I be afraid of the Gestapo?"

"Well then, why won't you let me report you to them?"

The man opened his eyes and opened his mouth to speak, but she didn't let him.

"I can help you. I want to help you. I went all the way into Freiburg today for you. I could have gone to a village closer to here, but they wouldn't have had the painkillers you need. Put the gun down, and let me help you, and then, when the roads open, I'll deliver you to the local authorities, and you can resume your recovery in a Luftwaffe hospital."

The man looked at the ground and put the gun in his lap. His voice was weak, drained of life. "Why are you doing this for me?"

"Because I'm a nurse. Because you needed help." *Because I needed to be valuable again. I needed to do something useful, something good.*

"You don't need to deliver me to the authorities. I can look after myself."

"Whatever you wish, Herr Graf. I really don't care. Think of this as a recovery ward in a hospital. I'm here to do a job, and once you're gone I'm no longer responsible. Does that sound fair?"

"Yes, it does. Thank you, Fräulein." His body drooped. The color had drained from his face.

"You're welcome. You must be half-starved. Have you had anything to eat?"

"I didn't make it to the kitchen."

"You wouldn't have found much in there."

Franka let out a deep breath. She still didn't know who he was, but that conversation could wait. Right now she needed to be a nurse again, and that felt good. She reached into the bag and removed a small bottle of morphine. He didn't speak as she drew out the syringe and filled it full of the clear liquid.

"This will help you with the worst of the pain. I have enough for the next three days or so, and then you'll be back to aspirin. You might feel dizzy, faint, or drowsy, and we'll keep a bucket for your vomit, but you'll be spending the next few days in bed anyway. There's no reason for you to be out here."

"I understand."

"You're not my prisoner," Franka said as she flicked the barrel of the syringe with her fingernail. "I'm a friend. You'll come to see that in time. You're free to go as soon as the roads open, or you can stay a little longer should you wish to continue your recovery here."

"Thank you."

"Now how are we going to get you back into that bed?"

"I crawled out here. I can crawl back in."

"And how exactly do you suggest crawling back into the bed? You won't be able to haul yourself up."

"I can manage it."

"I have a better idea." Franka went around behind him and tilted the rocking chair backward so that his legs were off the ground. He stifled the pain, biting down on his fist. She put a hand on his shoulder. "I'm sorry. I need to get you back into the bed first, and then I'll give you the painkillers."

"It's just a little discomfort. I'm fine."

Franka took her hand off the man's shoulder and pushed the rocking chair. He kept the gun on his lap. She didn't reach for it or even ask for it back. Pushing him proved harder than she'd anticipated, and progress back to the bedroom was slow. Thankfully, it was only twenty feet away, and after a few aborted attempts, they arrived at the bed.

The man tried to haul himself up, his thick arms struggling with his weight until she reached under his armpits, helping him up and over. He reached back for the pistol and shoved it under his pillow. Best to let him keep it, to show him that she trusted him, that she wasn't the enemy. He lay back, the pain he was trying to hide etched on his face. He was sweating, panting, and she left to get him a glass of water before coming back and administering the drugs.

"It will take about twenty minutes for the drugs to start working, and then I'll set your cast tomorrow morning. In the meantime, I'll get you something to eat before any nausea sets in."

The man nodded. She smiled at him before going back to the kitchen and returning with a plate of fresh bread and cheese. He ate it in seconds and collapsed back onto the pillow.

It was after seven o'clock. "I'm going to leave you now. Try to relax and get a good night's sleep. We'll talk tomorrow." *I'll be the one asking the questions then.*

The man closed his eyes, the drug-induced euphoria kicking in. A tiny smile came across his face.

"Good night, Fräulein," he whispered.

She covered him with a thick layer of blankets, extinguished the oil lamp, and shut the door behind her as she left. He'd picked the lock once. Locking the door would be useless now. She would have to trust him, because she knew he wasn't giving up her father's gun.

The fatigue she'd denied all day came to bear, and she shuffled into the kitchen to get some ham and bread. As much as she wanted to go to bed, she knew that the fire wouldn't last the night, and the supply of wood was getting perilously low. She finished her meager meal, and after summoning the energy, she put on her hat, coat, and gloves and ventured back outside. Fortunately, there was just enough chopped wood remaining on the back porch to get them through the night. She would need to get more tomorrow. It was up to her. Everything would be.

Daniel Berkel haunted her thoughts as she lay in bed. His ice-blue eyes were the last thing she saw before she finally succumbed to sleep.

The house was cold when she woke. The fires had died overnight, and the air in the cabin was bordering on glacial. The mountainous layer of blankets on her bed was the only sanctuary, but she knew it was a temporary one. Hunger, and her desire to check on the man, drove her feet onto the floor. Her coat was hanging by the bed, and she put it on over her nightdress before emerging from her bedroom. With no sign of life from the other bedroom, she made herself a breakfast of liverwurst, bread, and cheese. The snow had come in earnest again last night, and the car was almost invisible now. Her footprints would be covered at least, and with the roads closed for a few more days the man would have some time to recover from the worst of his pain. The extra layers of snow outside would also offer some protection against any unwanted visits from Berkel. Perhaps by the time the snow had melted and the roads were passable, he would assume that she'd moved back to Munich. Wishful thinking. The Gestapo never assumed anything. She would need to finish that hiding place under the floorboards as soon as possible.

Franka went to the man, pushing his bedroom door open with two fingers. He was still asleep, lying on his back, snoring.

"You sleep, whoever you are," she whispered. "That's the best thing for you." She stayed in the doorway for another minute or two, listening to the sound of him breathing, hoping to hear him say something in English again, to cement her convictions. He didn't say a word, in English or German. She left him. The matter of warming the cabin was more pressing.

The snow was three feet deep beyond the back porch. She took the sled and dragged it into the woods, ax in hand. Her father had taught her these things when she was a child. He hadn't loved her any less because she was a girl but hadn't babied her either. He taught her how to gather wood, season it, and set the fire. He taught her how to shoot, set traps, and skin and prepare the kill. He'd also introduced her to the works of Goethe, Hesse, and Mann, as well as the now-banned novel by Remarque, *All Quiet on the Western Front*. She thought about her father for the two hours she spent collecting wood. The Allies had killed him, and now one of them was asleep in his cabin. She tried to mentally separate the stranger in the spare room from the men who'd dropped those bombs. She knew that the Nazis were the aggressors, but where was the justice in carpet-bombing civilians? Tens of thousands of innocents had already died, and the bombings were only intensifying. Then again, the enemy of her enemy was her friend. Despite what they'd done, the Allies had to have some kind of right on their side, and helping the man could afford her the chance to get some measure of revenge on the Nazis.

Franka piled the wood inside the back door in crisscrossed open stacks to ensure minimum drying time. It would need to dry quickly, because it seemed that the winter weather, like the war itself, would only get worse before it got better.

It was almost eleven in the morning when she went back to his bedroom. His eyes flicked open as she entered. They were murky, full of pain.

"How are you feeling?"

"I'm fine. I think I could use some more painkillers. I slept through the night, but I fear they might be wearing off now."

"Of course." She had the prepared syringe in her hand as she went to the bed. He took his arm out from under the deep layer of blankets and presented it to her. He took the shot wordlessly and, without flinching, watched her push the needle into his arm.

She brought him a light meal afterward and waited to speak until he'd finished it.

"I'm going to set the casts on your legs now. They'll give you a far better chance of making a satisfactory recovery, and it shouldn't be too painful while you're under the morphine."

His eyes were half-closed, but he nodded.

"I'm going to have to wash your legs first; then I'll put on the stockings."

His answer came in the form of another nod, his eyes closed.

Franka warmed up some water and formed a good, soapy lather in an old basin she'd found under the kitchen sink. She removed the primitive wooden splints and saved the wood for that night's fire. Franka washed the bottom half of his legs. She knew he probably needed an all-over sponge bath, but he would have to do that himself. That didn't seem proper here. She slipped on the stockings, which ran from his knees to his ankles, and then wrapped the gauze bandages around them. As she mixed the plaster of paris, words tumbled out of her mouth, partly to make him feel more comfortable, partly to hear a voice in the cold silence of the room.

"I worked as a nurse for three years in Munich, at the university hospital. I saw a lot of broken legs. The injuries became worse as the war went on. I saw more and more young boys at the start of their lives, their whole futures ahead of them, with missing legs, or arms, or eyes. And then it wasn't just soldiers anymore—it was women and children too, crushed in their own beds or burned to a crisp by Allied bombs. Thousands and thousands of them. We hadn't enough room for the bodies in the morgue, not nearly. We had to lay them in the alley, pile them on top of one another."

She didn't speak for a few minutes as she dipped the gauze into the plaster mix and wrapped it around a leg.

"Did you ever work as a nurse around here?"

"No, I left for Munich after I graduated college. I took the opportunity to get out of Freiburg as soon as I could."

"Why did you want to leave?"

The sound of his voice startled her. His eyes were open, and he peered down at her.

"I was young. I broke up with my boyfriend. I wanted a new start. I shirked my responsibilities to my family, and I left. I thought somehow that people in Munich might be different."

"Were they?"

"Some, but not many."

She finished the first leg, leaving the plaster of paris to set, and moved to the other.

"It seems like I'm answering all the questions when I'm the one who found you in the snow."

The man didn't answer.

"Why did you bail out over the mountains, and what happened to the plane? I didn't hear anything. Why would you have bailed out there unless your plane was in trouble?"

He took a few seconds to answer, and when he did his voice was garbled and groggy. "I'm so sorry, Fräulein Gerber, but I cannot speak about my reasons for being here. That could compromise my mission and put brave soldiers on the front lines in danger."

Franka brought her eyes back down to the man's leg and bit her lip. "So then tell me something about yourself. Where are you from?"

"I'm from Karlshorst, in Berlin. Do you know the city?"

"Not well. I went a couple of times when I was a girl with my League of German Girls group. We saw the sights, Unter den Linden, the Reichstag, the Stadtschloss."

"It must have been exciting for a young girl to be at the center of the Reich like that."

She finished applying the gauze and began wetting the bandages in the plaster of paris. The other leg was already drying. She ran fingers over the surface of the cast. It was good.

"Do you trust me?" she asked.

"Of course. You're a loyal citizen of the Reich."

"Why were you pointing a gun at me last night, then?"

"I wasn't sure where I was. I'm trained not to trust anyone. There is too much at stake. I see the error of my ways now. I see the kind of person you are. I admire anyone who'd go to such lengths as you have for a member of the führer's armed forces. You're obviously someone who recognizes the value in every serviceman as we strive toward the final victory."

Franka almost laughed at the rhetoric the man was regurgitating but managed not to. What was he really thinking?

"Why didn't you ask me to contact anyone when I was in town? What about your wife and daughters? Do they even know you're alive?"

"That could compromise my mission. I need to ask that you not report to anyone that you've seen me, let alone the fact that I'm here."

Franka went to the window, stepping over the hole in the floorboards to get there. She threw back the curtain. The snow drifting down was just visible outside. "The snow is coming down again. The roads are going to be closed for days. Weeks maybe. You're not going anywhere for a long time. You need to start trusting me. I could be the only friend you've got."

She picked up the basin, threw in the medical supplies, and stormed out of the bedroom, shutting the door behind her.

A day passed, and then the next. The man lolled in morphine-induced delirium most of the time, and they spoke little. He emerged from his stupor on the third day. His pain was decreasing, and she had given him the last of his morphine shots that morning. It was two o'clock in the afternoon. His door was closed, but she imagined he could hear the radio programs she was listening to—none of them sanctioned by the National Socialists. If he was such a loyal subject, why didn't he object? What she was doing was illegal, and enough to land her back in jail. She sat in the rocking chair, staring past her book. She tried to reason that he was who he said he was, but there was no getting past what he'd said in his sleep, what she'd heard. If he were Luftwaffe, even a spy, he would have asked her to get in contact with someone when she was in town. Even if what he said were true, and he was nervous about the Gestapo finding out about his mission, there should have been someone to call. Surely someone would have wanted to know if he was alive or dead. She put the book in her lap and rubbed her eyes in frustration. She placed several pieces of wood on the fire and watched for a few seconds as the flames engulfed them. It seemed like there was only one thing to do.

He was awake and staring at the ceiling as she shoved the door open.

"I need to tell you who I am. If you are who you say you are, then you'll likely be disgusted with me, and the next week or two that we're forced to spend together is going to be difficult. But I need to tell you. Perhaps then you'll open up to me."

"Fräulein, there's no need for any loose talk. The less we know about each other, the better. I'm most grateful for all that you've done for me, but I can't let you compromise my mission."

"What mission? What mission could a Luftwaffe airman possibly be on in the Black Forest Mountains in wintertime? I think you're here by mistake. I also believe that you're planning on trying to escape as soon as you're well again. That's your business as long as it doesn't compromise my safety."

The man seemed shocked. "I would never do anything to hurt you. Not now that I know—"

"Do you have any idea why I was prying up the floorboards when you woke?" The man didn't answer, just looked on. "I was prying up the floorboards so I could hide you. So when the Gestapo come, which they inevitably will, you won't be lying in this bed."

"Fräulein—"

"The Gestapo will come," she repeated. "I ran into an old boyfriend of mine, who's a captain in the Gestapo. I didn't tell him that you were here, but he will come, particularly if they're already looking for you." She leaned over the bed, both hands on the blanket. "I'll tell you who I am, and at the end of my story, if you still insist that you're a Luftwaffe airman, I'll look after you here for the next few days, and you can limp away when the weather clears. Or else you can trust me, and I can help you."

The man didn't answer. His face was pale. He reached for the glass of water she'd left for him by the bed and then looked at the hole in the floorboards. Silence filled the air.

"I'm listening," he said.

Chapter 6

The arrival of another new chancellor in 1933 didn't seem momentous or noteworthy. There had been many, and little seemed to improve. Life was still hard. The worldwide depression was getting worse, and Germany appeared to have been stricken the hardest. The newspapers said that more than fifteen million people, 20 percent of the population at the time, were living at subsistence level. This new man, this Hitler, was regarded as an upstart, a bad joke. His National Socialist party had never achieved more than 37 percent of the vote, but the president had named him chancellor. Either way, the "little Austrian corporal," as his political opponents had referred to him, could never last long. He and his brown-shirted rabble would be run out of power once the republic had solved the infighting that had split the political powers apart. And besides, Hitler could not have really meant what he said in his speeches about his intention to tear the republic apart and start again, or about his determination to avenge Germany's defeat in the world war, or about the Jews. A statement released to the papers by one of his spokesmen was largely ignored: "You must realize that what has happened in Germany is no ordinary change. Parliamentary and democratic times are passed. A new era has begun."

That same week Franka learned new words like "lymphoma" and "metastasized" and saw her father cry for the first time. Fredi didn't understand, and his mother hugged him tight to her breast as he smiled that beautiful smile at her. She urged them to be brave. They had been through so much already. The future held only wonderful things. She would beat this cancer, and they would go on together. This was only the beginning of their lives. She wasn't even forty. It didn't matter what the doctors said. Faith would bring her through this, just as it had before, just as it had when Fredi was born, and all of the times with him after.

The cancer spread.

Within weeks, Hitler had consolidated his power. The rights of free speech, press, and public assembly were abolished, and thus the German experiment with freedom and democracy ended. The German citizenry ceded absolute power to Hitler and his Nazis without so much as a whimper. The people didn't seem to feel oppressed by the new regime. They had no great faith in a dysfunctional and poorly designed democratic system. Kids began to wear Nazi armbands to school, and the new greeting of extending one's arm while saying "Heil Hitler" became a way of signaling loyalty to the party.

The enthusiasm for a leadership that promised to place Germany back on its pedestal as one of the great nations of the world was contagious. Franka felt it. Almost every young person she knew felt it. It seemed like the German people were on the brink of something momentous and incredible. The support for the new National Socialist system came from all sides. Franka even noticed in the paper that an organization called the Association of German National Jews had voiced their support for the new Nazi regime.

Franka saw the change almost immediately. A new ruling class was rising in cities and towns throughout Germany, and they were determined to make their presence known. Fortified by the party emblems in their buttonholes, the party-membership cards in their pockets, and the swastikas on their sleeves, the previously obscure and unnoticed group began to assert themselves. Josef Donitz, a local grocer, began wearing a storm trooper's uniform to work. Within weeks he took over the local government without the formality or troubles of an election. The local fire chief, a lifetime friend of Franka's father, was elbowed out of his job by a junior fireman who was a known alcoholic and just happened to be a member of the party. Employees with party credentials spoke sharply to management, who began to listen respectfully. On every level of social and political life, the National Socialist revolution manifested itself as a kind of seepage upward—the scum rising to the top.

Franka's mother's determination pushed her past the timelines that the doctors laid out for her. For Sarah, "six months to live" meant "I'll see you next year to make you eat your words." She wanted to spend her time outside, in the wondrous natural playground that seemed to stretch without boundary all around them. Franka's father, Thomas, bought the cabin in the mountains from his uncle Hermann, who had used it as a hunting lodge on his expeditions to shoot red deer and boar. Franka and her mother took to refurbishing the cabin while Thomas worked on making it habitable in time for the warmer months. They spent most of that summer of 1933 up there, luxuriating in their time together. Franka grew to adore the sight of her family sitting outside the cabin as she returned with her friends from a hike in the mountains. On those warm summer nights when the sun set behind the cabin, bathing the sky and trees in orange and red, when the smell of food on the stove mixed with the smoke from her father's pipe, it seemed like they'd found their own little piece of heaven. At the end of that glorious summer, when Sarah declared that she was going to see the same again the next year, Fredi wrapped loving arms around her. Franka and her father remained silent. Only Fredi seemed to believe it was possible, but time would prove him right.

School changed. The Nazis were determined to be the party of youth. Commanding and controlling the allegiances of Germany's youth was a fundamental goal. The influence of the National Socialist revolution was evident when Franka returned to Freiburg after that summer. The Nazi flag was hoisted in every classroom, and suddenly portraits of Adolf Hitler, the demigod at the head of the nation, appeared in place of crucifixes on the walls. The visage of a man she wouldn't have recognized a year before was now in every classroom. Books from the school library that were deemed subversive were taken out, piled high, and burned in the yard. Franka asked the librarian what they had taken and was told that the local party members had removed any books, fact or fiction, that expressed a liberal idea, or suggested that the people themselves, rather than the führer, should control their own destinies. New books on how the National Socialists had rescued Germany from the abyss of the Weimar Republic soon filled the gaps on the shelves. These new books were written in childish, simple language, but none of the teachers complained. They all became members of the National Socialist Teachers League. Eager to retain their jobs, and under pressure from the local government, they began championing the new ideas of the Nazis. Franka's favorite teacher, Herr Stiegel, was one of the few to protest the new ways, insisting that his lessons remain the same as they had been before the new government came to power. He lasted two weeks, and when Franka and some of the other students went to visit him at his old house outside town, they found it empty. They never saw him again. Nina Hess boasted afterward that she had informed on him to one of the local Nazi leaders. She was rewarded with a red sash signifying her loyalty to the National Socialist regime, which she wore every day for the rest of the school year.

No one wanted to be left behind, and Franka found herself swept up in the tidal wave of enthusiasm for the new dawn of the Aryan people. The Nazis had started using that term, "Aryan," to describe the characteristics of ideal Germans. Franka was undoubtedly one of the superrace they described. There was something gratifying in being told by the government that your blond hair and blue eyes were perfect, that they made you the ideal German. She didn't know any other races, but the National Socialists insisted that she and her friends were blood born into a master race, and that they were superior to all others. It felt good. She felt part of something important.

The decision to join the League of German Girls came easily. All her friends already had. She was almost seventeen then, and a bit old to be a member, but the promise of possibly being a group leader spurred her on. She didn't want to be left out, and besides, this was not a time to stand on the sidelines. This was a time for bold action. So she joined, despite the protestations of her parents, who seemed wary of the Nazi Party at almost every level. Franka Gerber was the model of the magnificent youngster that Hitler prophesized would help Germany dominate the world, and she wasn't going to let any old-fashioned notions stand in her way. She was going to do her bit for the cause of the German people.

Franka cherished her uniform of a white blouse with a loose black tie, pinned tight with the emblem of a swastika, over a navy skirt. The girls of the league marched in much the same way as the boys in the Hitler Youth who eyed them. They performed drills and did calisthenics and went on long hikes, often camping out under the stars, where they sang songs glorifying the führer and longing for the day when they might provide strong sons for a future war effort. A sisterhood developed between the girls. Their common goals and focused efforts brought them together. It felt wonderful to be accepted, to be valued, to be superior.

Daniel was a troop leader in the Hitler Youth and led the drills as they jogged through town in swastika-emblazoned singlets, singing "the old must perish, the weak must decay." Truly they were the finest of German youth, slim and lithe, as fast as greyhounds, and as hard as Krupp steel, just as Hitler himself had demanded. And Daniel was the finest of them all and directed the younger members with a strict but fair countenance. With flushed cheeks, all the girls talked about him and whispered behind their hands as he strode past. He and Franka came together like magnets—all that was strong and beautiful about the new Germany encapsulated between them. His father, who had been unemployed before the National Socialist revolution, was now a leading member of the local council. Franka never saw him without his Nazi pin on his chest, or the Nazi armband adorning his bicep. His son was the realization of his dreams, the promise of a new and better life for the Aryan race.

Daniel was stern with his recruits but reserved a tenderness that he seemed to show only her. He was ambitious and forward-looking, serious and determined. He was the perfect boyfriend for the exciting times she was living through. She found herself drawn in deeper and deeper. It was the end of school, just before graduation, when she took him home to meet her parents for the first time. Daniel was respectful and polite. He wore his Hitler Youth leader's uniform to dinner and gave the Nazi salute as Franka's father opened the door to him. Franka's mother stepped forward, doing her best to smile as he greeted her. They made their way to the table, and Franka sat down next to him. Fredi sat in his usual spot at the end of the table. Daniel greeted him with a nod. He wasn't shy toward her parents, however, and spoke of his plans to join the newly formed Gestapo, the elite police force, and about the need to protect the revolution from spies and malingerers. That was the first time Franka ever heard the phrase "enemies of the state." Her parents retained their polite demeanor, but she saw them glancing toward one another during the meal through slit eyes, could feel their judgment. She knew what was coming after he left.

Franka's father carried Fredi up to bed. Her mother waited until he got back downstairs before she sat Franka down. She put a pale hand on Franka's leg. She looked tired all the time now, her beauty dulled by the unseen enemy within her. Her bloodshot eyes were earnest but calm.

"How serious is it with Daniel? I know you've been seeing each other awhile."

"I love him, Mother. You were only a little older than I am now when you met Father."

Thomas sat down, rubbing his eyes. "I was twenty-two, your mother nineteen. You're just seventeen and still in school. We're wondering if Daniel is a distraction to your studies. You're so involved with this League of German Girls now. It seems that you're spending all your free time with them."

"I love my troop. I'm part of something. You don't know anything about what's going on in this country. You're stuck in the old world of the kaiser and the Weimar idiots who ran Germany into the ground."

"The old world?" Sarah said. "Who taught you these things?"

Franka fought back the sympathetic emotions telling her to comfort her mother. That wouldn't have been the patriotic thing to do. This was an opportunity to convince her parents that every German had a duty to help with the National Socialist revolution.

"We're worried about you," her mother said.

"Worried about what? I have the comradeship of the other girls in the league. Even my teachers all express the glory of the new movement. Everyone seems to but you."

"So tell me about your glorious revolution," Thomas said, his voice low.

"You only have to look at the statistics in the newspaper. Hitler is ending the depression. Unemployment is dropping to levels no one could have dreamed of before the führer swept to power. The German workman is productive once again. Surely that is an achievement worth lauding?"

"Yes," said her father, "but think about how it's being done. The wheels of industry are beginning to turn again—war industry. Hitler is taking us on a path to war. And those statistics you're talking about don't include women, or Jews—two groups that have been frozen out of the labor force."

"Hitler is making Germany strong again."

"For the people, or the Nazis themselves? This will end in war."

"The führer is being praised all over the world. Inge, my troop leader, showed us an article in the paper where David Lloyd George, the British prime minister during the last war, called Hitler a great leader. He wishes the British had a statesman of their own like him."

"He sounds like a fool," Sarah said.

"I know the Nazis better than he does," her father said. "They are wolves preying on the German people, and I'm afraid, Franka. I'm afraid of the effect they're having on you. Being with a boy like Daniel is only going to exacerbate that effect."

"I've found my place within the revolution, Father. The National Socialists are instituting policies for the good of all Germans—you included."

"What about women?" Sarah repeated. "They've been barred from many sections of the workplace. And the Jews? They're being frozen out of German society."

"I don't know about the Jews. They'll find their place in our new society."

"Have you not listened to Hitler's speeches? This man you follow proudly preaches hatred against the Jews. And what about your brother? What place is there for him in this new, perfect Aryan world?"

"I don't know anything about that." Franka stood up. "I think we've had enough political discourse for one night."

She left them there, and her determination to follow the path of National Socialism only strengthened within her. She wasn't going to let their quaint notions hold her back. This was her time, not theirs.

The next day, as Daniel held her in his strong arms, he asked how she thought the dinner went.

"It went well," she said. "My parents thought you were an upstanding young man, and an ideal partner for me—the very picture of a young, Aryan National Socialist."

Franka, like all the others, had been encouraged to report on her parents' opinions and thoughts. All contrary thinking had to be rooted out at the source. She knew that any word to him would be reported to the local authorities. They would have dinner with his parents from now on.

Sarah proved everyone but Fredi wrong and indeed lived to see the summer of 1934. And though Franka was busy with her troop, she tried to make it up to the cabin to see her family as much as she could. Fredi's body was growing, but his mind remained mired in childhood, as they had always known it would. The sweetness of his nature and the purity of his soul overwhelmed anyone who met him. He was perfect, untouched by the evil swirling all around him—above it. He and Sarah grew closer and closer as her health deteriorated. They all still hoped for the miracle she'd promised them, but with the passing of time, its possibility seemed more remote. Franka missed much of that idyllic last summer with them. There always seemed to be something to do with her troop, and there were so many young girls who needed guidance from someone as experienced and committed as she was. She knew her parents understood, even if they voiced their disapproval.

Franka was named troop leader at the end of the summer. Her mother missed the ceremony where she received her sash, had been too ill that day. Daniel was there, however, leading the applause, shining in the sun.

Those last few months of her mother's life were agonizing in their beauty, miserable in their wonder. Her mother slipped away with effortless grace. They had the escape of one last Christmas together, and then the new year came with a ruthless reality. Sarah wanted to be at home. Her sisters came with their plethora of children but eventually went home to Munich. Sarah clung to life, defying expectations, and when the end finally came it was a surprise. Franka had somehow hoped—no, believed—that the doctors were all wrong, and that miracles could happen.

Sarah was with her family as she lay dying on that freezing January morning. Franka remembered her grandfather explaining that it was up to her to look after Fredi now, and that her brother could never truly understand, but she knew he was wrong. Fredi sat by the bed, resting his head on his mother's chest, never crying and never moving. He knew exactly what she needed and was selfless in giving it. No one else knew what to say, or think, or do. Only he truly understood.

Sarah asked to speak to Franka alone, and the others left the room. The light of the morning was dull through the window and shone white against her mother's pale skin. Her hair was gray now, the fire in her eyes reduced to embers. Her hand was cold as Franka took it. Somehow Franka wasn't crying.

"My beautiful daughter," she said, squeezing Franka's hand with surprising strength. "I'm so proud of the young woman you are, so excited for the strong, mature woman and mother I know that you'll become. You're going to be a wonderful nurse. Don't let anyone dictate to you who you are, or what's in your soul. Only you know that. Remember that you're my daughter, my beautiful, intelligent girl, and you always will be. I'll be with you always. I'll never leave."

Franka had to wipe away the tears to see her mother's face.

"Don't let the new ideas of the National Socialists change you or let hatred twist your soul. Remember who you are."

The funeral was five days later, attended by all of the members of Franka's troop, as well as most of the local Hitler Youth. Franka wore her League of German Girls uniform, and Daniel held her as she cried afterward, her mother's final words echoing through her.

The rest of the school year passed in a blur, and summer was hollow and joyless. Her family tried to re-create the times in the cabin from summers past, but Franka found more comfort in the comradeship of the troop she now led. With her mother gone, her father had to take time off at the factory to look after Fredi. Franka couldn't be expected to give up all of her commitments to look after her younger brother. She helped out where she could, but with the promise of university beckoning, she didn't want to create a precedent. She had her own life to live, her own cause to dedicate herself to. Her father had always encouraged her independence, so he allowed her to shirk her commitments to her family, to her own brother. University began in September 1935. She started her studies, and Daniel was with her every step of the way. It was then that he began his Gestapo training.

Her family life now fractured, it was painful for Franka to spend time at home. She wanted to break away from the painful memories of her mother's passing that haunted her there. Franka realized that Fredi had drawn strength from their mother, and no matter how much she or her father tried, they could never replace her. Fredi was still his same cheerful self, a bright light in the darkness, but his body betrayed him more and more.

In October of 1935, her father ordered Fredi's wheelchair as a temporary measure, although they both knew that he'd likely never walk again. Fredi delighted in his new mode of transport, seeing it as a game. Franka often pushed him through the town, where he waved to everyone he saw on the street. Almost everyone returned his smiles. The party members were the only exception, strutting along with their chests out, brandishing their armbands and pins on their lapels. They seemed annoyed by his cheerful demeanor. Franka grew to despise their glares.

Later that fall her father came to her. They had just finished dinner and cleared the plates away. Evening meals were not the same now. Franka's father insisted on preparing the same recipes her mother had, but he cut corners and had no flair for cooking. She was reading to Fredi, one of those fairy tales he loved so much. The book was dog-eared and frayed, yet he never grew tired of hearing those same stories, over and over. Her father put on the radio and tuned it to one of the Swiss stations that reported the news with some semblance of accuracy. He sat down beside his children.

"Thank you for not reporting me for listening to the foreign stations."

Franka felt her cheeks flush. "Oh, Father, I would never report you."

"I know they put pressure on you to tell them what I'm doing, and since Daniel is preparing for life in the Gestapo . . . I realize the strain you're under."

Franka sat there, remembering Daniel's words from just a week before. "The German people are your family," he had said. "And your loyalty should be to them."

Franka knew that he wanted her to report something, to give him a crumb of information to feed his new masters with, but she didn't say a word. She knew that her father could be jailed for listening to the foreign radio stations, or for reading the books he'd insisted on keeping despite the new laws, or for the casual remarks he made about the regime. There were so many things. Several girls she knew had already reported their parents. Gilda Schmidt's father had spent weeks in jail for a derogatory comment he'd made about the Nazis and was being monitored by the Gestapo now. Gilda had reported him for saying that Hitler was a dangerous warmonger.

"The führer is eager to have everyone support his brave intentions," Franka said, hearing the words of her instructors coming out of her own mouth. "He is determined that enemies of the state be identified so that they can be educated in the correct ways of serving the German nation."

"That doesn't sound like you," her father said.

"What are you talking about?"

"That sounds like Daniel or one of the Nazis who stomp about downtown speaking. Remember who you are, Franka."

"I do, Father."

"I have something I want to show you." He placed the newspaper, the *People's Observer*, on the table in front of her. The headline spoke of the heroic new laws created to subjugate the threat of the Jews in Germany. "The Nazis have said that Jews cannot be German citizens. They've had their citizenship stripped from them and are not allowed to intermarry with Germans any longer. This is the brave revolution to which you're so committed."

It took her a few seconds to answer. "I'm sure that the führer knows what's best for Germany. I asked some of the local leaders of the league just the other day. They assured me that it was better to focus on the bigger picture and to leave the details to the führer."

"And that satisfied you?"

Franka didn't answer. She picked up another book to read to her brother.

Her father interrupted her before she had a chance to begin. "I have something else to show you." He took another newspaper out. "This paper is called *The Striker*. It's controlled and published by the Nazi Party, just like the *People's Observer*, but this one is less surreptitious with its intentions."

Franka took the paper. She'd seen it on newsstands but had never picked it up before. The pencil-drawn picture on the front cover was of a caricatured Jewish man, his long curls hanging down over his dark suit, strings of saliva dripping from his razor-sharp teeth. He held a curved dagger in his claw as he bent over a beautiful Aryan-looking woman asleep in bed. The headline read "The Jews Are Our Misfortune." Franka could feel tears welling up in her eyes. She turned to Fredi, but he was playing with a toy train he'd found.

"This is a rag," she said. "This is a ridiculous rag."

"This newspaper has a circulation of several hundred thousand. Hitler has spoken many times of its journalistic integrity."

"I don't know what to say. The system isn't perfect, but . . ."

The words fell away. She had nothing.

"We didn't raise you to turn your head away from injustice. We always taught you to—"

"Remember who I am."

"Exactly. I think the reason you've taken to this regime so readily is that you're eager to change the world, just like many children of your generation. But you have to realize what you're subscribing to."

"I don't agree with the policies toward the Jews, but I'm sure the führer has a reasonable plan for them."

"Reasonable? Is that what you call denying their citizenship? Have you heard of a place called Dachau, Franka?"

She shook her head.

"I hadn't either. It's a little market town, fifteen miles from Munich, not far from where your mother was born. I had a business meeting with a man from there last week. He told me of a camp the Nazis founded there."

"What kind of camp?"

"A place that is a crime against the German people. The man I met with supplied some of the materials for the new buildings there, back in '33, and has been back several times. The camp is the first front in the war that the Nazis are already waging against their own people. Dachau is where they house the political enemies of the system. Socialists, and communists, leaders from the unions the Nazis outlawed, pacifists, and some dissident clergymen and priests. There are thousands there, being worked and starved to death, guarded behind wire fences by SS men with death's-head insignia on their helmets."

"This can't be. Does the führer know about this?" Franka felt the repulsion rising in her but still wondered what Daniel and the other group leaders would make of this.

"How could he not know? Herr Hitler makes every decision that the country is run by. He could abolish it any time he wants to. My guess is that there are many more camps coming."

"Who is this man you met from Dachau? Why is he spreading these vicious lies?"

"They're not lies. Open your eyes, Franka. See who you're pledging your loyalty to."

Franka closed her eyes. She felt as if her head were about to explode. Hot tears ran down her face as she stood up. "I can't believe you'd spread these disgusting lies in front of Fredi, who can't possibly see through them. We have a responsibility to him, Father. We have to be better than this."

She stormed out of the kitchen and up to her room, the poison of doubt swirling inside her.

College was an extension of the Nazi propaganda system that had engulfed Franka and her friends in high school. Intellectuals were on the same level as Jews and merited the same treatment. Hundreds of professors across Germany were dismissed for being too liberal, or Jewish. Among them were some of the greatest scholars in the country, and several Nobel Prize winners. "Culture" became a dirty word. The universities were transformed into vessels for the Propaganda Ministry. There were no student activities save for the Nazi-sponsored rallies and pep talks declaring the greatness of the regime. Franka found that in her courses, with their focus on human physiology, she could avoid the minefield of classes such as Racial Hygiene and Folk and Race.

Franka left the League of German Girls. The other troop leaders questioned her decision, but she convinced them that she hadn't the time anymore, with college and her brother to think about. It was true that she had a lot of work to do both at college and at home, but there was something else. She couldn't stop thinking about the story of the camp in Dachau. It explained a lot. Where had Herr Rosenbaum, their neighbor from down the street, gone? Where were Herr Schwarz and his family, and her old teacher Herr Stiegel? They had been taken away for questioning by the Gestapo. They had never returned, and no one seemed to care. Franka knew that even mentioning their names could get her thrown in jail, so she kept the questions and the maelstrom of doubt to herself. She could trust her father, but no one else—least of all Daniel.

Daniel's devotion to the cause turned to obsession under the tutelage of his professors in law school. The Gestapo was a police force first and foremost—with the same entry paths, pay scales, and lengths of service that had always been in place—but the police force, like almost everything else, was unrecognizable now. Daniel reveled in his immersion in Nazi teachings. It became harder and harder to be around him. He spoke of enemies everywhere, of the communists and the Jews. No one was beyond the scope of his suspicion. The hatred that drove Daniel left him bereft of joy. He became impossible to love, and the feelings she once had for him crumbled and died. It was February 1936, and Franka was coming from dinner with Daniel. He had insisted on paying—as he always did, only adding to her feelings of guilt about what she had to do.

"You're quiet tonight," he began.

"I've a lot on my mind."

"What is it? Your mother? Or is it your brother again?"

"It's us, Daniel." A look of surprise she wasn't used to seeing came over his face, but he didn't say anything. "I think we've grown in different ways. We're taking different paths in life."

"What are you talking about?"

They stopped walking. She was aware of strangers' eyes on them as they passed but knew that she had to press on. She steeled herself for the next part, ready now to say the words that had been dormant inside her for months. "I think we need some time apart. I'm not sure I want to—"

"You're breaking up with me? What? You can't do that."

"I think you're a determined, courageous young man, with so much to offer . . ."

"Don't be ridiculous. We're not breaking up. We're going to be married in a few years, and we'll settle here and raise a family. We decided that together."

"That's not what I want anymore."

"All right," he snarled. "Have it your way. Don't think I'll be waiting when you come crawling back in a few days, you bitch!" He stormed off.

A few weeks later Daniel received a letter from the Reich Labor Service and was called away for six months to toil, unpaid, on behalf of the Reich on a farm in Bavaria. The letters from him began after a few weeks. Franka's father, who had been subtle in his satisfaction at her breaking up with Daniel, held the letters at first but then relented. She was an adult and could make her own decisions now. Franka took the letters her father had hidden from her and went to her room. She tore the envelopes open and let them drop to the floor as she took the letters in hand. Daniel declared that he was sorry, that he had been upset. She didn't reply, but still the letters came. Daniel was laboring on a massive farm, lodging with dozens of others. He spoke of the wonderful feeling of serving the Reich, and of the comradeship that had engendered between him and his fellow workers, all aged around nineteen. A sense of curiosity drove her to read each of the letters once before burning them in the fire. She knew from his tone that he wasn't finished with her, even if she was with him.

Her father's reading habits hadn't changed since the inception of the National Socialist state. Many of the dusty and worn books that clogged the bookshelves in his study were now banned and would result in questioning from the local Gestapo, and even a few nights in jail. He shrugged when she reminded him of the prohibition on subversive literature, and he promised to take them down. Weeks passed. The books remained. Franka took the matter into her own hands and was halfway through clearing off his shelves when her father arrived home from work.

"What are you doing?" he asked.

"I'm doing something you should have done long ago," Franka explained. "We can't afford for you to go to jail or lose your job, and just for a few books?"

"These aren't just any books." He plucked the book she was holding out of her hand. "You see this? Heinrich Heine?"

"I know Heine. Anyone who knows German literature knows Heine."

"Yet he's been banned by our National Socialist overlords. His incomparable lyrics have been officially declared both forbidden and nonexistent. I remember reading through his *Book of Songs* with you as you sat on my knee as a girl."

Franka nodded. She remembered the lines glittering on the page, dancing from her father's lips to her ear.

He riffled through the pages. "Were you planning on having a bonfire, like the Nazis do?" He found the page he was looking for and pointed at a line as he stared at her.

"No, Father. I was going to put them under your bed."

"Does it not seem absurd that suddenly a great poet is no longer a great poet, because he belonged to the wrong race, because he was a Jew? The man's been dead for almost eighty years."

"Of course it's absurd, but it's also his political views they're concerned with. I was just trying to protect you, Father."

"Read out the line I'm pointing to. Read it."

Her eyes found the words. "'Where they burn books, they will also, in the end, burn people.'"

"Perhaps they've already begun," her father said. He handed her the book and left without another word.

Later that night, after Fredi had gone to sleep, she was sitting on her bed when her father brought the rest to her.

"These books are precious now. You are privileged to read these words so many are barred from. And why are they barred? Because the Nazis know that their real enemy is the independent thinker, the true German patriot who questions their ways and speaks up against their injustices. I'm not suggesting you go around preaching the writings of Heine, but keep the ideas he speaks of in your heart, and use them. Analyze what's going on, and remember that he never knew of Hitler or the National Socialists. He understood human nature and the nature of the German people, and that's why his writings still matter. That's what the Nazis are afraid of."

Two weeks later Hitler marched his troops into the Rhineland, an area of Germany on the French border that had been demilitarized by the Treaty of Versailles, in a flagrant snub of international law. That night, Franka sat on her bed, reading the words Heine had written almost a hundred years before. The poet said that once the moral rule of law was broken in Germany, the savagery of the ancient berserker warriors that the Nordic bards sang of would blaze up once more. And this new fury, this thunderclap of German rage, would be like none that the world had witnessed before.

Franka lay back on the bed, knowing that it had already begun.

From then on, Franka did her best to ignore the intrusions into her life by the National Socialists. She immersed herself in her schoolwork, paying little attention to the omnipresent flags and the posters wallpapering the hallways proclaiming the greatness of the regime. There were things the Nazis couldn't touch. There was music, art, the books she now kept hidden under her bed, and the wondrous playground of the forest and mountains that surrounded her. She took hikes every weekend with her friends and walked away when they referred to "handsome Adolf" with coquettish laughs and blushing cheeks. Women had been known to swoon in his presence. Franka found the attraction hard to see, in any circumstance. Some of the local boys grew tiny mustaches in tribute to the führer, but even the most fanatical supporters of the regime looked in the mirror once in a while. The cult of facial hair as a tribute to the demagogue didn't last long.

Nazi ideology and paranoia permeated every human relationship, to the point where friends could no longer be trusted and family members informed on one another for the good of the cause. The old society crumbled piece by piece. Even the most committed supporters of the regime were under the Nazi microscope at all times. In Freiburg, as in every city and town in Germany, an agent of the National Socialists was put in every apartment block, and on every street. They were known as the *Blockwarte*. The *Blockwart* on Franka's street was Herr Duken, a gardener who'd joined the party back in the 1920s when they were little more than a rabble of loudmouths espousing anti-Semitic propaganda and deriding the "November criminals" who had signed the armistice at the end of the Great War. Herr Duken was a licensed nosey neighbor, a paid snoop with terrifying power. He reveled in it. Now he was an important man, respected and feared by his neighbors. His job was to report any misconduct he witnessed or any hearsay that might be relayed to him. He reported on his neighbors for not putting out a swastika flag on gala occasions or for not contributing to the party with the requisite gusto. Franka, aware that the thoughts in her head were reportable as crimes against the state, smiled at Duken when she saw him on the street. Dozens of *Blockwarte* operated throughout the town and in the surrounding countryside. The summer cabin was the only place isolated enough that they could escape.

Daniel came back from his service to the state more committed than ever to the cause of the fatherland, and, seemingly, to Franka. His fumbled attempts to win her back proved little more than an annoyance, but she was wary of the advances of other boys now. She knew the power that Daniel held, and didn't want to make trouble for any poor, unsuspecting boy that merely wanted to take her out for a beer or dinner. Daniel explained to her once, in a misguided attempt to impress her with his new connections, that the Gestapo was the real power in the German state. The shadow of the thousands of agents peppered throughout the country, along with the *Blockwarte* who reported to them, loomed over every German citizen. Soon Daniel would have the power to ruin lives on a whim. The critical analysis of the regime—even the mere expression of disapproval of it—was enough to merit arrest, imprisonment, torture, or even death. Franka was amazed at herself for ever being attracted to him and was determined never to let him touch her again.

She wondered what he could have amounted to if the Nazis hadn't corrupted him. What would he have become if he'd dedicated his talents to a just cause? It was a tragedy, one of the concurrent millions happening throughout Germany.

She spent much of the summer of 1938 at the cabin with her family, and that was the place they spoke freely. Nowhere else was safe. Outwardly, Thomas Gerber was a loyal citizen, and although not a committed Nazi by any means, he paid his dues in terms of both money and respect to the party. Resistance was pointless—it would only mean enduring even closer scrutiny and possibly jail time. His responsibility was to his family, and some futile show of rebellion would only exacerbate their problems. Some family friends expressed the same views in surreptitious whispers. Not everyone subscribed to the Nazi ways, but no one spoke out. Those who didn't agree with the National Socialists went about their daily business just as Thomas and Franka did. They tried to live independently from a regime that viewed independence as dangerous. They knew that punishment awaited any cross word. Hitler himself had stated, "Everyone must know that if he raises his hand to strike at the state, then certain death will be his lot." There was nothing to do. All intolerance was internalized. Franka learned to maintain her composure outwardly while screaming inside. But her complacence was eating away at her. The brave words that she and her father spoke behind closed doors were just that—words. When she put it to him that they should try to execute some kind of change, he laughed in her face.

"That's impossible," he said. "The Nazis are nothing if not meticulous, and while they may be uneducated and backward, they have an innate talent for propaganda and suppression. The system they have set up is perfect in its dysfunctional functionality. Everyone is a spy. I could count on one hand the people I can trust in this entire world now."

"But what use are we, then? Surely there is something we can accomplish, no matter how small."

"Nothing good can come of protest. The notion of free speech is as dead as the kaiser. How can we accomplish anything when even publicly disagreeing with any decision the führer passes down is a treasonous offense? Last week a man was jailed for two years for refuting the notion of expelling all Jewish children from school. Two years!"

Seeing his daughter's downcast face, he went on. "I'm proud of you for wanting to fight, Franka. But the best thing to do is just hold on. The National Socialists are not going to last forever. They're steering us toward war. It's as inevitable as the sun coming in the morning, or the dark at night. It's going to take a lot to oust them, but they will lose in the end. And when they do, our victory will be our survival. As long as we remain true to ourselves and don't let them scar our souls, then we will have won."

"But at what cost, Father?" Franka shook her head. "I'm tired of feeling afraid all the time."

"We will get through this, as a family. I promise you. Your mother is watching over us every day."

Franka wanted to agree with him but didn't feel her mother's presence in her life anymore. The memories were slipping through her fingers.

The facade of Nazi civility crumbled when they unleashed their attack dogs on Kristallnacht. They used the murder of a German diplomat by a seventeen-year-old Jewish boy to unleash the full pent-up rage of their thugs. The Propaganda Ministry organized a series of demonstrations that spread throughout the country like a disease. From the roof of her house, Franka watched with growing horror the mobs and storm troopers attacking Jewish-owned businesses. Almost every local Nazi turned out to throw bricks or firebombs, to intimidate or even to kill. And she saw Daniel, a swastika on his arm, directing the mob into Greenberg's bakery. Herr Greenberg was dragged onto the street and beaten until his body went still.

The next day the newspapers spoke of the justified vengeance of an outraged people. The journalists gloated that at last the Jews were receiving the punishment they deserved for years of unspecified abuses against the German people. The editorials warned against the squeamish opinions of people who disapproved of the heroic actions of the mobs. Such liberal opinions were dismissed as delicate and sentimental. The journalists warned their readers to report to the proper authorities any cross attitudes and decried any German who could not recognize the glorious times that they were living in.

Two days later the government levied a fine of one billion marks on German Jews for the destruction of Kristallnacht.

Tens of thousands of Jews were sent to concentration camps—mysterious prisons known in whispers as KZs by the Germans who dared to speak about them. Franka's father reminded her of the stories he'd heard about the first camp, at Dachau, stories that seemed beyond doubt now. The Nazis had revealed their savage nature but did not lose support. The Hitler Youth still sang their songs as they jogged through town. The members of the League of German Girls still sewed their swastika flags and giggled about "handsome Adolf," the monster in chief. The lackeys of the National Socialists still strutted through town with their heads held high and their Nazi badges shining in the sun. Millions throughout the country still greeted one another by saluting the führer. The German people still seemed entranced by the hold the Nazis had taken of them.

Life went on, despite the injustices and horrors that were now the daily currency in Germany. Franka had finished her training and been offered a job in Munich. Somehow, people were still graduating college, looking for jobs, and contemplating moving between cities. With everything that the Nazi regime had imposed upon them, the Gerber family was still trying to function, but even that was about to change.

Fredi was getting worse.

At the end of that summer in 1939, they talked to him about the hospital—they couldn't avoid the topic any longer. The sun was setting, beaming ethereal light over an infinite horizon, casting the leaves of the forest all around them in gold. Fredi was in his wheelchair. He was almost as tall as Thomas now, but his limbs were thin and bent, his legs almost beyond use. He was playing with a toy train, running it on his thighs. His choo-choo noises were interrupted every few seconds by the sounds of his own chuckling.

"Fredi?"

"Father, what's wrong? Why are you crying?"

"It's because I love you so much, Fredi." He turned to look at Franka. "We both do."

"More than anything else in the world," she said.

"And I love you," he said.

Franka hugged him, felt his spindly arms gripping her and his soft kiss upon her cheek. She tried to speak but couldn't get the words out. She couldn't believe they were giving charge of Fredi to an institution. She couldn't fathom that this would have happened if their mother were still alive.

"How do you feel?" Thomas said.

"I feel great." Fredi smiled.

"Your arms—they don't hurt?"

"No, I feel good."

Fredi was always happy. It was all he knew. The world could not sour the wonder of his spirit. His smile remained through the pain, and through the hospital stays, through things that almost no one else could endure. His smile never left. Everyone knew him on his all-too-regular visits to the hospital. The nurses adored him. Some of the doctors—the ones with Nazi badges on their lapels—stopped just short of openly dismissing him, of expressing their resentment at having to treat someone that the government had deemed an "idiot" and "unworthy of life."

Franka knelt beside him. The sun was still warm, even as the dusk settled in. He seemed to know something was going on. His intuition was sharper than hers. She went to speak, but he beat her to it.

"Franka, I love you. You're so beautiful. You're the best big sister."

"We need to talk to you about something," she managed.

Thomas knelt beside her.

"You've been getting sick more and more lately," she said, "and Daddy doesn't have the time that he needs to look after you anymore."

"I'm so sorry, Daddy."

"Oh no, don't be sorry, Fredi, never. It's not your fault. You're the best boy in the world—the best son a father could ever have. We're so lucky to have you, our own angel on this earth."

"You love the nurses, don't you?" Franka said.

"Oh yes, they're so nice."

"And you know that I'm going to be a nurse, just like they are?"

"Yes."

"I've been offered a fantastic opportunity—a job in a hospital in Munich. You know Munich, where Mummy was from?"

"Yes, I remember the lollipops we bought there."

Thomas laughed. "Yes, when we visited two years ago. We bought lollipops and ate them as we sat in the park."

"Well, I'm going to work there."

"It's far on the train."

"Yes, it is—too far from here. I'm going to have to find somewhere to live there."

"You'll be the best nurse in the whole hospital. You're going to help so many people."

"I hope so." It was hard to get the words out.

Thomas spoke up. "The nurses and doctors in our hospital want you to come and live with them, in a special house, where they can take better care of you."

"Daddy can't look after you alone anymore."

"Will you visit?" Fredi asked. "You're not going to leave me there?"

"Oh no. Never. I'll come every day, and Franka as often as she can, whenever she's home."

"Nothing's going to change," Franka said. "We'll still love you just as much as we always have. We're still going to be together. We'll all live together again soon, and forever."

Franka thought about those words many times after she said them. Fredi accepted them, as he accepted anything she said, with a smile and an open heart. But time and circumstance made her a liar, and that was the last thing she ever wanted to be, especially to him. Fredi moved into the home the week after. They left him with the nurses and walked away empty and alone. Franka moved to Munich on the third of September, the day Britain and France declared war on Germany. By the time she arrived at the platform in Munich, her father's prophecy had come true, and the mad berserker fury of the ancient warriors was unleashed on Europe once more.

Chapter 7

The hurricane of agony had reduced to a gale-force wind. It was still the first thing he felt when his eyes opened with the coming of the morning. He reached across for the bottle of aspirin, popping a couple of tiny white pills into his mouth before downing them with water so cold that he was amazed it didn't have a layer of ice across the top of it. He wondered about the bottle. Was it some kind of Nazi truth serum? It hardly mattered. Submission to her was the only option. He needed her. There was no other way.

The snow painted a spiderweb of ice on the windowpane. The door was open, but there was no noise from the living room. He thought to call out, to ask how she was, or to inquire about the fire, but he didn't. He brought the covers back over his face until only his eyes were exposed. He thought back to the story she'd told him the night before, and the haunted look in her eyes as she told it. If she was Gestapo, she was one hell of an actress. He brought a hand to his face and rubbed the sleep out of his eyes. The decision to tell her the truth would have to come soon. His legs still rendered him immobile. He'd be stuck here as long as the snow took to clear, and that could be weeks. What could he do while he was laid out in bed? He was miles away from his target. He was useless and possibly being prepared for torture and a grisly death.

He reached back under his pillow, feeling for the cold metal of the gun. She had saved his life. No matter what else, that much was true. Killing her would be tantamount to murder. But what was murder in war? He had killed men, had seen the look of terror in their eyes as they realized that they were about to draw their last breath. It was easy to dismiss what he'd done, to lose the sense that he'd ended their lives, to veil his actions in the fog of war, but he thought about those men often. Most days. They were enemies. They would have killed him. The only reason they hadn't was that he was faster, stronger, better. He thought of the man he'd killed when his pistol had jammed, the feel of warm blood running over his fists as he plunged the knife into the man's chest. He remembered the noise as he pulled the knife out. He knew that there would be no escape from that horror. Not now. Not ever.

Sounds from the living room jarred him back into the present—logs being stacked in the fireplace, the popping and cracking of the unseasoned wood struggling to ignite. What if she was who she said she was? But what were the chances of being found by someone who'd been immune to Hitler's mass hypnosis?

There had been no allowance for nuance in his training. The Nazis were to be wiped out. His mission was paramount, and anything or anyone who stood in his way was to be eliminated. Nothing was more important. Not him, and certainly not Franka Gerber. He thought of her face and the earnest beauty of her eyes. He couldn't let her charms sway him. He had to remain strong. He heard the footsteps coming to the door.

"Good morning," Franka said. "How are you feeling?"

"Better, thank you."

She seemed embarrassed for having revealed too much the night before.

"Would you like some breakfast?"

"Yes, please."

Franka walked out, and he listened as she rustled around in the kitchen for a few minutes before returning with some meat and cheese, as well as a hot cup of coffee. She left him there eating it, returning to collect the plate from him only once he'd finished. A part of him longed for her to sit with him again, for her to tell him the rest of her story. Where was Fredi now? Was he a real person? It was getting harder to believe that this was just an elaborate ruse to gain his confidence. She left the room without a word.

A few seconds went by before he heard footsteps tramping across the wooden floor once more, and she came back into the bedroom, toolbox in hand. She passed by the bed without looking at him and sat down beside the hole in the floor. He watched as she took a hammer and began prying up the floorboard adjacent to the opening.

"What are you doing, Fräulein?"

"What does it look like? I'm opening up the floor."

She didn't look at him, just kept on. He waited until she'd pulled up the floorboard to speak again. It felt wrong to watch her doing all of this work while he lay there useless in the bed.

"Why are you doing that?"

She stood up and pushed out a breath as she stretched out her lower back. She got back down on her knees and peered into the hole she'd made. She seemed to be measuring out the width. It was about three feet wide and six feet long. Franka stood up and left the room, again without making eye contact. A couple of minutes later she returned with several blankets under her arm. She knelt beside the hole and laid out the blankets, lining the space under the floorboards. She stood up again. It seemed she was going to say something, but instead she made for the tiny corner between the bed and the wall where his rucksack and uniform still lay. She folded the uniform and placed it inside the hole.

"Fräulein, I really must ask what exactly you're doing here. That's my uniform."

"Is it?" She threw the rucksack down on top of it. She picked up one of the floorboards she'd left against the wall and slipped it back into place.

"Fräulein Gerber?"

She laid the other two floorboards back into place. She got on her knees once more and pushed the floorboards down as hard as she could. She ran her hand over the surface of the boards, making sure that they weren't protruding, and then stood back to examine her work, her fingers on her chin. The scuff marks at the end of the floorboards told an unwanted story. She walked out, and he heard her going through the cupboards for a few seconds before she returned, a pot of wood varnish in her hand. The floors in the old cabin had been well tended. The varnish on the floor was smooth and even, probably not five years old. Franka got on her knees and began to dab fresh varnish on the ends of the floorboards to mask the flecks that had flown off. Within two minutes or so it was impossible to tell that the floorboards had been disturbed at all.

"That's for when the Gestapo come. If they find you here, we're both dead, and I'm not going to live in denial, even if you are. They're not going to come while the snow is as thick on the ground as it is, but once it melts they'll start searching for you. Someone saw your parachute or heard the plane you jumped out of. The longer you keep up this ridiculous charade, the longer you're jeopardizing both our lives. If you don't start trusting me, we're both going to die."

She walked out of the room.

He lay alone through a dreary afternoon. The window let in little light, and the door remained closed. He heard sounds every so often but didn't see her. There were no answers—only more questions. There was nothing he could do trapped here in this bed. The pain in his legs was bearable now, but he wouldn't be able to walk out of here for weeks. Could he trust this woman? Had she disavowed the mindless obedience that the Nazis had instilled in so many Germans? Or were there more like her than he thought? What would she be willing to do if he did trust her? The pressure was building inside him. Every day alone and useless in this bed was a day closer to failure, and that was something he couldn't accept. He cursed his legs, cursed the Nazis, tried to somehow sleep to escape the agonizing possibility that he might fail this mission. He bit down on his fist so hard he almost drew blood. Sleep would not come. There was no escape.

The cuckoo clock sang seven times, and a few seconds later the door opened. She came in and placed the tray on his lap as he sat up. He didn't touch the food, even though he felt as if he were starving to death.

"Fräulein? Franka?"

The wind howled outside the window.

"Do you have pictures of your family? Do you have a picture of Fredi?"

"Yes, some."

"Can I see them? I didn't see any pictures when I was outside."

"There were pictures once. I took them down just a few days before I found you."

"Do you still have them?"

"I do."

She disappeared through the door and came back a minute later, two dog-eared photos in her hands. She held them as if they were an injured bird she'd found. He took them between two fingers. The first photo was of the four of them posing together on the steps of what he assumed was their house. Franka was younger, perhaps sixteen at the time. She had short blond curls and was wearing a white dress. She had her arm around her father, a stout, handsome man with a brown beard and smiling eyes. Her mother's long blond hair was carefree about her shoulders, her smile radiant and her eyes sparkling even in the colorless old photo. She had her arms draped around Fredi, who was nestling into her. He looked about eight. His weak, lank arms and legs protruded through his T-shirt and shorts. He was looking up at her lovingly. He turned over the photo to reveal the date—June 1933. Franka handed him the next picture, taken outside the cabin on a warm summer day in 1935, just the three of them. Fredi still smiled as he sat on his father's lap, but it seemed for the benefit of the camera. Thomas was gazing at his son, the adoration clear. Franka sat beside them, staring with a seriousness uncommon in a girl that age. He handed the photos back to her.

"Thank you for showing me."

She nodded and left, taking the pictures with her. He'd almost finished the meat and vegetables she'd served him when she came back into the room. She had a chair with her and sat down beside the bed, waiting for him to finish eating.

"I wanted to thank you for sharing your story with me last night," he said as he finished. He took a drink of water as he waited for her to answer.

"I haven't spoken about my family for some time. It opened up some wounds that had barely begun to heal."

Restrain yourself. Let her be. She'll tell you in her own time. He put the empty glass down on the tray she'd brought, nodding his head. She took it from him and left without speaking.

Hours later, he sat listening to the wind as it rattled the windowpanes. It was dark outside now, and she came back to light the oil lamp beside his bed. She sat down beside him. He didn't speak, waiting for her to begin.

"I want to tell you the rest of my story. I've been debating back and forth, wondering what I should say, what I should censor, and if you really are who I think you are. But then it came to me. I realized I don't have anything left to lose. If you're not who I think you are, and telling you my story costs me my miserable life, then so be it, but I'm not holding back. Not anymore. I don't care. You can kill me. Your side killed my father. The others killed almost everyone else I love."

It was all too easy to forget the reason he was here. Best to stay quiet, let her reveal her true self if that's what she was so determined to do. He had enough food to last a week or more. If she were to leave, he could survive on his own. It wasn't his job to save this German woman from the demons of her past. There simply wasn't time for attachment or sentimentality.

He lay back as she began to speak. The wind died outside, and darkness fell. The room filled with golden light from the oil lamp burning on the table. She stared out into nothing as if the past were all around her and she had only to reach out to touch it.

Berlin was the capital, and where Hitler resided, but it was a city he never liked. Munich was Hitler's heartland. He often spoke of his boundless love for the place where he'd arrived as a penniless artist, sketching picture postcards to sell on the street. This was where the National Socialist revolution had begun with the unsuccessful Beer Hall Putsch in 1923—where the bodies of the men who died that day were encased in massive stone sarcophagi, guarded by granite-faced SS men in black uniforms. Munich was where Hitler had found his first supporters—disenfranchised soldiers, rejects, and castoffs of a society scarred by war. In those early days, they marched in step, dressed in coats and windbreakers, not able to afford uniforms. His followers multiplied until he was known as the "King of Munich" just a few short years after his arrival. It was something Hitler never forgot. Munich was his.

The Nazi takeover had tempered the luminosity and charm of Munich by 1941. There was even less escape from the ubiquitous Nazi flags than in Freiburg. The Nazi bullyboys controlled the city, as they did everywhere in Germany now, and the lack of freedom felt like a vise. But the Nazis could not snuff out all life and beauty from this vibrant place. Franka found refuge in the arts and attended concerts regularly. She found the ultimate escape in music, and that in itself was a protest. Music gave life to the part of her that the Nazis could never touch. She found peace in this subtle form of protest, for to declare an interest in the arts was to be anti-Nazi without declaring it. Hitler scorned the intellectual and the pursuit of the aesthetic. Showing love for such things was a sign of weakness, not the iron-willed toughness that the National Socialists demanded. The concert hall offered a sanctuary, and Franka felt at one with the others in the seats as the ambrosia of sound swept over her.

The hospital where she worked was filled with joy and dread, horror and beauty. The soldiers from the front filled the beds, their wounds a glimpse into a hell she could never have envisioned before the war. Young boys lay broken all around her, their futures stubbed out by bullets and bombs, their eyes or legs missing, their faces burned to cinder, their lifeblood leaking onto the marble floors. So much waste. She sat with boys whose only wish was that she hold their hands and smile. They showed her pictures of wives and girlfriends, who'd come to visit with flowers in their hands and wet eyes. Going from bed to bed, being there for them, imbued her with a happiness she'd thought impossible. Those soldiers lit a candle in the darkness inside her. Sometimes they spoke of the Reich, and their hopes for the future once the final, great victory was won. Through broken teeth and torn lips they spoke of magnificent glory on the battlefield. Their loyalty to the regime that had destroyed them was unwavering. So few of them realized they had been chewed up and spat out in the service of a lie. Few seemed to recognize the vilification that lay in wait for them once the history was written. They remained convinced that they were doing right, even at the end. She didn't have the heart to tell them any different. Nothing could have been crueler.

Hans Scholl wore the gray uniform of the Wehrmacht, but with a lively charisma that was all too rare in those days. He was a year younger than she, with dark blond hair and a face that could have graced the movies he loved. The other nurses nudged each other to look up as he strutted past. He was a student medic taking classes at the university. He didn't use the Nazi salute, instead proffering a handshake. He asked her out thirty seconds after meeting her. She was powerless in the face of his charm and gave an almost-immediate yes. They went to a concert together the next night. He held her hand as Beethoven's Fifth Symphony boomed, and she knew he was different. She knew he was like her. The moon shone bright over the city that night, and they sat in the park after the concert, sipping red wine in the warm summer air. It was almost enough to forget. Hans made her laugh, made her feel beautiful. His eyes sparkled in the silver light. Tyranny and terror were forgotten. The barbs of the past melted away. And she knew something had begun.

He was from Ulm, a small town she remembered visiting as a child, one hundred miles from Munich. He spoke about his family often. His father was a local politician and business owner, as well as an ardent critic of the Nazi Party, and had been arrested by the Gestapo for seditious thinking. He often mentioned his siblings, especially his little sister Sophie, who was to follow him on to the university the year after. He was a former member of the Hitler Youth. He should have been one of the bright lights in the movement—yet he wore no Nazi pin and spoke about the government evasively, always eager to change the subject. Instead, he told stories he'd heard from his fellow soldiers who'd served in Poland. He talked about civil liberties and freedom with a passion and vehemence that left her in no doubt as to where his allegiances lay. There was a liberty in being with him. He was someone she could discuss art and politics with and who agreed with her that the machinations of the National Socialist regime would ultimately lead to the destruction of the German nation. Some of the other nurses stopped talking to her when it became public knowledge that they were together.

At the end of the summer of 1941, Hans invited her to a gathering of a group of his friends. Ostensibly, he said, they were meeting to discuss philosophy. In reality they met to vent their political frustrations. The gathering took place not at a bar but in the study of a private home. Cups of coffee and glasses of beer lay on the table along with stacks of papers and books. Hans introduced Franka to his friends Willi and Christoph, and she sat around the table with a handful of others. All were students and younger than she, except for the owner of the house, Dr. Schmorell, whose son, Alex, sat beside him. After brief introductions, Hans began to talk.

"We've all heard stories from the front. Franka and I see the German victims of this useless war every day in the hospital." The men glanced over at Franka before fixing back on Hans. "I heard just yesterday from a trusted friend who saw with his own eyes the sight of Poles and Russians being herded into concentration camps on the eastern front, to be executed or worked to death providing slave labor."

The feeling of escape was overwhelming, almost giddying. Franka hadn't heard anyone speak like that other than her father. Not even Hans had been this frank with her before. A fire had been set within her.

"Girls are rounded up," Willi said, "and sent to whorehouses to service their new SS masters against their will. It's more than the mere subjugation of a people. It's rape and murder on an industrial scale. It's horror that mankind has hardly known before, and it's being perpetrated in all our names."

Christoph stood up. "The treatment of the people in the occupied territories is an abomination, even more so than the regime's treatment of its own citizens. The question is, do we act? Can we sit back and watch this happen? It's all well and good sitting around this table, voicing ideas that, if known outside, would land us all in jail." He turned to Franka, who felt the spotlight glare on her. "Franka, Hans has told us what the Nazis did to your brother. You've suffered terribly at their hands."

All waited for her to speak, but the words caught in her throat. She'd only told Hans of what had happened to Fredi in stuttering sentences, hadn't revealed the depth of the pain behind it, and she wasn't ready to share with these strangers, like-minded though they were.

"I'm not ready to speak about that here and now, but suffice to say that the Nazis have destroyed, or attempted to destroy, all that was once virtuous and true in this wonderful country of ours, and you ask should we do something? My unequivocal answer is yes. It is our moral duty."

"But what can we do?" Willi said. "If it's our moral obligation to do something as loyal Germans, then what? The scope of the military is certainly beyond us. We're not assassins or rabble-rousers. We're not military strongmen or bullies like the Nazis themselves."

"We use our strengths," Hans said. "We channel our ideas onto paper, and we spread the truth as we see it. The Nazis are quick to proclaim their might and the fact that the empire they're building will last a thousand years, but they're so afraid of their own people that they suppress with terminal effect any denunciation. They're terrified of one thing: the truth. If we can spread the truth among the people—about the horrors the Nazis perpetrate in their name—we will win. The Jews left in our cities are marked with a golden star, but where are the others? We know now. We know, but most people don't or pretend not to. If we can force the German people to face up to the truth, we have a chance of real and sustained change. We must be the conscience of Germany. We must speak for the Jews, the homosexuals, the clergy, and the other enemies of the state who have disappeared. We need to let our people and the rest of the world know that there are Germans who are appalled at the actions of the Nazis and demand that they desist." The political discourse lasted a few more hours, until, exhausted, Franka went home. The words she'd heard at the meeting buzzed around inside her head for days, drowning out the Nazi propaganda that would have otherwise dominated her daily life.

The steps to turning these words into actions took time. In the Nazi state, the necessities of their mission, such as typewriters, paper, and a duplicating machine, were hard to come by without drawing suspicion. Hans procured a location to house the tools they acquired, and they began to work out an outline for their leaflets. They came up with basic arguments, which were smoothed out and sharpened at their regular meetings.

They called themselves the White Rose, and their first mail drop was scheduled for a few months later, for that summer of 1942. There were no set rules or regulations for meetings or membership of the White Rose. No members list was formalized, and no one was sworn to secrecy or forced to place their hand on a Bible as they joined. It was understood that Hans was the driver of the organization and, as such, made the decisions about what direction the group was going. New members joined, always vetted by the existing ones, more on feeling than anything else. A Gestapo mole would mean arrest and prison, or worse, for all of them. The yoke of the Nazi state hung heavy on them, yet they laughed and had fun. They were still young.

None of the activities of the White Rose focused on the university, where most of them were enrolled. The group was an island in an ocean of Nazi loyalists, and they refused to take part in the university's activities, all of which were sponsored or approved by the National Socialists.

Franka and Hans spent all their free time together now. There was more to their lives, more to their relationship than the politics of the White Rose. There was still time to be young and in love even as Germany sank deeper into the abyss.

In April 1942, weeks before the first mail drop, Franka and Hans walked hand in hand along the banks of the river. Other couples strolled past them. Some were teenagers, some were married couples with children scampering along in front of them, but none seemed fundamentally different from Franka and Hans. They passed an elderly couple sitting on a bench and staring out at the setting sun with contented looks on their withered faces.

"Do you think we'll be sitting there together in fifty years?" She passed the words off as a joke, though the question behind them was quite deliberate.

"Of course," he replied. "I could never imagine wanting to be with anyone else." She was just about to say something when he spoke again. "In a way I'm jealous of other couples. They seem to be oblivious to the horrors around them. I can imagine there is some bliss in being able to remove yourself like that."

"You could never do that, Hans. It's not who you are. That's part of the reason I love you so much."

"That and my incredible good looks, right?"

"I didn't want to say that first. I didn't want to seem shallow."

"Too late, I know now."

"You're different when we're alone," she said. "Lighter, somehow."

"You see the real me, Franka—the person I want to be all the time." He looked around to make sure no one could hear them before he continued. "You see the person that I'll be for the rest of my life once the scourge of the National Socialist regime has been vanquished for good. That's all I want—to live a quiet, simple life where I can be myself, with you."

She believed him. She believed every word he said.

The leaflet was around eight hundred words. Franka spent her time poring over it like a starving person wolfing down food. Franka's eyes clung to the third sentence, which read, "Who among us can imagine the degree of shame that will come upon us and upon our children when the veil falls from our faces and the awful crimes that infinitely exceed any human measure are exposed to the light of day?" It urged all those who adhered to German Christian tradition to "offer passive resistance—resistance wherever you may be, prevent the continuation of this atheistic war machine before it is too late." The page ended with a poem of freedom, followed by directions to pass it on and to copy it as many times as possible. Across the top, the heading read: "Leaflets of the White Rose."

It was Franka's job to distribute a portion of the thousands they printed. She took a train back to Freiburg, the seditious papers in her suitcase. The leaflets were enough to have her executed. Nerves replaced the usual joy she felt on her trips home, but the train ride went without a hitch. Once back in Freiburg, she mailed the flyers to the list of addresses she carried. The mail from Munich was just as good, but the authorities wouldn't be able to pinpoint where the White Rose was from if the letters were sent from Freiburg, Berlin, Hamburg, Cologne, and Vienna. Franka returned triumphantly a few days later. No one was caught. Another leaflet followed, and then two more. They followed the same protocol, took the same precautions. Thousands of leaflets of the White Rose scattered across Germany. The authorities didn't recognize their effect, but soon she began to hear whispers on the university campus and beyond. People were talking about the White Rose essays. The conversation that the members craved had begun. The typewritten sheets were passed hand to hand, leaving excitement and disquiet in their wake wherever they went. The readers were astonished by their content. Some people met the leaflets with disgust, others amazement or disbelief. A ripple spread from Munich across the country. More than one person went to the Gestapo—after all, it was best to report things such as this straightaway. No sense letting someone else take credit for reporting such seditious words. The Gestapo began the search for the originators of the leaflets, but the members of the White Rose remained untouched. Hans was determined that this was only the beginning.

Franka had first met Hans's little sister Sophie after she enrolled in the university in May 1942. She came to live with him. It was awkward at first. Franka had grown used to a certain sense of intimacy, which having Hans's little sister there interrupted at times. But she was sweet and kind—if a little serious. Hans had never spoken of her joining the group. He thought it best to hide his illegal activities from her, but it wasn't long before she came across some of the leaflets hidden in the apartment they shared. She demanded he let her join. Franka helped convince Hans. She felt emboldened by Sophie's courage, and by her clearheaded determination to stand for what she thought was right. It was infectious.

Any refusal would have been futile, and Hans gave in after a few days of fighting. Within weeks, she had become Hans's equal in spearheading the group. She took over completely while he, Alex, and Willi were sent to the Russian front with their units at the end of that summer.

Franka continued working in the hospital, her secret life as a seditious traitor hidden from all but her closest confidants. Doubt and suspicion overtook her relationships with her colleagues and casual friends. She examined every word they said, every gesture they made. No one could be trusted. And within this isolation, Franka felt the lack of Hans in her life even more. Her regular letters, coded and repressed as they were, referred to their work with the White Rose as "the building project." There was much to tell him. The writing and publication of the White Rose leaflets had gone into hiatus pending their return, but still the activity continued in the background. A Hamburg branch of the White Rose had been founded to help distribute the leaflets. She closed every letter to Hans with a paragraph only about her, only about them. No matter what else, she wanted him to know she thought of him every hour of every day and was counting down until his safe return. There were some things she knew the Nazis wouldn't censor in the letters to soldiers at the front.

Her father didn't return to the cabin that summer. The heartbreak was too much for him. He came to Munich at Christmas, a pale reflection of the man he'd been before the National Socialists had broken him. His job in the factory had been given to a local Nazi half his age. He had been demoted and was considering early retirement. Father and daughter met on the platform of the train station. His face was unshaven, his skin sallow, and he smelled of whiskey. They went to dinner but spoke little, afraid of what the other might say. They went for long walks in the city, passing the rubble of the bombed-out buildings that were becoming more and more common, and past the air-raid shelters that were being constructed all over. They spoke about the old days, the golden times in the cabin, and her mother. That was all. They barely mentioned Fredi's name. It would have been too painful. It had already drained so much from them. They had no more left to give.

She left her father at the train station late at night on that Sunday in January. The tears came again as she hugged him.

"Will you be all right?" she asked as she drew back.

"Of course," he said, but his eyes spoke a different truth.

"Would you consider moving here?"

"No, thank you. I'll stay in Freiburg, where my work is, where your mother and brother are. I still visit her grave most days. I only wish I had somewhere to go to visit him. We'll never know what those animals did with his body."

Her father broke down on the platform, the tears gushing down his face. She offered to stay with him, to come back to Freiburg for a while, asked again if he'd stay, but he refused. They sat on a bench, waiting for the train, holding one another until the train finally arrived and she said goodbye.

When Hans came home from the Russian front, he was more determined than ever to spread the ideas of the White Rose. In his time as a medic on the front he had witnessed how the German soldiers had been stripped of any chivalry, mercy, or humanity. The career army officers who had once followed a strict code of honor now fully subscribed to the Nazi racial dogma that drove the Wehrmacht and SS forces alike. The war on the eastern front was sold as a defensive crusade against communism, but, Hans told her, it was actually a ploy to provide the living space that Hitler had promised the German people. The real crusade was against the Jews. Hans had spoken to dozens of soldiers who had witnessed the mass murder of thousands of Jewish civilians, lined up along the edge of mass pits that would become their graves. He was changed by what he'd seen. Franka held him as he lay shaking in bed on the first night he returned.

The newspapers were full of stories of heroic victories against the communist hordes on the eastern front. The Russians were portrayed in caricature as beasts, dismissed as uneducated subhumans unworthy of existence. Only the Jews were a lower form of life. Only they were more beastly, more inferior to the Russians, whom the dashing Aryan soldiers would vanquish with ease. The Battle of Stalingrad changed perceptions that the Nazis were invincible. The members of the White Rose took careful note. Hitler refused to give the order to let his men retreat, condemning them to death in a frozen city over a thousand miles from home. The German Sixth Army was wiped out. The official reports held that the hundreds of thousands who died were heroes, and stated that their sacrifice would lead the Reich on to greater victories to come. The members of the White Rose knew better. They knew that Nazi victory was no longer inevitable and that for the first time, Germany was looking defeat square in her cold, gray eyes. Hitler had tasted his first major loss. The White Rose wasn't going to pass up such an opportunity.

Stories of the regime cracking down on any defiance, no matter how inconsequential, littered the newspapers. A man was put to death for stating that Hitler should be murdered for allowing so many German soldiers to die. The Gestapo beheaded a waiter for making fun of the führer and executed a businessman for daring to state out loud that the war was going badly for Germany. In Berlin, fifty people were executed for transmitting sensitive information to the Russians in what became known as the Red Orchestra affair. The men involved were not executed by guillotine—the official method of the Nazi executioners. They were hung on meat hooks and left to die in agony. The women, who were sentenced by the court to life in prison, were executed by guillotine on Hitler's personal orders.

Franka knew several people arrested by the Gestapo for careless words, or writing the wrong thing in letters. The Nazi grip on Germany was tightening, even as it entered its death throes. Somehow the White Rose managed to avoid the sprawling tentacles of the Gestapo, but they all felt the pressure of what they were doing. Franka felt the fear of arrest in everything she did now. They all did, but it only made them more determined to press on. There was no talk of backing down. That would have meant giving in.

They wrote and printed more leaflets. Franka played her part once more. She read through the latest paper as she sat in the bathroom on the train to Cologne to distribute the latest set of flyers.

"We will not be silent," the leaflets read. "We are your bad conscience. We will not leave you in peace!"

Thousands were mailed all over Germany.

The excitement she'd once felt was usurped by terror at the thought of her capture. Surely it was a matter of time. It was a question of who would capitulate first, the White Rose or the regime itself. The tides of war were turning against the Nazis—Stalingrad and the defeats since had proved as much—but the Gestapo was as formidable as it had ever been. Thoughts of leaving the group had been germinating inside her for weeks. They began to sprout. She made up her mind on the train back to Munich to take a break, to go away for a while, and to convince Hans and Sophie to do the same. They were operating with an abandon that would lead to their deaths. Nothing else seemed logical. Telling them was going to be the hard part. Hans and some of the others had begun a graffiti campaign on the walls of the University of Munich, daubing anti-Hitler slogans in tar on the walls and roads of the old university. They were going too far.

It was February 1943. The Allied bombers had taken the night off from their relentless pounding. Franka stole down the street in the darkness, came to the studio where they printed the forbidden leaflets. She gave the secret knock. Willi answered the door and greeted her with a kiss on the cheek. Sophie sat at a desk in the corner, writing. Hans was operating the stencil machine, his sleeves rolled up, his face red and sweating.

"Can I speak to you, Hans?"

He nodded and gestured to Alex to take over. Franka led him into the back room, where they sat down.

"I want you to stop," she said.

"What are you talking about?"

"The Gestapo is closing in, and you know it. They're asking questions all over the university. They know we're based here. It's only a matter of time before they find us. Perhaps it's time to stop while we're all still alive. You are no use to the resistance if you're dead."

His hand was shaking as he picked up his coffee mug. "We can't stop, not now that we have the nation's attention. Perhaps the Gestapo is getting closer, but that only raises the stakes. We have a platform that we must use while we can. No one has ever had the chance to do what we're doing. We can't waste that. That's exactly what the Nazis want."

"Everyone admires what you've done."

"What we've all done. We've all played our part, you included, Franka."

"Of course, thank you. I'm proud to have been a part of this, in some small way, but what can we achieve if we're dead or in jail?"

"You don't think I know the risks? A child knows that anyone who speaks out against the regime is dead. But does that not necessitate our work even more? Does that not inflate the importance of what we're doing? We're the only people spreading ideas of freedom in a country that needs them more than any other. We're giving bread to the starving minds of the masses. If we disappear, then so does the dream of a better nation."

"Do you really think that you can bring down the most powerful regime in Europe with a few leaflets?"

"Do you appreciate anything we've been trying to do here?"

"Of course, I do . . ."

"I don't think that we can change anything alone. We can only change if the entire German nation stands with us against the Nazis. That's what this is about. That's what this has always been about—spreading the idea of freedom and planting the seeds of truth in people's minds."

"I don't want to see you die, Hans. I love you."

"And I love you, Franka, but this is bigger than us. We're creating a dissonance that has the power to challenge the greatest evil ever to befall our country, or maybe even the world."

"Can't you just stop for a while?"

"Not now. Perhaps the Gestapo is closing in, and perhaps I will die soon, but history will not judge me kindly if I don't take this opportunity we've been given. And how could I leave my sister to do this alone anyway? You've seen her. If anything, she's more passionate about this than I am. There's only one way for me, and for the White Rose, and that's forward."

"It seems that nothing I can say will change your mind."

His bloodshot eyes remained unmoved.

"Just promise me you'll be careful."

He stood up to embrace her. She held him against her and kissed him one last time. He walked her to the door as the others said good night, and then he closed it behind her.

Hans and Sophie were arrested at the University of Munich on February 18, 1943. A handyman, empowered by the Nazis, and in his spare time a goose-stepping storm trooper, saw them tossing leaflets over the balcony like confetti. He had been briefed by the Gestapo to watch for any suspicious behavior—even more so than usual. It must have seemed like the best day of his life when he saw the two students tossing the forbidden flyers off the balcony. He arrested them himself, doubtless excited about his upcoming promotion and the cash reward that awaited him. Hans and Sophie were taken from the university campus to the Gestapo headquarters at the Wittelsbach Palace, the former royal palace of the Bavarian monarchs in the center of the city. They were charged with high treason, violent overthrow of the government, the destruction of National Socialism, and the defeat of their own army in wartime. Christoph was arrested a few hours later. The Gestapo found all the evidence they would ever need in their apartments, and any trial would be a sham.

The news of Hans and Sophie's arrest spread throughout the university. Franka was at work that night when Willi came to tell her. She cried all night. There would be no mercy, only retribution, and it was just a matter of time before the Gestapo came for them too. The newspapers reported the arrest of the traitorous students the next day. The editorial trusted that swift justice would follow, and so it did. Roland Freisler, the notorious chief judge of the People's Court, which only tried cases of treason and subversion, was brought down from Berlin. The trial began just four days later, on February 22. Franka waited along with the other members, praying for some form of leniency. The trial lasted a few hours. Hans, Sophie, and Christoph were convicted and sentenced to death. They were taken from the courtroom to jail, and guillotined. Christoph's wife, who was sick in the hospital at the time, didn't find out that he'd been executed until several days later. Hans and Sophie's parents, who were present at the trial, went home to Ulm after the guilty pronouncements, planning their next trip back to see their children a few days later. They were not told that their son and daughter were to be executed that very day.

Franka was in her apartment when the Gestapo came for her a few weeks later. Her trial was set for April, along with several other members—the panic that had overtaken the Nazis upon the initial arrests had seemingly subsided. The Gestapo questioning she underwent was milder than she'd imagined. She realized after a few minutes that they thought she was too gentle, too pretty, and too much of a girl to have had anything to do with an organization as reprehensible as the White Rose. It seemed like the investigators had already made their minds up about her, and all she had to do was play along. They knew that Hans and Sophie were the driving forces behind the movement, and that Willi, Christoph, and Alex were the other main actors. The interrogators merely wanted Franka to corroborate the story that they'd already formulated about the group and about her role as the leader's unwilling girlfriend, the loyal Aryan girl misled by the traitorous dissidents. Her role seemed vital in the narrative the National

Socialists were trying to spin to a fascinated, shocked German public. The lawyer her father hired could barely believe their luck.

"I don't think they'd go so easy on you if you weren't so pretty," he said.

"The important thing is to get out of this alive," her father said. "Say whatever you need to say to get out of this with your life. Denounce the organization. Save your skin."

Franka wanted to speak up for the cause, wanted to tell the court that she was proud of what they'd done, and that Hitler was the murderous traitor. "How can I denounce my friends? That would mean turning my back on everything I believe in. How could I live with myself?"

"Don't do it for yourself. Do it for me. I need you now, more than ever. Don't leave me. Live on. For me."

So she did. She denounced the White Rose in front of the court, stating that she'd been led astray by the dangerous revolutionary her boyfriend had turned out to be. Her heart was ragged inside her, every denial tearing another strip away. Her father smiled at her across the courtroom, giving her the thumbs-up as she declared her loyalty to the Reich. She thought of Hans, and the rousing final speech in support of freedom he'd given in that same courtroom. But as her father said, he was dead now, and so was the White Rose. She didn't have to die with them. So she sold out everything she believed in to be there for him so he wouldn't be left alone. Franka got six months in jail. The judge proclaimed that he hoped it would give her pause to reflect on the choice of company that she kept and that once she got out, she should fulfill her duty in marrying a loyal servant of the Reich, preferably a soldier serving on the front, and bear him many children to serve the führer. She cried as the bailiff led her out of the courtroom. The shame was more than she could bear. Willi, Alex, and the professor from the university they'd drawn inspiration from, Dr. Huber, were all executed also. They were the true heroes.

Franka avoided the dreaded KZs, the concentration camps, which had become the unmentionable horror in Germany, the truth that even the most hardened Nazi supporters didn't want to admit to. She was sent to Stadelheim Prison along with several other former members of the White Rose, where Hans and the others had been executed. She sank into a deep depression. The ghosts of the fallen heroes of the White Rose haunted her dreams. Time passed. Her depression deepened. Her father regularly sent letters, and the promise of the next one was the only thing that kept her alive. His kind, hopeful words were the only sign of love or beauty in a world that had been stripped of such things. The letters stopped in October. Her father had been killed by a stray bomb dropped from an Allied plane. She was due to be released three weeks later. Her family was the victim of both sides in this useless, disgusting war. They had taken everything from her.

She lingered in Munich for a week or two after her release. There was little to remember from that time. She didn't belong there anymore. She couldn't pretend to be a part of their society anymore. The flags still flew over bombed-out buildings, and the swastika still adorned the countless coffins shipped home from the eastern front. A letter arrived from her father's attorney in Freiburg. Her father's will was ready. No one else would be in attendance. That was when she decided that she would end her life. There was nothing left for her. It seemed fitting to go back, to do it there in her hometown, near the place she'd known the most joy.

She heard the lawyer read her father's will, endured his disapproving glares under the portrait of Hitler that hung above his desk, and the next day visited her parents' graves. They lay nestled beside each other on a hill overlooking the city they'd lived in. Immediately after, she retreated to the cabin. The worst of the memories came at night, and sleeping alone was an unendurable torture. The pain became more than she could bear. She set out that night with no destination in mind, never thinking that she'd walk as far as she did, but there was always another hill to climb, another tree line to pass, and then she found him.

Franka finished her story. The candle, almost burned down, flickered in the room. The night was still outside—absolutely silent.

"Franka, what happened to Fredi? How did he die? What did the Nazis do to him?"

"I can't talk about that now. I have to go."

She shut the door behind her, leaving him alone in the half-light of the bedroom.

Chapter 8

It had been a week since she'd found him. The pain in his legs had reduced to a simmer now, but he was still bound to this bed, trapped in this cabin. The light of the day outside was dying, the sun tossing out bright oranges and reds that cut through the snow-dusted glass of the window in his room. He ran through Franka's story again and again, searching for inconsistencies that weren't there. He hadn't seen her since last night, since she'd walked out after telling him about her past. It had been hard not to tell her what he knew about the activities of the White Rose. He thought back to his training, to the interrogation techniques he'd learned. Her eyes betrayed a profound truth. He knew she wasn't lying, but he also knew that she was holding something back. She'd told him most of her story, but there was something else, a missing piece. Regardless, it was almost impossible to imagine she was a Gestapo agent. If she knew he wasn't German and had reported him, he would have been in a windowless room, staring into a spotlight. She was a traitor to the cause, had served time for activities against the regime, and had escaped the guillotine only by being underestimated by the men who'd tried her. Had she somehow worked out who he was? How? He reached over for the glass of water beside his bed and took a cool drink. If she had worked out that he wasn't German, what else had she worked out?

Today's weather was fine. It wasn't easy to tell through the frost-encrusted window, but it hadn't snowed. The cabin was likely accessible now. The world could encroach on their hidden place. He looked around. There was no room in the cabin for a listening place, for clandestine Gestapo men peering at him through holes in the wall. He heard everything that went on when she brought wood in, when she made herself a cup of coffee in the kitchen. He'd heard her take a bath earlier and knew that she was reading in the rocking chair by the fire in the living room right now as she listened to the radio. She acted with absolute abandon in front of him. She listened to illegal radio stations and often spoke about her disdain for the regime. If he were a Luftwaffe officer, as his credentials said, then she could expect harsh treatment from the Gestapo if he reported her illegal activity. She was telling the truth when she said she knew. There was no other explanation. Somehow she knew.

A noise from the living room told him that she'd gotten out of her seat and was in the kitchen now. Her footsteps came toward his door, followed by a knock. The door opened. Her face was colorless and drawn. It was rare that he saw her during the day unless she had a specific reason for coming into the room. She usually came only at mealtimes, but it was still at least an hour until dinner.

"Are you well?"

"I'm quite comfortable, Fräulein."

It was a discipline, a learned behavior, to fight back his instincts, to not reveal himself. He had heard her bedsprings creaking through the night and saw the rings under her eyes now.

"Franka? You've nothing to feel guilty about."

"What?"

"It's not your fault you're alive and they're not. And you shouldn't feel shame for not wanting to die." The words came without thought or ulterior motive. He was surprised at himself.

"I sold out the last thing I believed in." She turned to him, her voice muted, her eyes on the floor. "I had nothing else in this life. At least if I'd spoken out—"

"You'd be dead now, and so would I. What good would that have done? Who would that have served? Hans is dead, but that doesn't mean that you can't live on."

"It's ridiculous—I've never revealed this much to anyone before. I don't even know you."

"Confidants are hard to come by these days."

Could he trust her? Was her story real? What were the chances of finding someone like her? He wanted to believe her, but he couldn't, not while he knew she was holding something back.

"Franka? Is it all right if I call you that?"

"Yes, of course."

"I want to thank you for telling me your story."

"Are you going to report me?" she said.

"For what?"

"For listening to banned radio stations? For making seditious claims against the führer?"

"I'm not a Nazi."

"Who are you, then?"

"Not every German in uniform is a Nazi. You should know that better than most."

"And not everyone in a Nazi uniform is a German."

"There is no room for questioning the government in time of war," he said, feeling the hollowness of his words.

"The White Rose felt quite the opposite."

"And you consider yourself a true patriot, for speaking out against the government?"

"I did once. I'm not worthy of the name now. Not after what I did. Hans, and Sophie, Willi and Alex. They were the true patriots."

Silence hung heavy in the room. This was the time. The opportunity was dangling in front of him.

"There's something you're not telling me," he said.

"What are you talking about?"

"I know people. It's part of my job. I was trained to recognize when someone is hiding something, and I see you are."

"What about you, Herr Graf?" She spat the name out as if it were sour. "What are you hiding from me?"

"This isn't about me."

"Oh, isn't it?"

He was aware of the gun under his pillow and knew what effect reaching for it would have on this conversation, on all of this.

"There's something in you that you haven't told me about."

"You've told me nothing!" she shouted.

"I can't divulge the details of the mission that I'm undertaking—"

"I know, for the good of the Reich. You reach inside me, and when I give, you only ask for more." She stood up. "You say you're not a Nazi, but you're just like them. Maybe you're the one who's hiding something."

She made for the door and slammed it behind her, but the lock didn't catch, and it came ajar. The entire cabin quaked as she stomped to the kitchen. He heard her pull a chair up to the table and then the sound of her weeping.

He fought the weakness he felt within himself.

She wept alone.

What could he do stuck in this bed, in this cabin, in these mountains? Could he trust her? It was the same question, over and over in his mind, unchanging. Could she do what he couldn't now? It was true that she'd revealed much of herself, but he could tell there was something else lurking. He could feel it. What had happened to Fredi, her brother? She'd glossed over him in the story as if he'd faded into nothing. Why wasn't she visiting him if he was in an institution nearby? It was the last part of the riddle, the final puzzle piece. Once revealed, secrets could not be unsaid, and the pistol he'd stowed under his pillow might be his only recourse. He had to be sure. Her life depended on it.

Hours passed. Dinner never came. His water glass ran dry, and his chamber pot remained. He could hear her outside, could hear every footstep, but he didn't make a sound. He knew they were at a tipping point, and she had to be the one to make the next move. He waited. The cuckoo clock in the hallway chimed eleven. The impenetrable black of night had turned the window into a mirror, reflecting the yellow glow of the oil lamp.

The sound of her footsteps came. She stood at the door a few seconds, the light of the oil lamp dancing through her blue eyes. He didn't speak.

"I'm going to tell you what you want to know, but not for you, for me," she said, her voice faded and dull. "I've been carrying this around with me for too long. Hans was the only person I told, but there were some details I couldn't share even with him."

She stared off into nothing, the words tumbling out of her mouth.

Fredi was almost fourteen when they took him to the institution in 1939. His size was beginning to work against him. He was already almost six feet tall, and as his body grew, his limbs seemed to wither. The sight of him walking was a memory now, and Thomas was struggling to lift him in and out of his wheelchair each day. Franka was going to Munich to begin her new life. Her father had encouraged her to the point of almost forcing her to take the job. He insisted that she had her own life to live and that Fredi was going to prove too much for either of them. It was best that the professionals look after him. Franka accepted her father's wishes without protesting, but deep down she knew that it was her selfishness that was driving her away, her own wish to live a separate, independent life. She was twenty-two. Daniel was the only love she'd ever known. She wanted more. Freiburg seemed poisoned to her now. Munich, the big city, would offer a new hope.

Fredi was better than any single person she had ever known. Hatred, malice, vindictiveness, and spite—the emotions that formed the bedrock of Nazism—were beyond him. Love was all he knew. Those who knew him felt the radiance of this love. It was impossible to resist. He took with typical optimism and good grace the news that he was moving into the home, declaring that he'd have a chance to make hundreds of new friends. And so it was. When Franka came back to visit in November 1939, a few weeks after he'd moved in, it seemed as if he'd been there his whole life. Everybody knew him. Everybody loved him, and he spent almost an hour introducing her to his new friends there, from the nurses who greeted him with beaming grins, to the patients who couldn't move, or talk, who greeted him with a nod or a raised hand. No one was immune to his spirit.

Franka came back to visit as often as she could. She returned to Freiburg every three weeks or so, visiting Fredi each time with her father, whom the staff all greeted by name. Fredi seemed happy and in the best place. Her father reiterated that so often that she began to believe it, and the guilt of her moving to Munich eased. His condition stabilized. The doctors offered no hope of a cure, but the degeneration in his limbs slowed. Fredi could get around the institution with ease in his wheelchair, and he always had somewhere to be, someone to see and cheer up.

Franka knew several of the nurses from her time in school and kept in touch with them about Fredi's progress in between visits. The more time went on, the more at ease Franka and her father became. Their new life with Fredi was better than ever. Their father could relax for the first time in what seemed like many years. Franka's peace of mind over Fredi's welfare allowed her to launch into her new life with verve and passion. It seemed as if equilibrium might be possible.

The news came without warning. It was April 1941, and Franka was called to the phone at work. It was one of the nurses she knew from the institution, crying as she spoke.

The black SS vans came without warning on a Tuesday afternoon. It was a fine day, and all the patients, even those in catatonic states, were brought outside. The older patients who were able to stand were told to line up. The head nurse objected but was pulled away and arrested. Men in white coats who didn't identify themselves as doctors examined the older patients' mouths. The staff were assured that it was all routine and would soon end. The patients were put into groups, some with an ink stamp on their chests from the attendant. One group was allowed to return inside, while the other, much larger group was herded to where the vans were parked. The patients were loaded into the vans, some in their wheelchairs, others hobbling on crutches, and some carried on stretchers. One child asked the SS commandant where they were going, and he told them they were going to heaven. They went to the vans with reassured smiles on their faces.

Fredi was nervous. It was as if some instinct told him that they were lying. Fredi fought, flailing at the nurses, begging them to let him stay. Screaming nurses who tried to come to his aid were held back with the flat edge of rifles and thrown to the ground. A smiling SS man put a hand on Fredi's shoulder and told him that they'd soon return with wonderful stories to tell, and that where they were going to be offered free ice cream. Soothed by lies, Fredi began to calm. The same SS soldier took the handles of Fredi's wheelchair and pushed him to the black van to take his place with his friends. The SS men started the children in song as if they were sending them on a day trip to the fair. Fredi waved as the door slammed behind him, and the sound of the children singing lilted through the air as they drove away.

Franka's father made frantic inquiries as to his son's whereabouts and was met with a wall of feigned ignorance and denial. A few agonizing days passed before he was informed by letter that Fredi had died of a heart attack and his body had been cremated. The letter was accompanied by a death certificate, and at the bottom was the official salute of *Heil Hitler*.

The ruling came from Hitler himself. The führer was inefficient and lazy and prone to giving vague directives, which he expected to be followed in quick order. He had spoken in the past about the "useless eaters" at home who wasted resources while the flower of German youth was being sacrificed on the battlefield. People "unworthy of life" were to be cleared from their hospital beds in order to make room for the wounded coming home from the front, or for the mothers whose children could make up for the losses in battle. What use were the incurably ill, the physically and mentally disabled, and the senile, in this time of war? "Disenfranchising" them would make for a healthier, more vigorous nation, and go toward securing the future of the Aryan race. Hitler appointed a panel of doctors who were to decide who should live and who should die. Countless thousands were selected to be murdered.

Thomas Gerber was destroyed. Fredi's death sucked any life or love or joy out of him. The vitality and mirth he'd once been known for disappeared. Franka never heard him laugh after that. It was as if he didn't know how to anymore. He lost his job soon after and retreated into a drunken stupor. The depth of agony was beyond anything Franka had ever felt. She cried for days, unable to eat or sleep, the hatred for the Nazis burning like molten glass inside her. Fredi's murderers were glorified as heroes, and the man ultimately responsible deified. There was no escape—Fredi's murderers were everywhere. They were everyone who wore the Nazi armband or sported a Nazi pin. They were every SS man, and every loyal Aryan. They were every Hitler Youth and every wild-eyed hysteric screaming the Nazi salute at countless rallies. Who knew how many thousands had been slaughtered under the National Socialists' euthanasia program or subjugated because they were Jews, Gypsies, communists, trade-union leaders, political dissidents, or just citizens caught saying the wrong thing? Franka realized that a line had been drawn in German society between the perpetrators and the victims. There were thousands to share in the collective guilt that Hans wrote about, but there were so many more victims of the regime—those whose families had been sent to concentration camps or murdered as "unworthy of life." Their whole lives were lived in the open prison that was Nazi Germany under the rule of those who had committed heinous crimes against them.

They had no body to bury, and no one would ever face prosecution for Fredi's death. Franka went back to visit the institution, hoping for some closure. The nurses broke down upon seeing her. Franka's friend who'd called her fell into her arms, begging forgiveness for something she had no power to stop. Franka didn't stay long. The place was haunted now, and the staff reckoned it was only a matter of time before the SS came back for the rest of the patients. Franka returned to Munich, tried to immerse herself in music, work, anything to distract her from the ever-present pain inside her, anything to stop remembering. She met Hans. He understood, and they joined together in outrage, willing to die in service of the German people.

Fredi never left her. She saw his face every day, heard his laugh everywhere she went. He had been too good, too pure for the sewer of prejudice and hatred this country had become. This country wasn't for angels anymore. Only those twisted by hatred and fear could prosper here now.

The wind rattled the windows, then died down. A wordless two minutes had passed since she'd finished her story, and only the sound of her crying filled the air.

"I said too much," she said. "It's time I left you to get some sleep. There's nothing to be gained by—"

"Franka?"

She was walking toward the door but stopped at the sound of his voice.

"My name is John Lynch," he said. "I'm from Philadelphia, Pennsylvania, and I need your help."

Chapter 9

The island of Guadalcanal, November 1942

The wind brought some respite from the relentless heat, and John took his helmet off and brought his wrist up to his forehead to wipe away some of the sweat that seemed to cover his entire body. The men around him took off their backpacks and rifles, many using their helmets to sit on. The long grass on the hill above them hissed and danced in the breeze. John reached for the canteen on his hip. His hands were dry, cut to shreds, and shook as he held the water to his lips. He drank just enough to quench his thirst and screwed the cap back on. They hadn't been resupplied in several days, and water was running low. It didn't seem to be a priority for the top brass. A thousand tiny agonies wracked his body, and even crouching down seemed like a luxury after the day's march. He let his rifle rest against the wall of the ridge his platoon sat on. Some of the men peeled the tops off tin-can rations and dug in with filthy fingers. The smell of cigarette smoke drifted past. Men groaned. Few spoke. They knew what was coming. They knew that this was only a brief respite. This hill had to be taken.

Albert King, a farmer from Kansas, offered him a cigarette. John shook his head.

"Too good for my smokes, are you?" King said. "And that silver spoon up your ass's preventing you from sitting down, I see."

"I'm just waiting for the valet. It's so hard to get good service these days."

They heard the major's voice before they saw him stalking the line of exhausted soldiers, eyeing them each in turn. He stopped where John and King were sitting.

"I need volunteers," Major Bennett said. "I need five men to go up and take a look at what's up on that hill." He walked on a few feet, the weight of his stare on each of the men. "We're sitting ducks down here. If the enemy has a gun up there, which I think he does, he'll cut us apart like a scythe. I need five men to take out whatever's up there. The artillery came through earlier, so there's a good chance the only thing you'll find is a bunch of yellow bodies. Who wants the job?"

Tired, reluctant hands went up, John's among them. Bennett picked him first. The five men corralled around the major. "Lynch is going to lead you. If there's a gun up there, take it out. Report back to me."

The men followed John as he stuck his head up over the ridge. Waves of grass flowed with the wind three hundred feet up to the crest of the hill. The sun was setting. The sky turned orange and gold, daubed by some celestial painter. The light seemed to be thickening, as if they could reach out and feel it. John wiped sweaty palms on his faded fatigues and motioned for the others to follow him. He crouched, his eyes barely above the line of thick grass that hissed all around them. The men fanned out, King and Carpenter on his left, Smith and Munizza on his right. They moved in silence, their legs pumping through the thick grass. A hundred yards separated them from the rest of the company now. He motioned for the men to stop. They crouched as one, instantly invisible. He took binoculars from his belt. Nothing. The crest of the hill was just beyond his view, hidden by a ridge.

John motioned for the four men to follow him as he rose to his haunches, inching forward. The men were level with him, spread out thirty yards on either side. The company behind them was invisible now, hidden by the slope of the hill. John, his breath stilted and ragged, felt his heart beating faster. Each footstep was more painful than the last. His feet were blistered and raw, his socks crusted with blood. There was nothing here. They could signal the others to come up. He just had to see over the ridge in front of him. The crest of the hill was almost in view. He turned to look at the men with him, and in that split second they reached the ridge first. The clatter of machine-gun fire ripped through the air, and Munizza's chest opened up and sprayed a fountain of crimson. Rifle fire cracked, and Smith's head spurted blood, his body flopping backward. John threw himself to the ground. Bullets chewed the dirt in front of him, and he rolled to the side, where King was lying ten yards away. John crawled to him, the rattling of the machine gun filling his ears.

"I'm going to die here," King said. He was lying on his back, the fatigues on his chest stained red.

John took his hand. "You're not going to die, Al. I'll get you out of here."

John raised his head again, just enough to see the bunker a hundred yards away. He held the binoculars to his eyes, could make out the gun spewing fire. The ground in front of him erupted again, and he dropped his face to the dirt. A few seconds passed before he dared raise his head again. The others were dead. Carpenter's body was lying thirty yards to the left, Munizza beside him. Smith had rolled down the hill, his body punctured and pouring crimson blood. A bead of sweat ran down John's face as he opened up King's shirt. The wound was on the right side of his chest, below his lung. It wasn't a death sentence if he could get him some attention. How was he going to get him back down the hill? That machine gun would open up on them the second they moved. He could have crawled back down himself, but what about King, and the men who'd be cut down by this same gun later? They had to take the hill. There was no getting around it.

He took King's hand. "I have to go up and take a look. I'll be back. I'm going to make them pay for what they did to you and the others."

King's grip gave way, and John crawled below the line of the ridge, past Smith's corpse. He stuck his head up, could see the bunker, but no bullets came. The machine gun fired a few indiscriminate shots toward where King was lying, and a few rifles cracked, tearing up the ground where John had been. None came toward his position. He climbed up over the ridge and began crawling forward, using the two-foot-high grass as cover. His hands were shaking, his throat so dry that he longed to go back to Smith's body to check his canteen. He had left his own with his backpack and the company. He ignored every instinct crying out inside him to run back down the hill. Every movement forward felt unnatural, insane, but still he kept on.

John moved out to what he hoped would be an open expanse on the right. For all he knew, there would be a whole battalion of Japanese up there, and these would be the last few seconds he'd ever have. He thought of Penelope, remembered the way the sun had illuminated her skin in that hotel room in Honolulu before he'd shipped out. He could almost feel her touch again, could almost hear her voice. He thought of his father, his mother, his brother, and his sister and fought back the bitterness he still felt. He didn't want to feel that way. Not now. He remembered fall in Pennsylvania, and how the red leaves carpeted his parents' backyard, and how he and Norman had kicked through them as children.

The shower of bullets didn't come. He slithered forward on his elbows, rifle in hand. The bunker came into clearer view, a hundred yards away on his left, and just beside it, a mortar position. They were waiting. They would tear the company to pieces. Three Japanese soldiers sat readied at the mortar position, staring down at where King and the others were. The bunker was built into the ground, and a heavy machine gun protruded from its dark window. The Japanese were moving the gun from side to side, searching for any movement. John rolled onto his back and held the rifle above his chest. He thought about King. Should he return to him and try to make it back down to the rest of the company? The Japanese hadn't noticed him slipping through. He was in a perfect position to flank them. The machine gun wouldn't be able to stretch around to where he was at this angle. He was likelier to be picked off if he tried to make it back down. The Japanese would make sure he didn't have the chance to report their positions.

He crawled on, fifty yards from the mortar now. The Japanese soldiers were still staring down the hill, unaware of him. He was close enough to hear the men talking. One of them laughed. John jumped up, brought his rifle to his shoulder, and fired. He ran toward them, squeezing the trigger again. One of the soldiers went down, hit in the neck. The other two reached for their rifles as the roar of the machine gun began again, shooting at nothing. John saw his bullets strike one man in the chest. The last soldier raised his rifle, but John already had him and loosed off his last two rounds, hitting him in the head with both. John was still running, hot breaths thundering in and out of his lungs. He reached for a grenade on his belt, stopping at the mortar position to heave it toward the entrance to the bunker. It landed just as two Japanese soldiers were emerging, and they disappeared in a shower of mud and gore. He ran to the bunker, unhooked another grenade, and tossed it into the opening from six feet away. He hit the dirt as the concussion rocked the earth around him, almost lifting the roof off the bunker. A scream rang out as the figure of a man stumbled out, samurai sword aloft, his crazed eyes protruding from a blackened face. John reached for his rifle, pulled the trigger, but the hammer clicked—empty. The bloodied and burned soldier stumbled toward him, slicing down on the ground as John rolled away and reached for his knife. Half the man's face was gone, the skin hanging off like ribbons. He swung the sword at John again, but his swings were languid and weak. John grabbed at his arm, pulled him on top of him, and thrust his knife into the man's stomach. Hot blood spurted, and the soldier's eyes widened, life ebbing from his body. All fell silent. John pushed him off. Coated in the man's blood, he raised himself to his knees. The hiss of the wind in the grass came again and a deep darkness fell, the silhouettes of the company advancing up the hill to support him barely visible against the evening sky.

Washington, DC, February 1943

They had overstarched his shirt.

"Stop pulling at the collar," Penelope said, radiant in her red-sequin dress. "You're going to mess it up, you idiot." She seemed livid.

"It's fine, Penny. What does it matter?"

"It matters because people are watching."

She took him by the hand and led him into the ballroom. He felt out of step, as though he weren't there at all. The men in his platoon were in his thoughts always. The memories seemed to drag him back. The part of him that truly mattered was still there, would always be there.

He looked at his wife. She was as beautiful as she had been in his daydreams. Though they were together now, holding hands, she was nevertheless inaccessible. Something was lurking behind her smile, behind the kind words she'd offered upon meeting him at the train station. Her obsession with what others thought and felt seemed more alien to him than ever. Had she been like this when they'd first met in college? That fall evening in Princeton came into his mind. It had been a meeting of two great families—the ultimate merger. It had seemed forced at first—a ball at her parents' nearby mansion arranged almost specifically for them to meet. His first impulse was to reject the whole charade, but her beauty, and the urgings of his parents, drew him in. And he had loved her for a time—until he realized that the man she wanted wasn't the man he wanted to be. He felt her grip on his hand loosening as they weaved between the tables to where his parents were standing, waiting for them.

His father was friends with senators and congressmen, had met the president once, back in '38 when he'd toured the factories in Philadelphia. The photograph still hung above the desk in his study. He'd used his connections to get John home for a month's rest he had never asked for.

John still bore the marks of his time in the jungle, but the scabs were healing. It had taken him days to get clean, to scrub the dirt out from under his fingernails, to make himself presentable. People were watching. His father greeted him with a handshake. He hugged his sister, Pearl, and shook his brother Norman's hand, though he couldn't quite look him in the eye. This was the first time he'd been seen with them in public since he'd been back. This was their chance to show him off in front of their peers. Penelope kissed each of her in-laws and waited for John to hold out her chair before she sat down. Pearl sat on one side of him, with Penelope on the other. Pearl's husband was with the air force, stationed in England. The bombing raids on Europe had begun. Her eyes betrayed the worry she was working to hide.

The time for speeches arrived, each speaker proclaiming the urgent need to purchase war bonds. John's father took his turn and, motioning to his son from the podium, asked John to stand. He did his duty, holding up the Silver Star he'd won in Guadalcanal for clearing the machine-gun nest and saving King's life. The entire room of more than two hundred people stood as one to applaud. He felt Pearl's hand on his shoulder, saw Penelope standing back, clapping with the rest. He sat down once the applause had ended, the weight lifted.

Dinner ended, and a steady stream of family friends and well-wishers, some of whom he knew, came to shake his hand and tell him how much they admired the job he was doing out there, how they'd be right beside him if they weren't so damned old. His wrist hurt from shaking hands. His face ached from smiling. Penelope charmed them all, and old men opened their checkbooks.

The music had begun when John's father called him over. He was standing beside a silver-haired, rather dumpy man in his sixties wearing a tuxedo.

"John, I'd like you to meet someone. This is William Donovan. Bill, this is my son John."

"Pleasure to meet you," Donovan said, offering a bone-crushing handshake.

"John wants something more than I can offer him."

"What are you talking about, Dad?" John had a sense of where the conversation was going—it was one he and his father had often had, one that always left him feeling guilty.

"I planned for him to take over my business," John's father explained, "but he didn't want it—almost broke my heart. But my other son, Norman, is doing a great job."

"Why didn't you want to continue your father's work, son?" Donovan asked.

"It wasn't for me."

"It's truly a shame, but John never wanted to become the captain of industry I groomed him to be. He wants to make his own way."

"Can we talk about this later?" John said.

"Yes, perhaps that would be a better time. I'll leave you men to talk."

Donovan waited until John's father was gone to begin. "Firstly, I just wanted to thank you for your service."

"Thank you."

"Do you know who I am, John?" Donovan's tone left John in no doubt that he was military, yet he was wearing civilian clothes.

"I'm not sure, sir. I don't want to make any presumptions. My father seemed eager for us to meet."

"There's a reason for that, son. I'm an old friend of your father's. We served in the last war together, when you were a baby."

"Why haven't we met before, sir?"

"Your father and I lost touch for a while. We hadn't seen each other in years, until we met at a dinner like this just before Christmas last year." Donovan reached into his pocket for a cigarette case and offered one to John. When he declined, Donovan put them back in his pocket without lighting one for himself. "Your father told me about you, and your incredible exploits in service of our country. He told me you're a true patriot."

"That I am, sir."

"You speak German too, don't you, from your time over there?"

"We lived in Berlin for a few years back in the twenties, before things got too crazy. My father set up some factories over there."

"How is your German now?"

"I might be a little rusty, but I'm fluent. I was my family's translator for the first couple of years there. Pearl and Norman are older than me. They stayed in boarding school over here and came for the summers."

"So why the Pacific when you've so many connections with Europe?"

"I just wanted to serve, sir. I knew that someone with my background would most likely be expected to join the officer elite. I knew that, but I wanted to—"

"You wanted to prove that you could get down and dirty, that you could serve with the other grunts."

"I suppose you could put it that way, sir."

"Have you heard of the Office of Strategic Services, the OSS?"

"I heard some things," John said, now understanding the real reason he'd been summoned home. "I heard whispers about an agency set up for spies."

"It's more than that, but spying is a part of what we do. I set up the OSS last year to coalesce the various intelligence departments of the army, the navy, and the air force. Our job is to coordinate espionage activities behind enemy lines for all branches of the armed forces. We have more than ten thousand men and women working for us now."

"What was in place before the OSS?"

"A few old ladies who looked after some filing cabinets at the War Department."

John knew more than he'd revealed. He'd heard about "Wild Bill" and his pet project. It had just taken him a while to realize that was who he was talking to. The OSS was a place where the well connected could play at war. Donovan used his connections in the old-boy network to staff the agency, with the personnel recruited from Ivy League schools, prestigious law firms, and big banks. It appeared to be a club for a privileged caste John was trying to escape.

"We're neck-deep in both conflicts right now. We have agents in the Pacific and behind enemy lines in Europe. These men and women volunteer to walk among the predators, with no reception committees, and often no safe houses or friends in the most hostile territory imaginable. These are the bravest, finest men and women in the armed forces, providing us with vital intelligence on a daily basis."

A gray-haired woman in a black dress tapped Donovan on the shoulder, and he greeted her with a kiss on the cheek. Donovan told her he'd see her in a few minutes, waiting until she'd gone to continue speaking. "This is a new type of war. The old days of arranging a fight in a field are long gone. This war is going to be won by the side who knows more about what the other guy is thinking, and who knows what he's going to do before he does it."

"Why are you telling me all these things, sir?"

"I've spoken to your father a lot over these last few months. His eyes light up with pride when he mentions your name. He told me he wanted to leave the reins of the family business to you, but you wanted something else. He also told me how you and your brother have fought since he took over."

John wondered how much this man knew about him. There could be only one reason why Donovan was so curious.

"My father told you I didn't approve of what my brother was doing with his business?"

"Among other things. We spoke about you at length. He said you weren't as comfortable as your brother in this world." Donovan gestured around the room. "I know you joined the marines because, deep down, you wanted to prove you could make it on your own. I know because I see myself in you. I was a lawyer before the last war, but I wanted more. I wanted to serve, but not just my country. I wanted to prove something to myself."

The man's magnetism was undeniable. He was soft spoken but carried an unquestionable authority.

"Do you think joining the OSS would be something you'd be interested in?"

"What kind of men are you looking for, sir?"

"I'm looking for a cat burglar with a conscience. I need a man who can work with his intelligence before his heart. I need someone who's honest yet devious, inconspicuous yet audacious. I need someone who's hot-blooded and cool, all at the same time.

"With your skillset and the manner in which you've already proven yourself in the field, I know you'd be an ideal fit for our organization."

"I assume you've already been through my service records?"

"We're meticulous, John. We have to be. Our role in this war is too important to be left to chance."

John turned around. His father was forty feet away standing at the bar, drink in hand. Donovan was right—he did look proud.

The letter from Penelope came three months later when John was entrenched in OSS training in a park in rural Virginia masquerading as the Reich. The instructors were teaching him, and the other recruits, how to survive behind enemy lines. Without a training facility, the fledgling organization had taken over segments of Prince William Forest Park, turning former summer camps into secret training grounds. John was coming back from several nights with little sleep in the field. A hot shower and a bed seemed like luxury beyond measure. Mail call came, and he was handed a letter. The postmark on the envelope was from two weeks before. John sat on his bunk as he opened it. He hadn't seen her in almost six weeks, had barely felt the lack of her. He knew what was coming before he opened it. He would have done the same in her position. He read the first two words of the letter and almost laughed. It was the ultimate cliché of war, and it was happening to him.

> *Dear John,*
> *I met a man. A captain in the air force. I want to marry him. I'm asking you for a divorce as the last act of love between us. I don't love you anymore. You're not the man I married. I love someone else. Please help me leave you. Please do this for the love that we once shared. I know we'll always care for one another. A love as strong as the one we shared never truly dies. But our time is done. You have another life now, separate from mine. Our souls are no longer joined, are no longer indivisible from another as they once were.*
>
> *I'm sorry. Please forgive me, and grant me the divorce I need to leave you with my soul intact.*
>
> *Sincerely,*
> *Penelope*

It had been years since he cried. He didn't even know he was still capable of it. His emotions felt alien in a place like this, and he looked around to make sure no one was watching. The letter was still firmly in his grip. He couldn't let it go. He had no idea he still loved her. He knew that he had stowed his feelings for her until it was convenient to revisit them. Perhaps once the war was over—maybe then there would have been time to love her again. But now it was too late. He reached for the pencil he kept beside his bed and scrawled down a few words on a piece of paper. He could never hate her, not when it had been his fault. He read and reread the letter and then wrote her back—*You can have your divorce*—and mailed it to her the next day.

December 1943, over southwest Germany

The rumble of engines rendered almost any other noise irrelevant. John could feel every vibration through his body. He was taut as wire, his heart galloping. He thought of the words of his superior officer, who'd spoken with unvarnished honesty about the fact that they weren't sure of the strength of the false documents he carried, nor of the cover story they'd concocted for him. They had little precedent to judge the current circumstances. The OSS had never parachuted an agent into Germany before, let alone one unaided and alone. He knew the risks. He was a volunteer and had beaten out many more agents for the honor of fulfilling this mission.

The crewman cupped his hands around his mouth and spoke up over the engines: "We're coming up to the target. We should be there in thirty minutes."

John nodded, and the crewman disappeared back inside the cockpit. John moved to the window, a few feet from where he had been sitting. The clouds swirled by in the dark night, and only a few lights dotted the vast quilt of black on the ground below. He ran his hands over the Luftwaffe uniform he was wearing and went over his cover in his head for what seemed like the millionth time. He felt as if Werner Graf had taken hold of his soul now, that he truly *was* him. It felt like John Lynch was a cover, or at best, a memory of a life he'd once known. There seemed no point in being John Lynch anymore. Reminiscing could jeopardize the mission, could cost him his life. He would return to himself one day, when Werner Graf had served his purpose.

The plane jigged as it hit turbulence, and he was thrown forward, but his seat belt locked him in place. One of his instructors had warned him that the Gestapo would check for strap bruises across his chest and thighs. He dismissed those thoughts as soon as they came. No use in worrying. No use at all.

A rumble came over the din of the engines. John raised his head up. Another rumbling sound came, and then another. John knew they were over Germany now. He'd never reckoned that flak would take down the plane before he reached his drop zone. He'd thought through almost every other scenario. He'd gone over every conceivable question he might be asked, practiced his accent and his cover story more times than he could remember, but he hadn't negotiated for being shot down. The crew chief stuck his head out of the cockpit again to tell him they were taking flak on both sides. John gave him the thumbs-up, and the chief disappeared back inside. He was just closing the cockpit door again when a loud explosion ripped through the air. The force of the blast opened up a gash in the side of the plane a few yards from where John was sitting, and cold air rushed in. John gripped his pack, his knuckles white. The wing was torn like paper. The engine poured smoke, hacking like an old man clearing his throat. John felt for his parachute, knew that the drop zone was probably a hundred miles away. The plane shuddered and fell as more flak exploded on each side. The explosions came louder and louder, and the plane shook with each concussion, tossing John back and forth in his seat. Another jolt rocked the plane, this time on the other side, but it limped on. The flak continued.

The crew chief opened the door again, surveying the damage as the aircraft continued to drop. The flak was beginning to level off, the explosions sporadic now. John looked out the window again. The engine was billowing thick black smoke. It sputtered to a halt. The man stuck his head back into the cockpit, and John could just about make out the shouting. The chief made his way over to him.

"We're never going to make it to the dropping point!" he shouted, but John already knew that. "We're crippled. The starboard engine's gone. We'll never make it back. We're going to have to turn around and try to get to Switzerland. If you want to jump, it's going to have to be now."

John nodded and unbuckled his safety belt. Were they high enough? The plane seemed to be losing altitude by the second. They were miles from the target, but he could make it there if he got to the ground in one piece. If he stayed on board the plane, the best he could hope for was to report back that he'd failed—if they made it that far at all. The flak had stopped, for now. They'd passed whatever city the flak had been defending, and now a tapestry of darkness lay below him.

The crew chief shook John's hand. His good wishes were lost in the roar of the wind as the jump hole opened. John moved to the jump hole, felt the surge of the airstream. The dispatcher checked the static line on his parachute and gave him the thumbs-up. The green light flicked on as the plane bumped and jerked. He forced himself to concentrate on the task at hand, remembering to jump straight, legs together, and tuck his chin into his chest. He felt the plane slowing, and the dispatcher pounded his shoulder. He jumped. The cold air crashed into him, as if water from a waterfall. He felt a tug at his thighs and armpits as the chute opened. The plane disappeared into the black. The night was still, and he was alone. The roar of the engines dissipated, leaving only the sounds of his own breathing and the rushing air. The parachute flapped as he hurtled toward the deep-black ground below. There was no way to know where he was landing, but the dark told him he was somewhere remote, somewhere unpeopled, and that might give him a chance. He realized he was too low, but there was nothing to be done. He thought to pray, but his numb lips fumbled the words as the ground rushed toward him like an unseen, soundless express train. He felt the agony in his legs as his body collided with the snow-covered ground. He opened his eyes, the spread of snow all around him, and felt his body go slack as everything faded to nothing.

Chapter 10

Franka sat frozen to the chair. The fire had gone out in the living room, and the temperature in the cabin was noticeably lower. He was motionless before her, helpless. She knew the truth now. She felt vindicated. She wasn't going insane. Her suspicions were correct. This man in her father's cabin, whom she had rescued from the snow, was an American. A spy. She'd known he was American or English, had been sure of the fact for days now, but to hear him say it was still a revelation. She thought of Daniel and the Gestapo. There would be no leniency this time. Sheltering a spy meant the guillotine, but only after tortures that would make death seem like a mercy. Yet somehow she felt free. For the first time since she'd delivered those leaflets, seen the enthusiasm and pride in Hans's eyes, she felt like she was living again. Truly living. Not just eating and sleeping and breathing. Not just killing time—living a consequential life.

"I must tend to the fire," she said, and left him there.

Thoughts bounced around inside her mind and collided. She knew everything now, everything except why. Why was he here? What was his mission? What was this help he'd asked her for? The logs crackled as she tossed them onto the glowing embers in the fireplace. She stood for a few seconds, warming her hands before going to the kitchen. She was hungry. Little food remained. Stretching her rations for two people was hard and would only be more difficult now that the reserve of canned food they'd had was gone. She thought of going to town tomorrow. No need to go all the way to Freiburg. She stopped and rested against the kitchen table, her arms folded across her chest. She closed her eyes, then walked back toward the bedroom.

"So now you know everything," he said.

His accent was unchanged, but she could see the cracks in it now. She wondered how he would hold up under questioning—wondered if those trained to weed out such details would notice more quickly than she.

"Your German is excellent, not rusty at all."

"It was a little before my training. It came back quickly. That was the easy part."

"What was the hard part?"

"Learning to resist interrogation techniques. The simulated torture."

"I was interrogated by the Gestapo."

"Of course."

"They didn't need to torture me. They knew everything already." She paused for a few seconds and went to the window. "Do you still think of your family, of your home in America?"

"I've tried not to. I tried to be Werner Graf, but John Lynch kept rearing his ugly head."

"You were thoroughly convincing."

"How did you suspect?"

"I heard you talking in your sleep when I found you. You were delirious, calling out in English."

"I had no idea I could ever meet someone like you. I didn't know someone like you existed."

Franka had heard how earnest Americans could be. It was a different experience.

"I do have a question for you—why did you hold taking over your father's business against your brother, when you didn't want it?"

"I didn't like what he was doing. He's going to run it into the ground. My father's life's work is in jeopardy."

"If that was so important to you, why didn't you take over yourself? You gave up the right to criticize Norman's decisions when you turned your father down."

"You don't miss a beat, do you?"

"You haven't answered my question."

"I didn't want to pursue a path that led only to making money. I wanted something more. Who knows what would have happened if it weren't for this war? I'd probably be home right now, working with Norman."

"Instead of fighting with him."

"I was trying to help."

Franka felt she'd pushed it enough. "You must be hungry. You haven't eaten all day."

"I'm famished."

"Food is getting low. I'll need to go to town tomorrow."

She went to the kitchen and heated the last of the stew and tore off a hunk of the bread she'd made to go with it. It took him less than two minutes to eat it all. She waited until he'd finished to ask the question.

"Why are you here?"

John took the napkin she'd laid on the edge of the tray and wiped the corners of his mouth.

"You deserve to know," he said, and put the napkin down. "I was never meant to be here. My drop zone was a few miles outside of Stuttgart. We mapped out the safest route to get us there, avoiding the major cities where we knew the ground-to-air fire was concentrated. I don't suppose they anticipated the installations around Freiburg. They must be new."

"They were installed after the bombing raid that killed my father. The city hadn't suffered too much before then. It was only a matter of time before Freiburg joined the other German cities the Allies have flattened."

"I'm sorry about your father. War has a habit of victimizing innocents."

"He was in bed when the bombers came. I don't suppose he ever knew what hit him. He never knew who murdered him."

"Your father's death was unfortunate," John said, immediately regretting his choice of words.

"Unfortunate? He was the last person I had in this world, and you took him from me. And now you're asking for my help?"

"The Nazis are your enemy, not the Allies. The bombers who came to Freiburg that night had no idea—"

"Are you going to tell me that they had no idea they were bombing civilians? What about the raids on Hamburg, Cologne, or Mainz? Thousands of innocents have died in firebombing raids."

"As thousands have died in London, and Birmingham, and throughout the occupied territories."

"But you imply that the Allies are the just cause? How can you justify the murder of hundreds of thousands of German civilians?"

"War is a foul beast. To tell the truth, I don't think the lives of German civilians matter to the generals who send those bombers, just as the lives of British or Soviet citizens don't matter to the Germans."

"What about to you?"

"What do you mean?"

"Do they matter to you, John? You lived here once."

"Franka, I see the newsreels of German citizens yelling allegiance to Hitler. Everyone back home did. The Allied bombing campaign is designed to break the will of the German people to fight."

"Don't you realize that the will of the German people doesn't matter? The Nazis subjugated the will of the German people years ago. The phrase doesn't hold any meaning anymore."

"That may be the case, but the Nazis started this. They started the indiscriminate bombing of Warsaw and London before the US even entered the war. If the Nazis are using the German people as a shield, then that's a pity, but that won't hinder the Allied efforts to win."

"Would you help me if German bombers had killed your father?"

"I don't see how that could be possible."

"But what if it did happen? What if your loyalties were torn between government and people? Would you go against the will of your government for the good of the people they're meant to serve?"

"That could never happen."

"No one thought it could happen in Germany—a modern industrial nation. A bastion of science and the arts."

"If you're asking me if I'd maneuver against my own government like you did, under pain of death, then the answer is that I don't know."

"Would you help a foreign agent against the apparent will of your own people?"

"If everyone I loved was dead because of them, and if they had warped the things that made America great, and noble, and just—yes, yes I would."

"Robespierre said, 'No one loves armed missionaries.'"

"I am not your enemy, Franka. You wouldn't have saved my life and kept me here these past days if you believed I was. There's a reason you took me in. Perhaps one day the German nation will grow to appreciate the efforts of the Allies."

"If there's a German nation left to consider the past."

"It may seem ironic, but the Allies are the only hope left for Germany. Use me, Franka. Give me the chance to help rid this country of the Nazis on your behalf."

Franka snatched the tray off his lap. A fork clattered onto the floor, and she had to bend down to grab it.

"I hate the Nazis. I don't want to feel that, but it's with me every day. I think about what they've done—"

John's voice was sharp as he interrupted her. "Leave the hatred behind. Do something for the future of the German people, for your father, and Fredi."

"I don't know. What do you want me to do?"

"Something simple. Something almost any adult could do."

"I need some time."

She went to the kitchen and set the tray on the table. Her heart felt like a stone. She dipped her hands in the water pooled in the sink before bringing them up to rinse her face. She thought of all the people she'd known who'd been swept up and seduced by the National Socialists and their lies. She wasn't like them. She was a criminal, a convicted enemy of the state, and now she was harboring another enemy. She couldn't be any less of a Nazi. It was impossible. Turning him in wasn't an option—she would rather die. So what then? She could let him go his own way and keep her silence as he slipped secretly into the belly of the Reich, but where would *she* go then? What would she do? Would she go back into the woods to finish what she started the night she found him? Or would she just do her best to survive the war? This man offered more.

"Continue your story," she said as she walked back in. "Tell me why you're here. If you want my help, I need to know everything."

"The flak hit the plane I was in, and I bailed out over the mountains. Then you found me." He paused for a long two seconds before continuing. "My mission is a man," he said. The tension seemed to evaporate with every word. "His name is Rudolf Hahn. He's a scientist—one of the most brilliant minds in the world. He's pioneering work in a new field of physics, which could change the war in Germany's favor. One of our German agents infiltrated his laboratory and made contact with him. Hahn agreed to defect to America. I'm here to get him out."

"Why couldn't the agent that contacted him do it?"

"He's a diplomat, and not suited to the more dangerous elements of the task. The Gestapo seemed to be onto him, so he had to melt into the background. Hahn is still in place. They haven't arrested him yet."

"So how did you plan to get him out of the country?"

"Let's slow down a minute."

"You need my help, don't you?"

"Yes, but—"

"You can't do anything, because he's a hundred twenty miles from here, and you're stuck in that bed with two broken legs."

John reached for the glass of water beside the bed and took a sip.

"So you want my help but still don't trust me enough to tell me everything," she said.

"Can you learn to trust me, and to agree with what I stand for?"

His question was met with silence.

"We were planning on traversing the Alps south of Munich and getting into Switzerland because the mountain passes offered the most secret way to cross the border. Although getting there would have been no easy feat. We had a guide, and the OSS trained me in mountain climbing, for all the good that's going to do me now." He looked at his legs and ran his hands over the casts that encased them.

"How is this scientist going to change the course of the war for Germany? What's he working on?"

"I can't meet him myself," John said, ignoring her question.

"What's he working on?"

"You're going to force me to tell you, aren't you?"

"If I'm going to risk my life for you, and your cause, I want to know why. I want to know what's at stake."

"Professor Hahn and his colleagues have been working on a new technology called nuclear fission. They published a paper in 1939 about the new process, and the Allies have been trying to monitor their progress ever since."

"And what's so special about this *nuclear fission*?" She fumbled the words.

"I wouldn't tell you even if they'd told me, but I believe it's enormous and that it could turn the tide of the war. Without Hahn, the project will die. He's the brains behind it. The Nazis don't realize what they're on the cusp of. The project has been underfunded and almost ignored by the hierarchy. Hitler's obsessed with jet-propulsion engines. They're more focused on that end."

"So why has this Hahn decided to turn?"

"He's not happy with the treatment of the Jewish population by the regime. Many of his friends and colleagues before the war were Jews. The Nazis excluded all Jews from the work on account of their race. Many of them are dead, or in exile now. We've taken some in ourselves. He's also frustrated with the lack of funding. The United States realizes how important his work is. He'll receive all the funding and support he could ever need once we get him back to the States."

"So the Americans can develop this new technology themselves?"

"We need to develop it before the Nazis, or even the Soviets, get their hands on it. It's a race that could determine the outcome of the war. If the Nazis realize what they could potentially have on their hands, it could change everything. That won't happen if Hahn disappears. We need his knowledge and expertise. If they've made a breakthrough, we need to know about it."

"Where do I come in?"

"The arrangement was that I make contact with Hahn, gain his trust, and then spirit him across the border into Switzerland."

"You want me to get him across the border?" Franka said, wide-eyed.

"No, I just need you to meet with him, to tell him what happened to me, and then . . ." It was hard to fathom it had come to this.

"What?"

"Then bring him back here so I can take him across the border myself once I recover."

"It's going to be a month before you can walk again, and you certainly won't be climbing any mountains then."

"Let me worry about the details."

"I would say that's more than a detail. You want me to go to Stuttgart to meet this man, don't you?"

"I can't see another way."

"I've no training in espionage. I've never done anything like this before."

"It's just the matter of meeting someone, hearing him out, and delivering a message."

"What if he won't speak to me, or if I get caught?"

"I don't see how you could unless you turn yourself in, and I'll give you the code words that will force him to listen to you. Will you do it? Will you help me?"

"I don't know—it seems like a lot . . ."

"It's much simpler than it seems. You can do this. You can make a difference."

"Okay," she said, her eyes closed.

"Thank you," he said, taking her elbow. It was the first time they'd ever touched without reason, and she felt a chill from it. It was ridiculous.

"The arrangement was to meet him in the public park. He was to sit on a bench reading the newspaper."

"In this weather?"

"He was to be there for a short time, between five fifty and six p.m., and only one day a week—on Mondays. He was there earlier today waiting for me."

"Will he be there next week? Should I go then?"

"With Christmas coming on Saturday? I don't think so. It's likely he'll go home to Berlin for the week. I think it's best if we go the week after, on January third. That way I'll have some more time to heal, and you'll be better prepared. You won't have to do anything too spectacular, just meet the man and tell him what happened to me."

"How will he know I'm not Gestapo?"

"The code words. Once he hears them, he'll know you're with me. You'll just need to make contact with him and perhaps give him the option of coming here once I'm better, but we can decide that later. We've plenty of time."

"Two weeks," Franka said. "I'll need to get you some crutches. No use in having you confined to that bed. You'll start to develop sores. The best thing for you is to get up and moving. I need to go into town to get some food tomorrow. I'll pick some up there."

"They'll have crutches in the store with the rationing going on?"

"No, I wouldn't think so, but I have some connections in the medical center there. I'll get them for you."

Morning came with a scythe of cold as always, but this one felt different. Sleep had been a long time coming the previous night. Many questions were still left unanswered. No need to bombard John now. They had other waters to navigate. They needed food first. She picked up the ration coupons John had given her. She knew they were forged, but would the shopkeeper notice? Without them, they would have only hers to rely on. It wouldn't be enough. They'd starve. She held his coupons up to the light, examining each letter printed on the paper. It seemed convincing enough, although upon close inspection the lettering looked wobbly and unsure in parts. She would try. The only other option would be to buy the food on the black market. The best food was available to those willing to pay for it, but that might attract attention from the police. It was too great a risk to take.

John was awake when she brought him breakfast.

"Good morning, Fräulein."

"I trust you slept well."

"I did. The best I've slept in a long time. How are you feeling about what we discussed?"

"Nervous. Bewildered. I feel I've been given a great responsibility."

"I wouldn't have told you about this if you weren't capable of it. I know I made the right decision."

She sat with him as he ate the breakfast of cheese and dregs of the stew from two nights before. She didn't tell him that there wasn't enough food for them both to eat. They spoke about the weather, the journey she was to make that day, and his health. There seemed nothing else to say about who he was, or his mission. The night before, she had promised herself that she wouldn't press him.

Franka went to the front door and pushed it open before stepping outside. No new snow had fallen in two days, but the previous weeks had brought so much that her car was still buried, the road impassable. Her breath plumed out in front of her. The cold sun shone down, good for nothing more than reflecting off the white of the snow below, and she slipped on her sunglasses.

Daniel Berkel's shadow hung over Freiburg. Her hometown was too dangerous. Even if she didn't run into him, there were too many people who could recognize her, too many people happy to help the Gestapo. There was no need to go to the pharmacy in the city like last time. Sankt Peter was just a couple of miles away. It was a small town but had a grocery store and a medical center. It would do for their needs this time. She strapped on her skis and set out. Franka thought about John Lynch, and what Philadelphia must have looked like. She thought about Rudolf Hahn, and what she was going to say to him.

She saw no one until she reached the line outside the grocery store. She joined at the back, resting her skis against the wall. No familiar faces gawked at her. Most of the people she knew from here were away at war or dead already. It was a relief to be anonymous. She mixed her ration coupons with the ones John had given her so the fakes wouldn't stand out. It worked. The shopkeeper didn't notice. She hid her elation as she left the store, her rucksack as full as her collection of ration vouchers allowed.

The narrow streets of the small town of Sankt Peter were deathly quiet. Franka kept her head down as she trudged along the sidewalk, all the way to the medical center. A teenager with his arm in a sling glanced up at her as she pushed the door open. Beside him sat two young men missing eyes and arms, one in a wheelchair, the other on crutches. The war had penetrated every inch of German society. No one was immune. A gray-faced old woman sat behind a drab wooden desk covered with papers. Franka went to her and waited her turn behind a mother with a baby in her arms. Once Franka's turn came, the woman behind the desk peered up at her with tired eyes.

"I'm here to see Martina Kruger; she's a nurse here."

"What's your business with Nurse Kruger?"

"I'm an old friend—it's of a personal nature."

"Nurse Kruger is busy, why don't you—"

"It won't take more than a few minutes," Franka said.

The woman grumbled under her breath.

"Perhaps she's due a break."

"Give me one minute." The woman disappeared through a door behind her.

Two minutes passed before the door opened again and Martina smiled, throwing her arms around Franka. They had known each other since they were children, had met in kindergarten and gone through school together. Martina had been in the same troop in the League of German Girls. Franka hadn't seen her since she'd left for Munich in '39. She looked almost the same, pretty, with long brown hair and shining green eyes. The woman glared at Martina, who scowled back before leading Franka outside. She lit a cigarette and offered one to Franka, who shook her head. They talked about Martina's family for a couple of minutes. She had two daughters, and a husband stationed in France. Franka trusted her, not enough to ask her for morphine, or anything she might get in trouble for—but surely a pair of old crutches wouldn't be missed?

"What are you doing back here?" Martina said.

Franka wondered how much she knew—probably everything.

"I came back to hear the reading of my father's will."

"I was so sorry to hear that he died. I saw his name in the paper. I couldn't believe it."

"Thank you. It seemed so random in a city that has hardly been touched."

"The bombs are coming. It's only a matter of time before the Allies try to murder us all."

Franka ignored the comment, although she felt a sharp spike of anger stab through her.

"I'm sorry not to see you for so long and then ask you a favor, but I need something."

Martina lit up another cigarette. "Of course, what is it?"

"I'm staying in my parents' old cabin in the mountains. You remember it, don't you?"

"Yes, of course."

"I'm there with my boyfriend."

Martina's eyes lit up. "You never told me you were seeing anyone. Is it serious?"

"I think it might be. He's a medic, but he's back from the front. We're taking some time together while we can. We have a problem, however. He broke his leg skiing, and we're snowed in."

"Oh, no."

"It's not been easy. I managed to set a cast on his legs myself."

"I thought it was just one leg?"

"No, it's two. I meant to say two."

Franka could feel her heart thumping in her chest. Martina's expression changed to grave seriousness.

"He's okay, and in casts, but he can't get around. I need some crutches. I was wondering if you had any old sets lying around that I could borrow for a few weeks until the snow melts."

"Does he need a doctor? Shall I ask—"

"No, that won't be necessary. I just need crutches. I was able to set his legs, and they seem to be healing well."

Franka stopped talking. Martina finished her cigarette and crushed it under her foot. She looked around to see if anyone was listening in.

"When do you need them?"

"Now, if possible."

"Give me a few minutes, and I'll see what I can do."

Franka waited outside in the cold for fifteen minutes and was just beginning to wonder if she was coming back, when Martina emerged, a pair of old crutches under her arm.

"These have seen a few winters, but they should do the job. I don't think they'll be missed either."

"Thank you so much," Franka said as Martina handed them to her. "This is going to mean the world to Tommy."

Martina stayed with Franka a few more minutes before duty called and they said their goodbyes. Franka tied the crutches to her backpack and made her way out of town, explaining to the guard who stopped her that they were for her war-veteran boyfriend. He didn't ask questions after that and handed her papers back.

Franka arrived back at the cabin, brandishing the crutches like a trophy. John slipped them under his armpits and pushed himself upward. Movement was still difficult, and he had to drag his legs behind him, but his situation now was miles ahead of being stuck in bed. His first journey was to the kitchen. They sat at the table together as Franka made up a meal of soup, bread, and cheese, and they ate it like it would be their last.

Later that day, Martina Kruger thought long and hard about the meeting with her old friend. Why hadn't Franka wanted her boyfriend to see a doctor? Even if the bones were healing well, surely it would have been better to make sure? The thought stayed with her through Christmas, and even into the new year of 1944. She couldn't shake the way Franka had looked at her and how unusual her request was. It was with some regret that she went to the local Gestapo office to report her friend. It was probably nothing, she reasoned, and surely Franka didn't have anything to hide, but it was best to let the professionals deal with it. She suppressed any feelings she had about loyalty to friends, because in times of war like these, it was more important to put the führer first. Franka Gerber was a criminal after all, and Martina couldn't risk getting involved. She had her family to think about. The Gestapo agent agreed with her—she had done the right thing.

Fear & pressure can deeply influence people, but not always to do the right thing.

Christmas came. They spent it together. They talked for hours on end. She went through every idea that the White Rose championed, and he told her he'd heard of the massive drops all over Germany of the Munich students' manifesto. That was her Christmas present—the quiet satisfaction that what they'd done hadn't been in vain. She told him of her childhood in the mountains. They had time to go through every summer she spent here, every memory she had. He taught her some English phrases—military language mostly. He told her of Philadelphia, his parents' house, and sunny days at the shore during the summer. He talked about his father's business and how uncomfortable he was with the privilege he'd been raised in. But the way he spoke about it was different from before. It wasn't something to hold a grudge over. There were far more important things to live and die for.

He told her about meeting his wife in Princeton, and about how happy their first few years together had been. She married her airman a week after the divorce went through, a month before John shipped out. He'd never told anyone his story this thoroughly before—his ex-wife, his childhood, his parents, and where he'd grown up. He'd never had the time. He went through every conceivable detail he could remember about Rudolf Hahn and told her everything he knew about his work, which wasn't much. There were parts of the mission shrouded even from him. He didn't need to know everything.

They talked about how they'd get Hahn back to the cabin. It would be best to wait until John's legs healed. That would be at the end of January. Only then could they strike for the border. With all they talked about, all the hours they spent together, they never mentioned the future. They never spoke about what Franka would do once John set off for Switzerland with Hahn. Only the mission mattered. He repeated those phrases over and over in his mind, until they became a mantra, words to live by.

Franka moved his bed above the pried-up boards in the bedroom. They developed a drill—what to do if the Gestapo did come looking for him. They went through it dozens of times. The only warning they would have would be the sound of a car pulling up. In that case John was to go to the bedroom immediately and slip the boards over himself as he lay in the space beneath that she'd made as comfortable as she could. The bed would cover the floorboards, which in turn would cover him. There would be no hiding if the Gestapo conducted a thorough search, but what reason would there be to do so? No word had come in the local papers of missing Allied airmen, or of spies. It seemed that they didn't know he was in the area, let alone hiding in her father's cabin.

The new year came. She had seen no one but him since her last trip to town almost two weeks before, when she had only spoken to Martina, the officer who'd asked for her papers, and the people working in the various stores she visited. John was spending more time outside the room. When she returned from her daily walk, she often found him sitting in the rocking chair by the fire, reading banned literature. He wanted to read only the books that the Nazis would throw her in jail for. The stiffer the sentence for having it, the more he wanted to read it. *The Magic Mountain* by Thomas Mann sat on the table where he'd left it, his bookmark jutting out. They only listened to illegal, foreign radio stations, reveling in the freedom of their solitude. She was fascinated as he told her about what was going on elsewhere in the war, the battles in Russia and Italy, the combat in the Pacific.

She cooked stew most nights, and he helped cut and dice the vegetables so thinly that they melted in her mouth. They had started eating together on Christmas Day, and it was a habit now.

They were silent as they ate that night in January. His table manners were exquisite. She tried to imagine him sitting down with his fellow soldiers and eating the C rations he'd described in such detail. It was hard to picture.

He raised his napkin and dabbed away breadcrumbs on the sides of his mouth before continuing with his meal.

"I see you looking at me with that smile on your face," he said. "What are you thinking about?"

"I'm just trying to picture you with your fellow soldiers, the 'grunts,' as you called them." She was proud of herself for using the English slang he'd taught her.

"It took a while for some of them to accept me in basic training. Once they saw that we were all on the same side, and prejudice against your own could cost you your life . . . I'd like to think I earned their respect."

He put his fork down, his meal unfinished.

"I know you're nervous about tomorrow," he said. "Everything will be okay. You only need speak to him for a few minutes. No one will suspect a thing. As far as we know, he's not under any suspicion."

"As far as you know . . ."

"Of course, there are things we don't know, but I wouldn't trust this job to just anyone."

"You don't have much choice."

"Of course I do. I could wait. Hahn might change his mind, or finish his work, or get caught, or something else could happen in the meantime. But I can't wait, and I can't go myself." He reached across the table and took her hand. "When are you going to realize what a valuable asset you are to this mission? I can't believe I found you. If it weren't for you, I'd be dead already."

Franka pulled her hand away and picked up the cup of coffee in front of her. "What makes you so sure I can do this?"

"I can see the strength in you. Who else could have done what you've done and still keep going?"

"The fire needs tending to."

"Never mind that. It can wait a few minutes." He reached for her hand again. His hands were warm, strong. "You can do this. You have every quality inside you to do this. You're brave, and—"

"I'm not brave. I'm a coward." She felt the tears coming and was ashamed to cry in front of him. "I sold out to save my own skin. I pretended I didn't know what was going on, and what Hans and the others were doing." She turned away from him, grabbing for the wood stacked in the corner. The fire under the stove crackled as she tossed on a couple of logs. "They were the real heroes, prepared to give their lives for what they believed in."

"The fact that they're dead doesn't make them heroes any more than you are. Don't you think they would have chosen life if they could have? What good would have come of your death? What would one more death have achieved?"

"I should have confessed to the truth of what I did, and what I knew. I played the 'stupid blonde.' I acted out the role of the 'idiotic girl.'"

"You did what you needed to do to survive. I would have done exactly the same thing in your place. You were brave, you were smart, and now you're alive. And because of you, so am I. You are blond, and you are a woman, but you're as far from stupid, or cowardly, as anyone I've ever met."

His kind words did nothing to halt the tears, which came harder and faster and dripped off the end of her chin. He used his crutches to struggle out of his seat and get to her.

"You might be the bravest person I've ever known, Franka Gerber."

"I left him," she said.

"What?" John said.

Her words were as faint as ash on the wind.

"It's my fault he died. I left him. My father couldn't care for him alone."

"Oh no. That's not true." John could feel the warmth of her on his skin.

"I should never have gone. It's my fault Fredi died. If I'd stayed in Freiburg, we could have taken care of him together. He would never have been in that home, and they would never have gotten their claws on him. He'd still be alive."

"It's not your fault Fredi died. The Nazis murdered him."

"Why did I have to go to Munich? Why did I leave him?"

"You wanted a new start. You were twenty-two."

"You say that but—"

"Fredi's death isn't your fault. Who's to say that they wouldn't have come to your house for him? There was nothing you could have done about it. There was no way you could have known."

"He would never have died."

"You have an opportunity to strike back at the heart of the regime that murdered your brother and your boyfriend. They don't realize how important this nuclear program is. We have to stop it before they find out. According to Hahn, they're ahead of us. If we let the Nazis develop their program first, they might never pay for murdering Fredi and so many others."

"It's too late. The damage is done."

"It's never too late, not while you've got breath in your lungs and life within you. The Nazis have left a trail of millions of victims throughout Europe. You've been gifted the chance to fight for justice on their behalf."

"Or revenge?"

"Either," he said. "Both. There are many different combinations of reasons for what we do. Revenge is one of them. I need to know if you're in this a hundred percent, Franka. Any less and you're endangering both our lives. Are you with me?"

"I am. One hundred percent."

Chapter 11

Franka was awake before the dawn, and she watched as the dark of night submitted to the dull gray of an overcast morning. She waited an hour to climb out of bed, wincing as the cold of the cabin bit at her face. It was a two-hour train ride to Stuttgart from Freiburg. The roads were still impassable, her car little more than a reminder of how she got up here and how she might leave. Hot coffee warmed her. She checked the food supplies for John, though she already knew exactly how much food they had. She checked again. His voice came through his door, and, with steaming mug of coffee in hand, she went to him. He was sitting up in the bed.

"You can do this. You're just meeting someone in Stuttgart."

They talked about the journey for a few minutes before she went to the bathroom to wash up. He was in the kitchen as she emerged, her hair stinging her scalp in the cold air. They sat and ate breakfast together. John went over everything again, even though she had it all memorized. She was packed and ready to go fifteen minutes later, and he propelled himself to the door to shake her hand as they said their goodbyes.

"I'll see you tomorrow," she said.

She tried to show the best side of herself, to hide the anxiety that seemed to be eroding her from the inside out, but she saw the uneasy look in his eyes.

Franka didn't move as the train pulled into the Stuttgart Hauptbahnhof station. Her mind was blank, as devoid of color as the snow that fell in the mountains. The soldier sitting opposite her offered to help with her bag. She clutched it tight and declined with a polite word. He tipped his hat to her and stood to get off the train. She forced herself out of her seat, aware of how pale she must have looked. She hadn't eaten, hadn't moved since she'd boarded. Her hands were shaking. She stuck them in her coat pockets and stood up. Franka followed as the rest of the passengers shuffled off the train and onto the platform. The train was on time. The clock on the wall read 3:15. There would be more than enough time to find a hotel before she went to meet Hahn. Several uniformed Gestapo men stopped members of the crowd to check for papers. They left her alone—seemingly more focused on men of military-serving age. They were looking for deserters.

The air was cold as she stepped out of the station. It was a cloudy, misty day. A line of massive Nazi flags flew on fifty-foot-high poles, barely visible through the murk. An enormous portrait of Hitler stood ten feet tall at the entrance to the station. Franka stuck her arm out for a taxi.

She forced herself to eat something after checking into her hotel and made her way down toward the Schlossplatz, the large square in the middle of the city where Hahn would be for those precious ten minutes. She ambled through the baroque gardens of the plaza to the statue of the Roman goddess Concordia jutting out of the center, almost a hundred feet into the sky. Bombing had scarred the buildings around the square, which faded into one another in the poor visibility. Some were under construction once more. Some were not. A massive Nazi flag billowed in the air, and several off-duty soldiers sauntered past. Her entire body stiffened at their glances. There seemed to be enemies everywhere, and she could feel the eyes of every passerby attach to her like leeches to skin. She took a seat on a park bench overlooking the square, wishing she smoked—to calm her nerves if nothing else. She resisted the urge to look at her wristwatch. A man across the square stopped, seemed to look at her, and then continued on. The seconds drew out like days.

And then she saw him. A man in his fifties in a beige trench coat made his way across the square and sat down on a park bench thirty yards from her. He was wearing a hat, but he had the gray mustache that John had described. He raised a newspaper in front of his face, just as John had said he would. Should she go straight to him? She looked over each shoulder, trying to make it look like she was expecting someone. A man in his thirties sat down beside her, glancing over.

"Beautiful place, isn't it?" he said, and Franka's heart froze.

"Yes," she replied, barely getting the words out.

She didn't bring her eyes to look at him, though she knew he was looking at her. She looked at her wrist, and then at the man in the beige trench coat. Hahn would be gone in eight minutes. Who was this man beside her? The sweet aroma of cigarette smoke filled her nostrils.

"Would you like one?" the man said.

He was holding the cigarette pack out to her. She shook her head. His smile betrayed crooked front teeth, and he had a deep scar down his cheek. His gray eyes were unreadable.

"I don't smoke," she said.

"Nasty habit. The führer himself has spoken out against it." He took a deep drag.

"I've never partaken myself. If you'll excuse me."

She stood up and ambled away without another word. The man in the beige coat was still reading his newspaper and didn't react as she sat down beside him. The man who'd offered a cigarette glanced at them.

"Fine weather for this time of year," she said. "It's a treat for the children."

Hahn whirled his head around upon hearing her words. It took him a couple of seconds to regain his composure. He had an umbrella by his side, just as John said he would.

"Fine weather for ice-skating, not for the farmers trying to feed our brave soldiers on the front."

His words were practiced, deliberate. They were the code words. He turned the page, keeping the newspaper in front of his face.

She knew she had to speak next but eyed the man smoking the cigarette. He was looking but averted his eyes as he noticed her peering back at him. A soldier in SS uniform walked past them.

"Is it safe to speak here?"

"Perhaps not," he said, but didn't move. "You're not quite whom I was expecting."

"There was a problem with the original operative. He wasn't able to make it." Hahn turned to her as she continued. "He's alive and well. He had some issues, however, and won't be able to travel for a few weeks."

She stared out in front as she spoke, aware that though his newspaper was in front of him, he was looking around it at her.

"I'm going to get up," he said. "I'll wait for you at the corner of the street over there. Come in five minutes, and we can walk together."

He folded up his newspaper and tucked it under his arm as he stood. She tried not to check her watch more than a couple of times. The man who'd offered her a cigarette was talking to someone else on the bench now, seemingly oblivious. As soon as she'd counted out the five minutes, she made her way over to Hahn, who greeted her with a handshake.

"You know who I am, but I don't know you. What do I call you?"

"Franka. I'm German."

"Do you speak for our Allied friends? Can you make promises on their behalf?"

"Yes, I can." John had assured her of that much.

"You say that your man cannot travel. What exactly is the problem?"

"He has two broken legs. He's recovering in a cabin near Freiburg."

Hahn waited until they passed a soldier and his girlfriend walking arm in arm.

"That could be a problem. There's been a change of plan."

"What change of plan would that be?"

"I want to get my wife out with me."

"I thought you were divorced, with a daughter living in exile in Switzerland?"

"Heidi is in Zurich, yes, but I can't in good conscience leave my wife behind. The bombing has stepped up in recent weeks. It seems that the Allies have absolute rule over the skies of Germany now. Thousands are being slaughtered, and God help us all if the Soviets come. I can't leave her to face that fate alone."

"I'll see what we can work out."

Hahn stopped. "If she doesn't come, I don't either."

Franka tried to picture John hobbling on legs barely healed and trying to lead a couple in their fifties through the frozen forest to Switzerland. It didn't seem plausible.

"I'll talk to our friend about it. I have a number of questions for you too."

Franka looked around. No one stood within earshot. They walked on.

"I trust you've organized the house I demanded. I want a house on the beach, and two cars, one German and one American." Hahn smiled to himself. "I want to be the leader of the team I'm working with, and I want control of the study."

"Everything has been taken care of," Franka said. "How is your work progressing?"

"We're drawing closer to a breakthrough."

"What about the Nazi leadership? Are they beginning to pay attention?"

"I had a letter from Himmler last week, praising me on the progress that we've made. The rumor is that he wants to make us his pet project. He's going to use our findings to curry favor with Hitler. He's in the process of scheduling a visit. If Himmler can get Hitler's approval, then we'll get all the funding we require, and we'll be able to develop our weapon."

The word "weapon" jarred her, and the questions multiplied, but she remained on task, remembering John's words. "Is there no way you can stop the progress?"

"I'm part of a team. If I were to make some kind of deliberate mistake, then the rest of the team would notice. I could be thrown off the project, and in that case, your people would have no one inside. I couldn't do that—it would harm my reputation, and besides, your masters want me to continue with my progress as far as I can before they steal it for themselves. They don't believe that the Nazi leadership is going to back us to the necessary extent we'd need to finish the job. They think the war will be over by the time we get to the stage of having something we could actually use."

"Are they correct?"

"Maybe. Maybe not. It's difficult to say. It's a dangerous game they're playing."

"Could the work continue without you?"

"Yes, but I am the spearhead and the driving force behind it. I am also the public face. Without me, people like Himmler will lose interest, and the project will be overlooked in favor of the jet-engine development Hitler believes can turn the tide of the war. Our project is one of many claiming to be the savior of Germany. It's just that I happen to know the true potential of what we're doing. It's been difficult to get others to realize it too. This meeting with Himmler could make or break our project."

It was hard to tell whether he was anti-Nazi or not. She was beginning to get the impression that if they didn't steal him away, he would see the project out to its resolution in Germany, and the Nazis would be able to make use of the potential of this weapon he'd mentioned. Perhaps he only wanted to make use of the Americans' superior facilities and funding. Perhaps the project itself was all that counted, and scientific discovery was all that mattered to him, not to what ends that science would be used. A man with no loyalties other than his work was a dangerous one.

They walked in silence for a few minutes, passing from the Schlossplatz into the streets beyond. Imposing stone buildings surrounded them, and the evening began to set in. Streetlights flicked on, some broken, some working.

"So what's your plan from here?"

"We want you to sit tight for two weeks and then make your way to Freiburg."

"And then you will take my wife and me to America so that I can continue my work?"

"What age is your wife, Dr. Hahn?"

"Fifty-three."

"Bringing another person along, particularly a woman in her fifties, is going to make getting across the border to Switzerland all the more difficult. I'm sure a brilliant man like you can appreciate that."

"That's the only way I'll go."

Franka tried to imagine what John might say. Perhaps John might get them across one by one, taking the wife first and coming back for Hahn. It was remote, but it might be possible.

"Have you any way of bringing the work with you?"

"I've made microfilm of blueprints and plans. Bringing it along shouldn't be a problem."

"And where is this microfilm?"

"Stashed safely."

She was just about to ask him to elaborate when the shrill sound of the air-raid sirens pierced the air.

Franka could see the fear in his eyes. "An air raid," he said. "We've got to get to a shelter."

"How long do we have before the bombs begin?"

"It's hard to say with the valley we're built into, and the foggy conditions. The planes could be right on top of us. Are you coming with me?"

"I've nowhere else to go."

People began running, and mothers dragged children along by the arm.

"There's a shelter a few minutes' walk away," Hahn said. A shrill whistle cut him off, and a loud explosion rocked the street behind them. A storefront several hundred yards away exploded, showering the street with rubble and debris. A burglar alarm sounded. The sirens still howled. People scattered. Franka looked back and saw bodies on the asphalt. Hahn grabbed at her wrist as the whistle of bombs came again. A hundred people or more were running down the street now. It was impossible to know how far away the bomb shelter was. She couldn't see it, could only see the scattered figures of people running. Hahn was slow. She was almost dragging him as another bomb struck, landing a hundred feet behind them. A man was flung into the side of a building as if swatted to the side by some giant hand, his corpse falling in an untidy heap. Another bomb, and then another, collided with the houses on either side of the street. Glass and debris sprayed out. Franka turned around and saw a man running behind her, his entire body consumed in yellow flames. He fell. People sprinted past, the sound of screaming left in their wake. Blind panic. Another bomb fell, and the building just in front of them exploded into the street, showering their path ahead with dust and rubble. There were dead all over the road in front and behind. And still the whistling of bombs filled her ears. Hahn slowed.

"How far are we from the shelter?" she screamed.

"Half a mile perhaps. Usually, there is more warning. The clouds."

Another explosion rocked the air around them, and Franka could see that the street they'd just run down was now a trail of fire. Several bodies lay burning like torches in the dimming light. The sky above was blackening. The planes were invisible. She saw a bomb, caught sight of the flare of black before it hit the ground, obliterating a grocer's shop, scattering glass and wooden boxes of vegetables like confetti. Another bomb fell, and the mutilated body of an old woman skidded to the asphalt a few feet in front of them. Her clothes were burned away, her skin charred black underneath, her jaw sheared off. Franka ran around her as another bomb exploded behind them. She lost Hahn for a few seconds in the haze of smoke and then picked him out about fifty feet to her left. She made for him just as another bomb hit, scattering debris. Dozens of people were lying broken all around her, screaming. Dozens more ran on. Franka stopped, rubbing at her eyes. She lost Hahn again, scanned the ground for him.

Another explosion almost blew out her eardrum, knocking her off her feet. The buildings all around her were a sea of flames sending black smoke billowing into the air. She wiped grit out of her eyes, tried to focus despite the ringing in her ears. She checked her body. No blood. She could move. Only a little pain. She rose to her feet, falling behind most of the crowd now.

Another bomb exploded, but several hundred yards away this time. The thought emerged from the swamp of her mind that she was alone and still had to get to a bomb shelter. The crowd in front of her was still running toward the air-raid shelter, which she could now see was a few blocks away. Where was Hahn? She felt a warmth flowing down the side of her face, and her hand came back stained with her own blood. The cacophony of the sirens was changed now, mixed with the agonized moans of the wounded. She stumbled across rubble and broken glass, searching for Hahn. She counted seven dead within fifty feet of where she was standing, some missing arms and legs, others crushed under bricks and mortar. The whistling of the bombs came again, farther away now. The bombers had passed over, but that didn't mean they wouldn't come again. She still needed to get to a shelter. Staying out in the open meant death.

Franka screamed as she saw him. Hahn was on the other side of the street, lying on his side in a pool of thick crimson. She stumbled to him and passed the outstretched hands of several wounded and begging for her help. It was against every instinct in her to ignore them, but she did. A faint voice inside her head reminded her to focus on the mission.

"Hahn," she said. Her voice seemed to echo within her, as if inside a deep black cavern. More explosions rocked the earth as she bent down to him. People were still running past. A young man shouted at her to come, tried to grab at her, but she shrugged him off. Hahn opened his eyes and lifted his head. Blood oozed out the sides of his mouth. He coughed, brought his eyes to hers. His clothes were wet with blood, the pool in front of him thickening by the second. His eyes implored her to help, though she knew there was nothing to be done. A loose piece of masonry lay on his legs, pinning him to the ground. She thought to drop him, to keep running toward the shelter. She remembered John, waiting for her in the cabin.

"Where is the microfilm, Hahn?"

His eyes flickered, and he managed nothing more than a grunt.

"Don't let your research die on this street. You said that the Nazis didn't value your work. Let the Americans finish what you started." He opened his eyes and was looking at her as she spoke now. "Where is the microfilm? Let me safeguard the work you've dedicated your life to."

Hahn tried to turn over, tried to move the concrete block off his legs. Franka reached under the block and strained as she attempted to lift it. It didn't budge, and Hahn, resigned to his fate, fell back to his original position. His breathing was getting shallower, the color running from his face. Franka knew he had only seconds now.

"Dr. Hahn? Don't let your work fall into Nazi hands. Let the Americans do something good with it."

Hahn curled his lips back in a bloody, macabre smile. "Like they've done here today? Do you even realize what I'm working on?"

"Nuclear fission? I don't know what that is. I know it could change the tide of the—"

"It's a bomb—the most powerful bomb in history. A bomb that could level an entire city."

"One bomb that could destroy a city?"

"That could incinerate thousands in seconds."

"Don't let it fall into the Nazis' hands. Think of what they did to your Jewish friends and colleagues. Think of what they could do with that power."

Hahn closed his eyes for a second and then opened them again for what Franka knew could be the last time. "It's in my apartment, 433 Kronenstrasse. It's close." He coughed again. "Make sure they complete it. It's all there. Go now, while the raid is on and the police are in the bomb shelter."

"Where is it hidden?" More bombs went off, only a few hundred yards away. Franka knew she had to move. The bombers would come again.

"The picture of my mother," he said, his voice weakening. "Look into it . . ."

His head fell back, his mustache coated in blood, his eyes open, staring into nothing.

People flashed past. Franka was the only person not running who was able. Hahn's apartment was being watched. Why else would he have told her to go there now while the Allied bombers rained death on the city below? This could be Franka's only chance to resurrect the mission, to do her part to defeat the evil that had killed Hans, and Fredi, and her father.

It took a few grisly seconds to rifle through his pockets for the keys. No one was watching. She left him lying there and ran with the others, the safety of the reinforced-concrete air-raid shelter coming into view at the end of the street. A haze of smoke and dust hovered in the air. The sirens were still blaring, and several of the buildings around her were ablaze. Dead bodies littered the way. She saw the name come into view—Kronenstrasse. The street was empty. No police. No soldiers. No Gestapo, and surely no Frau Hahn waiting for her ex-husband to come home. She'd never get another opportunity like this. She stopped for a second, her breath thundering in and out of her lungs, her hair wet with blood. The safety of the air-raid shelter was two hundred yards away. It could wait.

She ran down Kronenstrasse, glancing up at the numbers of the buildings as she went. The bombs came again, and several explosions rocked the ground behind her. Smoking hulks, which had been buildings just moments before, lurched over her, ready to collapse into the street. The mission. The mission. She followed the numbers 411, 413. A bomb fell to her right, hurling glass and concrete onto the road in front of her. She cowered down for a few seconds until she was sure there wasn't another one coming. She saw the apartment block and ran to the glass door, which was still untouched, and fumbled for the keys. She tried one—the wrong key—and then another, and the key turned. The door opened to a marble staircase. The elevator was a few feet away but would be far too dangerous to use. The postbox on her right told her that Hahn lived, or had lived, in apartment 2b. She made for the deserted staircase as the entire building shook with the concussion from a nearby bomb. Survival would be pure chance. She crouched on the stairs, waiting for the sound to pass, and then continued up. Red-faced and panting, she made it to apartment 2b. The key slid into the lock, and she pushed the door open. The thought arose that his wife may have still been there, but there was no time for hesitation. She ran into the living room, repeating the words he'd said over and over.

"A picture of his mother," she said, scanning the room. Old black-and-white photos filled frames on every table, and several hung on the wall. Who was his mother? And where would he hide the microfilm on a tiny frame like these? A closed door beckoned, and she ran to it. She pushed into the bedroom and saw above the bed the framed portrait of a traditionally dressed, stern-faced woman. Franka pulled it off the wall and placed it facedown on the mattress. More explosions tore through the air, and now she could hear the sound of flak biting back at the airplanes above. The back of the picture was covered in brown paper, level with the sides, raised an inch off the picture itself. Franka dug her hand into the brown paper and tore it away. A small black object was taped to the inside of the frame in the bottom-left corner. It couldn't have been anything else but the microfilm. Franka ripped it off and rammed it into her pocket.

The bombs came again as she made for the stairs, and she waited until the noise stopped before continuing down. She burst out the door of the apartment block onto the ruined street. A man who'd been calling out for her help minutes before was now dead. It was hard not to look at him as she ran past. She kept her hand in her pocket as she went, her fingers coiled around the microfilm. The front door of the air-raid shelter was shut, and she hammered on it with a closed fist and shouted to let her in. The door opened, and—panting, covered in dust and blood—she fell inside. Hundreds of people turned to stare at her, her hand stuck in her pocket as if cast in iron.

Hours passed. The bombing finally ended. The bandage the medic had placed on her head was itchy. He'd assured her that the gash was superficial, and that head wounds almost always looked worse than they were. She played dumb, nodding and smiling as he finished. The man beside her offered her his coat. She refused and asked directions to the hotel she'd booked into, hoping it was still intact. She thought of the Allied airmen dropping the bombs, wondered if they knew what they were doing, who their bombs were killing. Were they war criminals, as most of the people in the air-raid shelter would testify? Or were things like accountability for war crimes decided by the victors? She doubted that most of the criminals of this war would ever see justice. Those on the side that emerged victorious would likely be lauded as heroes, their crimes remembered as exemplary actions. Streets and railway stations all over the world were named after people who some would hold up as war criminals.

It was night when the crowd emerged from the shelter. Franka shuffled into an altered cityscape, the flames from the bombing still licking at the night. People said that it was the heaviest raid on Stuttgart so far. It would be days before the dead were all gathered and counted. Franka would be long gone by then. The citizens of Stuttgart walked like ghosts through the darkened streets, meandering around rubble and the bodies of those less fortunate than they. The howling of the sirens had ended for now, replaced by the wailing of tears and the silent guilt of those who had survived.

And what Germany did in
London & other cities was
much worse.
Camps, torture, ...

Chapter 12

John sat at the window for much of the time she was gone. He was thinking about Penelope. She pined for someone else now. Another man awaited her letters. He imagined the airman holding the envelopes up to his nose, smelling the sweetness of her perfume, just as he once did. He hadn't thought about her much since she'd written that last letter to him, which certainly had not been sprayed with perfume. He thought back on how they'd laughed together, on how proud of her he'd been, and on how they'd made love. The bitterness within him had faded away. He wished he could see her, tell her that he was sorry, that she was doing the right thing. Her happiness had been the most important thing in the world to him once, and he hoped she'd rediscovered it with her new husband. It was impossible to be angry with her. Everything was his fault. He'd never cheated or even wanted anyone else, but he hadn't been there for her. He knew there would be no perfect goodbye. They would see each other again, perhaps at some black-tie function where they'd glance across a crowded room at one another. Perhaps they could talk and wish each other well. It was something to hope for.

Thoughts of Franka seemed to intrude on everything else that crossed his mind. His attempts to wipe her from his consciousness were futile—she always came back. Her face seemed tattooed inside him. He fought the worry he felt for her. It was more convenient to treat her like any other asset—she would have her uses, but when he awoke that morning he felt the lack of her in the coldness of that cabin. It felt empty. He made his way out of bed, shunting himself out of the bedroom and into the kitchen. The coffee was on the stove where he'd left it. Everything was untouched except by his own hand. It felt unnatural. The feelings inside him were ridiculous—surely a direct result of being cooped up here for so long. It was true that he hadn't seen a woman like Franka in a long time. It was natural he'd feel some affinity toward her. She'd saved his life. She was brave and honest and beautiful. He couldn't blame himself for inconvenient thoughts he couldn't master. He couldn't help that he'd memorized every curve of her face. There were some things beyond his control.

He finished his breakfast of dried fruit, stale bread, and jam and made his way out to the living room. His book was lying on the table by the firewood he'd need to light. He estimated that the logs would get them through another three days before Franka would need to go out for more. It didn't feel right sending her out into the snow, yet she never complained. She never complained about anything. It took him a few minutes to get the fire going to the stage where he was able to sit back and relax. He wished he could do more around the cabin, but he was hobbled. He was more hindrance than help.

He wasn't using her—she volunteered. She was grateful for the chance to affect the outcome of the war against the regime that had destroyed her family and the country she loved. What were these feelings of guilt within him, then? Why did he feel like he'd sent her alone into the lion's den? He had told her how difficult Hahn was known to be. John was sure she could work it out for herself. She only needed to make contact, after all.

Lunchtime came, and John was still by the fire, his book untouched on the table beside him. The sun was shining outside, and he could hear the dripping of the snow as the long melt began. He shifted the blanket he'd spread over his chest, reached for the radio, and flicked it on. The royal-tinted accent of the BBC newsreader fluttered over the airwaves. John had met many Englishmen. Few of them sounded like that. The newsreader read through a list of bombing raids from the night before. John's blood froze when he mentioned the raid on Stuttgart.

"RAF bomber command conducted a stunning raid on the industrial stronghold of Stuttgart yesterday. Sources claim it's the biggest on that city of the war so far."

The raid had been small in comparison with the massive sorties that destroyed much of Hamburg and Cologne, but had been hailed as a major success. How many had died? He had sent her into the jaws of the Allied beast. Grisly thoughts consumed him. The newsreader moved on, giving little importance to the words that still echoed through John's mind.

"There's a war on, goddamn it," he said to no one. "She knew the risks."

He trained his eyes on the cuckoo clock in the hallway. It struck one. The minutes drew out like months until it was almost five. Darkness was descending when the door finally opened. John couldn't see her as she dropped her skis in the hallway. He didn't call out. Franka appeared at the end of the hallway. A large white bandage adorned her forehead. She dropped her bag and shuffled inside.

John stifled the instinct to express his relief upon seeing her. "Did you see him?" he asked.

"I saw him," she said. She made her way into the kitchen, emerging seconds later with a cup of water. "The bombers came when I was with him. The entire city seemed to erupt into flames."

"Are you hurt?"

She reached up and touched the bandage on her head. "It's just a scratch. I was one of the lucky ones. Hundreds were killed. Thousands maybe. Hahn died on the street."

"What? Are you sure?"

"I saw him. He died in front of me."

Barely able to hold her head up, she flopped down in a chair opposite him.

John tried to pull his thoughts together. Hahn was dead. That meant his work for the Nazis was too. But what if somehow the Nazi path toward nuclear fission continued unabated? Without Hahn's knowledge, the scientists in America might not catch up until it was too late. John's superiors would never be satisfied without Hahn's knowledge at their disposal. It took him a few seconds to regain enough composure to speak again.

"You aren't hurt?"

She shook her head.

"What happened? How long did you see him for?"

"Just a few minutes. It turns out he was more of a mercenary than a dissident. He seemed more eager to get the work finished than to use it against the Nazis. He didn't appear to care so much who finished it. He was convinced that the Americans would give him the funding and facilities he needed."

"And so we would have," John said. "I heard about the attack. I'm relieved you're alive. What happened?"

Franka went through everything from when she'd met Hahn to the moment he died.

"What happened to the microfilm?" John said.

"Give me just a minute," Franka said. She went into the bathroom and returned seconds later with the plastic container. Her face was stern, rigid.

He tried to get up, fumbling for his crutches. She went to him, and he slid back into his seat.

"You got it."

"I went to his apartment after he died."

He reached for the tiny container in her hand. She curled her fingers around it.

"He told me what his project was about," she said.

John sat back in the chair. The flickering light of the fire danced across the gentle lines in her face.

"I told you everything I know. It's not my job to ask questions."

"He was developing a bomb that could level an entire city. Hahn was developing the most deadly weapon in the history of the world." Her fist closed around the microfilm.

"I didn't know it was a bomb. I just knew it was a technology that could change the war. It's up to us now to get this film back to the Allies before the Nazis realize what they have on their hands. If they develop that bomb before we do . . . Can you imagine what they would do with it? They wouldn't hesitate to use it. Millions of innocent people would die."

"Millions of innocents are dying. I saw it with my own eyes. I witnessed what the Allied bombing raids are doing to the German people."

"This war is the Nazis' doing." He saw her move toward the fire. "Don't do that, Franka."

"You sound like a child arguing over who started it. This isn't some schoolyard brawl. Thousands of people are being slaughtered every day."

"What you have in your hand could go a long way toward ending that slaughter. The technology will be developed. Hundreds of the best minds in America are working on it every day. What you have in your hand could help them develop that bomb faster. It could end this senseless war."

"Or it could murder millions more."

"That's not for us to decide."

"Yet we are the ones who have that decision to make. I have it in my hand, so I am the one."

"Think before you do anything rash. Destroying that microfilm won't stop the research. Nothing will."

"At least I won't be contributing to the possible deaths of millions of innocent people."

"This is a race, between the Allies and the Nazis. What if the Nazis develop that bomb first? Do you think they'd hesitate to use it? On London, or Moscow, or Paris?"

"Who's to say the Allies won't use it? I've seen the destruction they've brought to Germany."

"We don't have a choice about whether the bomb is made—just who we help win the race to make it. Who do you want to win that race—the Allies or the Nazis?"

She uncoiled her fingers from around the microfilm and handed it to John.

"I know what you must be feeling."

"How? How exactly are you able to reach inside me?"

"I know this isn't straightforward, but it's not our place to make these decisions. We have to trust in our allegiances. You're doing the right thing."

"By helping with the creation of the most destructive bomb in human history? You'll excuse me if I don't see the sense in that."

"It is ironic, I'll certainly say that, but having a threat like this could force the Nazis to see that the war is unwinnable."

"You think that the threat of killing German civilians is going to bring the Nazis to heel? The Nazis care as much for the citizenry of this country as you might for something you dug out of your ear. They've used the people of this country for their own means since their inception. No threat against the people is going to end this, only the destruction of the Nazis themselves."

—She is mistaken. It does demoralize the entire war effort.

John placed the case of microfilm on the table beside him. He picked up his coffee, long since cold, and took a swig anyway.

"Thank you for what you did," he finally said. "Not just for the war effort, but for me too."

"What are you going to do?"

"I'll need to get this film across the border into Switzerland."

He looked down at his legs, encased in plaster of paris, jutting out in front of him.

"Your breaks are progressing well. We can probably take the casts off in another two weeks or so."

"There's no way we can expedite the process?"

"Not if you want your legs to work, no. I'm a nurse, not a miracle worker."

"I disagree, Franka. I think you are a miracle worker."

"Flattery? Is that all you have to offer me right now?" she said, and walked away.

Franka didn't quite get the warm bath she'd wanted, but the three inches of tepid water she managed to gather still felt like a luxury. The picture of the dead bodies burning on the streets of Stuttgart hung in her consciousness as she sat in the water. John would take another two or three weeks to heal, and then he'd be gone. What was there for her after he left? The thoughts of ending her life were blunted. He'd shown her that she was still useful and could still make a difference in people's lives. But what hospital would hire her now? She was a traitor to the Reich, had spent time in jail for sedition. There seemed little place for her in Germany. She had enough money for another year or so at least, but what then? What if she couldn't work? She had aunts and uncles in Munich and cousins spread in cities and towns throughout the country, but would they accept her? Would they treat her as the traitor that the Nazis had painted her as? She hadn't seen most of them in years. Her cousins on her mother's side were strangers to her now. It didn't seem enough.

This war would end soon. Everything was going to change. The act of living longer than Hitler and his regime would be her victory. It was more than millions of others would achieve. She longed for the day when the ideals that Hans and Sophie held up were the norm once more, when they would be revered as the heroes they were and she could at least be forgiven. Living long enough to see that time, whenever it came, would be enough.

John came into her mind again. It was ridiculous, but he was the closest thing she had to a true companion left in this life. She had no one closer. There was no one that she'd revealed as much of herself to in this entire world. And soon he would be gone. She thought of America. It was heartening that someone could believe in their country as he did and still retain themselves. His loyalty was to the people of his country, not to some regime that claimed to be working on their behalf. The "patriots" she knew were twisted and ruined by perverted ideals. Patriotism to the Nazi state was an abomination, and directly contrary to everything it should have stood for. The true patriots were the ones with a healthy suspicion of the government and every motive it acted upon. The true patriots were those who didn't let themselves be overtaken by the Nazi rhetoric, those who remembered who they were, like Hans and Sophie. Like her father. And perhaps the true patriots were the ones who would welcome the armed missionaries who were undoubtedly coming to her country.

The calendar on the wall read January 20, 1944. Daniel Berkel was hunched over his desk, where he seemed to spend the majority of his time these days. Most of his job was shuffling paper, checking sources, and investigating disputes between neighbors and former friends.

Because the act of denouncing neighbors could place them under arrest and potentially land them in jail, disgruntled citizens found themselves in a position of newfound power over the people they bore grudges against. All too often people condemned by their neighbors as enemies of the state were guilty of little more than encroaching on their land, or stealing their newspaper once too often. Just a week before, he'd dealt with a case of a jealous husband who had reported the handsome man next door. The agents tortured him just enough to get to the bottom of the matter, and the neighbor confessed to beginning an affair with the man's wife. The agents released him. There was an art to torture. If the agent went too far, the suspect would end up confessing to trying to assassinate the führer. The art was finding the right balance. Every man and woman had a breaking point. The experienced interrogator knew when to proceed and when to desist, which methods to employ and to hold back. They had beaten the handsome neighbor with rods but stopped short of hanging him up, and most certainly stopped short of attaching an electrical charge to his genitals. That was for more extreme instances, but such cases seemed to be the norm these days.

The orders from above were becoming more and more Draconian. Berkel harkened back in his mind to the days before the war started. Times were simpler then. The liberal, cosmopolitan attitudes of certain citizens, while never encouraged or accepted, could be tolerated before the war. These days there was no place for such attitudes in the Reich. The search for liberals and so-called free thinkers had become an obsession of the higher-ups. It was hard to believe that despite how many enemies of the state they'd disposed of, there were still more among the population, but somehow there were. The Gestapo was busier than ever. Archaic notions such as evidence and due process had long been dismissed. The Gestapo had absolute power over the populace, and Berkel never grew tired of the fear he could inspire in men who might not otherwise have paid him any mind.

Berkel was proud of the work he did. His only regret was seeing family so fleetingly. There simply wasn't time enough to do his job effectively and see his sons as much as he would have liked. Several framed photos of them adorned his desk. It was a difficult sacrifice but one he made for his country. His life was dedicated to a greater cause for which they would thank him one day. His was a generation that was willing to sacrifice itself for the good of the next, and what greater gift could he bestow upon his children than a peaceful and prosperous Reich? It was the ultimate duty of any father and something that motivated him on a daily basis.

Berkel reached over for his cold cup of coffee, then set it back down as he realized he'd dropped a cigarette into it hours before. He reached into his pocket for his cigarettes and lit one with matches he kept on his desk. The ashtray was full, so he used the coffee cup once more instead. The lamp on his desk pierced through the dark, shining down on stacks of papers to be pored over when time would afford. It was dark outside, but warmer than it had been. The snow was melting at last, and most of the roads were open once again. A knock sounded on his door, and he called out for the person to enter.

Armin Vogel, a Gestapo agent originally from a farm near Eschbach, appeared around the door. "Daniel, how are you?"

"Busy, Armin. I'm trying to prioritize whom to bring in next. Is a waiter who said that the war is lost more of a priority than a priest who is holding secret masses?"

"Sounds familiar."

Vogel sat down opposite Berkel and lit up a cigarette of his own. Berkel put the papers down, glad there was an excuse for a break.

"I did have something I wanted to tell you."

"What's that?"

"A report came across my desk you might be interested in. I remember you mentioning an old acquaintance that you ran into late last year. Franka Gerber?"

"Yes, an old girlfriend from my teenage years. What about her?"

"I had a report from Sankt Peter a few days ago. Franka Gerber was acting suspiciously there just before Christmas. She wanted crutches for her boyfriend, who'd apparently injured himself skiing."

"Is that right?" Berkel said, taking a deep drag on his cigarette. "She told me she was going back to Munich."

"Huh. Well, she's here. One of my men checked her papers here in town just the other day. Everything seemed normal, but I thought I'd tell you. It's likely nothing . . ."

"But suspicion is our business."

"Quite. I would have brought it to you sooner, but I'm as busy as you are."

"I understand. Thank you. I know where she'll be. I should pay her and this boyfriend of hers a visit, seeing that the roads are almost clear now. Nothing wrong with paying a visit to an old friend, is there?"

"Nothing at all."

Vogel stood up and gave the salute, which Berkel returned.

Vogel left, and Berkel sat back in his seat and waited a few minutes before going to the basement. He knew exactly where her file was and went right to it. It felt light in his hand—a life's work summed up in a few lines he'd read so many times that he didn't actually need to look at them anymore. She'd said she was leaving. She was still here. What did she need crutches for? His other cases were going to have to wait.

January had been warmer than expected, and her car was almost freed from its bondage. John was exercising the best he was able to when Franka returned with the firewood. She kicked the slush off her shoes before shouting to him, announcing her presence. He appeared a few seconds later.

"Just a few more days, and then we'll see how your legs are. You're through the worst of it," she said.

"Thanks to you," he answered before going outside to drag the firewood in. She pulled the sled, piled up with wood, inside. He did his best to help her, but as usual, she ordered him to sit down. She sorted through the firewood, tossing the driest pieces in the basket by the fire. It was the twenty-first of January. The six weeks she'd insisted on him wearing the casts would be up in four days, and then he'd be gone, never to see her again. She'd be just one more face who'd drifted into his life, then out of it. He made his way over to her and began sorting through the second pile of wood she'd not gotten to yet. The fire was crackling orange, the evening drawing near.

"What are you going to do after I leave, Franka?"

"I'm not sure—look for a job most likely." She continued sorting through the wood. "There's always going to be a need for nurses, especially with a war going on."

"Nurses with a history like yours?"

"I didn't say it was going to be easy to get a job, but chances are they'll be so desperate—"

"Have you ever thought about getting out?"

"Of where, the Black Forest? I did already—I lived in Munich."

"No, not the Black Forest—Germany. Have you ever thought about getting out of Germany?"

She put down the two-inch-thick branch she had in her gloved hands. "Of course, but where would I go? Germany's all I've ever known. And even if I had somewhere to go, how would I get there?"

"I have to leave in the next few days. You could come with me."

"To where, Philadelphia?"

"I wish. I won't be going home for a while, but I could get you across the Swiss border. You could start again. Someone with skills like yours is always going to be in demand. You'd get a job, and you'd be safe."

"Getting across the Swiss border isn't just a case of presenting your papers while the boys in the Gestapo wish you a pleasant vacation. The border's closed. There's no guarantee we'd even make it."

"I know about the border. It's going to be tough, no doubt about it, but what have you got to stay here for?"

"John, I've lived here my whole life. What do you mean by asking that? This is my home."

He struggled to his feet, cursing under his breath as he followed her into the kitchen. She went to the stove to sort through another pile of firewood she'd brought in. He sat down in the kitchen chair two feet from where she was kneeling.

"Why don't you think about it at least?"

"What am I to do in a country where I know no one and have nothing?"

"You could be free. You could start again."

"In Switzerland?"

"If you want, or maybe even in America. I could petition to get you a visa."

"How are you going to get a German citizen a visa in the middle of the war?"

"I have some powerful friends. If my father couldn't get it done, my boss sure as hell could."

The light outside had all but faded to black, and Franka stood up to light the oil lamp.

"You're the bravest person I've ever met. What are you so afraid of?"

"I've never been to America before. You're the only American I've ever known."

"I must warn you that not all Americans are as fabulous as I am."

"Are they all as sure of themselves? You're so confident about getting across the border, but you can't even walk."

"My legs feel good. You said that they were healing well yourself. I can't just sit here waiting when I've got that film. I have to deliver it to the consulate in Switzerland. I have to try."

"Do you know how ridiculous you sound? You can't go anywhere yet. You can't walk."

He stood up. "Let me show you. I can do more than walk. Come with me." He held out a hand to her, the crutches propped up under his armpits.

"What are you doing?"

"Just come with me."

She took off her gloves and threw them down but didn't offer him her hand. John shrugged and motioned her to follow him into the living room. He went to the radio, flicking it on. A news program in English came on.

"What are you doing?"

"Wait a few seconds," he said as he began to cycle through the channels. "You're always in such a hurry." He settled on a music station. "I can do more than walk," he laughed. He lifted his arms, and the crutches fell to the floor with a clatter. "May I have this dance, Fräulein?"

"You're being ridiculous. This is dangerous."

She took his hand, aware of the fact that she was still wearing her old woolen coat. He brought her body into his, their faces inches apart, one hand on her waist, his other together with hers. "I was quite the dancer once," he said.

He rocked back and forth on his feet, just able to keep his balance. His body was rigid, and she doubted he'd be able to balance without holding on to her.

"I can see that," she laughed. "You're very much the graceful mover."

"I call this the 'buffalo with a broken ankle.'"

He was perhaps six inches taller than she. Neither spoke for a few seconds, their faces illuminated. The song ended, and she broke away.

"Is our dancing over for the night?"

Franka heard the sound of a car pulling up the hill outside. Her insides collapsed.

"A car," she whispered. "Get to the hiding place." The crutches were on the floor. Franka got them for him, and he made for the bedroom without a word. He closed the door behind him and laid the crutches on the floor beside the loosened floorboards as he lifted them up. The car's engine died, the headlights dimmed, and she heard the sound of the door opening. John slid into the hole under the floorboards, his backpack at his feet, his Luftwaffe uniform inside it. The darkness of the hole consumed him.

Franka took a few seconds to respond to the rapping on the door. John's coffee cup was by the fire. His book. No other signs he'd been here. They'd been careful. All of his belongings were with him under the floorboards. She took a deep breath and went to the door. A howl of wind came just as she opened it. Berkel was alone.

"Heil Hitler," Berkel said through the scarf over the lower half of his face.

"Heil Hitler," she replied. She noticed her hand trembling and pulled it back down to hide it in her pocket.

"Aren't you going to invite me in, Franka?" he said, taking his scarf off.

"Of course, Herr Berkel, please come in."

He brushed past her and wiped his feet on the doormat before taking off his black trench coat. He handed it to her without looking, though he must have seen the coat hooks just inches from his face. He was wearing the full uniform of the Gestapo, complete with medals for outstanding service in defense of the Reich. She hung up his coat. He had already gone into the living room and was looking around the old place as she caught up with him.

"Amazing," he said, shaking his head. "How long has it been, eight years? The place hasn't changed, except for the lack of pictures on the wall."

"It could be eight years."

"A lot of memories." He took off his black hat.

"Yes, indeed," was all she could manage.

"So aren't you going to offer me a cup of coffee?"

"Of course, how rude of me."

He followed her into the kitchen and stood against the frame of the door.

"It was quite a surprise to hear that you were still here. You led me to believe that you'd be going back to Munich before Christmas."

Franka placed the kettle on the stove before turning to get a mug from the cupboard.

"Yes, I had a change of plans. The snow was so thick. I couldn't get the car out. I decided to stay another few weeks."

"I see the car is free now. And the roads have been open for several days."

She turned to him, almost able to feel his eyes piercing through her.

"Yes, it's high time I left. I've been lazy, I suppose."

John stilled his breathing, keeping his hand over his chest in an attempt to soften the beating of his heart. The jumbled sounds from the kitchen were identifiable as a conversation, but it was impossible to make out more than a few words. His hand was on the bag, reaching in for a pistol. The feel of cold metal told him that he'd found it.

"It must have been lonely up here all this time," Berkel continued. "You were always such a sociable girl."

"I needed some time to myself after what happened to my father. The cabin is the perfect place to get away."

"Indeed," he said, nodding. He watched her for a few seconds, letting her pour the scalding hot water into the mugs. Steam wafted through cold air. "Thank you, Franka," he said as she handed him the mug. "Can we go back into the living room? We have so much catching up to do."

"Of course," she said. It almost hurt to smile.

He led her back to the living room, taking the fireside seat John had been sitting in minutes before. His book, *All Quiet on the Western Front*, lay facedown on the table beside Berkel. It would be enough to land her in jail for several nights. Berkel took a sip from his coffee cup before placing it down beside the old, scuffed paperback. Franka sat opposite him and tried to keep her eyes off the book. Berkel rested back in the rocking chair, his fingers locked together in front of his stomach. His hat was on his lap.

"Yes, so many memories here. We had some good times, though, didn't we?"

Franka nodded, her head feeling like it was held in place by steel wires.

"We were so young then," he continued. "It hardly even seems real. They say youth is wasted on the young, but I'm not sure I agree with that. What do you think?"

"I regret many of the decisions I made in the folly of my youth. I think I can see where that saying comes from."

"I don't think I agree with that sentiment anymore. I mean, there are always cases of young people doing stupid things, but in my job you come to realize that you don't have to be young to act idiotically. I see it every day. Just last week I interrogated a man, a father of five in his forties, who got drunk and started shouting out to all around him that the führer was never going to stop until every last one of them was dead. He called the führer a liar, and a scoundrel—even a murderer. Can you believe someone would do that?"

"It is hard to fathom how anyone could think such a thing."

"Thankfully there was a plethora of people willing to do the right thing. I must have had ten separate eyewitness accounts. It was heartening to know how many loyal Germans were present, and how heavily good people outnumber the bad apples among us." He took another sip of coffee and placed his hat on the table where his mug had been. "One of my younger recruits crushed the man's fingers between two metal bars and pulled out his fingernails. The man confessed quickly. I think my man did it to gain a measure of revenge for saying that about the führer. We take such matters personally."

Franka pressed her hands down on her thighs to still their shaking. "It's an important role."

"Very much so. We're the only power that stands between the Reich and her enemies in the fatherland. The war within our own country started long before the one against the Allied forces, and we're winning it day by day."

Franka wanted to say something, but her lips weren't moving. The words wouldn't come.

"Yes, we've become quite different people, you and I, haven't we?" he asked.

"Have we?"

"Oh, I think we have. We were so similar once."

I recognized the evil. You embraced it, became it.

"But now," he continued, "many people would say that you represent the very ills that I'm trying to eradicate from the Reich. Some might say that you represent the worst of our society."

Franka fought the fear threatening to overtake her. This man had absolute power over her. He could drag her from this place and throw her into a cell, and no one would ever be told. He could kill her on a whim, and no one would question his motives. There was no legal process here, no higher power. The National Socialists had made Daniel Berkel a god, and he would exercise his power how he saw fit.

"I'd like to think that the Reich still has a place for people such as me who made mistakes. I've served my time—"

"I didn't say that I felt that way, Franka," he said, laughing to himself. "Oh, you always were such a silly girl. It's unsurprising that you were so easily led astray."

"I was confused. It was hard to be sure what was right or wrong after my brother died."

"Yes, I did hear about that," he said, staring down into the fire. The flames lit his eyes as he brought them back to hers. "An unfortunate, yet necessary business."

"Necessary?" She felt her true feelings spike inside her. The mention of Fredi was kerosene to the flame of resentment flickering within her, and she fought to keep her rage from exploding.

"Of course," he said. "The führer himself was first to point out that it would be more merciful to end the suffering of the incurably ill, the handicapped, and the idiots. The useless eaters who took food from the mouths of the brave soldiers fighting for our collective futures needed to be eliminated. It was merely common sense, and a vital part of the policy of racial hygiene that is returning our country to its rightful place among the greatest in the world."

"Excuse me, Herr Berkel," she said. She got up and went to the bathroom. She stood with her back to the closed door, letting the tears come, her body shaking. She had to get through this. This wasn't just about her anymore. Paranoid thoughts about the man who'd offered her the cigarette in Stuttgart flooded her mind. Did Berkel know about the microfilm somehow? Were more Gestapo men coming? Was Berkel toying with her before he took her in?

No, he can't know. He doesn't know anything. It's up to you to deal with this.

Franka reached for a towel and wiped away the tears. She looked at herself in the mirror. The hatred surging through her would cloud her judgment. She tried to shove it aside. He was still sitting by the fire as she came back out. His eyes seemed stuck to her as she moved to her place opposite him once more.

"To what do I owe this pleasure, Herr Berkel, particularly at this time of night?"

"We defenders of the Reich work all hours. Insurgency never sleeps. And please, call me Daniel. We have so much history together. We'll forever be part of one another's lives."

It felt like cockroaches were under her skin.

"Okay, Daniel. What can I help you with on this winter's night?"

"This isn't a social call, though I wish I had time for such things. Are you alone here, Franka?"

"Of course. Well, apart from you, but yes, I'm alone."

"And you've been alone the entire time you've been up here?"

"Yes."

Berkel reached for the cup of coffee and took another sip.

"So who were the crutches for?"

Franka's body tightened. "Oh," she said, trying to smile. "The crutches were for my boyfriend. He was here for a few days, but he left. I should have mentioned him. I'm such a scatterbrain sometimes."

"It's funny you keep referring to the fact that you're a scatterbrain. I must admit I feel quite the opposite. I know you and always found you to be most intelligent, and strong-willed. Certainly no idiot, or one to be led astray easily." He put down the coffee cup. "And who is this boyfriend?"

"His name is Werner Graf. He's from Berlin. He's a pilot in the Luftwaffe."

What if he found John—could they maintain his cover? No, not while he was hiding under the floorboards. She couldn't reveal anything. Lying was her only chance, but this man was trained to see through liars, and she was sure he was seeing through her.

"A flier in the Luftwaffe, eh?" he said. "I'm surprised one of our brave pilots would lower himself to be with a whore like you."

"He . . . he left several days ago," she said.

"You showed him that pretty ass of yours, did you? You fooled him into thinking you were a loyal German woman, instead of a dissident whore?"

He reached for the novel on the table beside him.

"Well, look here. The whore is reading a banned book. Do you know that this is more than enough for me to take you in?"

"It's an old book, Daniel. I was just looking at it. I'm so sorry . . ." She recoiled in her chair and looked toward the door. She knew she'd never make it that far.

"You lied to me. How can I trust a single word you say now?"

"I didn't want to mention him, because of our past together. I didn't want to make our discourse uncomfortable."

"I am an agent of the Gestapo. Do you think I put my personal feelings in the way of my investigations?"

"Of course not, but—"

"I must say I'm disappointed in you, Franka, but then I have been for the longest time, ever since you turned away from the word of the führer to embrace *liberal* thought."

"I always thought so much of you, Daniel. We just weren't right for one another."

"Because you were better than me? Well, who's better now? You know what I've done to people who lied to me? You know what I could do to you, here and now?"

"Of course, Daniel, but I've served my time. I've learned my lesson. Have you a picture of your wife and children? I'd love to see a photo of them."

He stood up, lurching toward her. "How dare you mention them, you filthy whore! How dare you mention them with that disgusting mouth!"

This interaction seems a bit much. It provides "provocation" but it is not very believable.

Franka stood up and backed away from him, terror overtaking her. "Daniel, please . . ."

"It's just you and me here. No one else for miles around." He inched toward her, and she away from him, but the wall was only two feet behind, barring her escape.

"Look into your heart. You're a good man. An excellent father, dedicated to his country, as well as his children. I'm a German woman. Don't do this."

"You're a useless little slut, only good for one thing, and that's being on your back. You were the sweetest piece I ever tasted."

The walls of the cabin seemed to be closing in around her, and her vision dimmed. Her father's old pistol lay in the cabinet by the front door, but that seemed like miles away. Franka screamed as he lunged at her, grabbed her by both arms, and dug his fingers into her biceps like talons into prey.

"Oh, you'll make quite the concubine. Perhaps I'll let you stay up here, and come and visit every few days. Otherwise, I'll take you down to the cells and lock you up and let anyone who wants to have a go. I'll leave that up to you."

He came close, and she turned her face, almost vomiting as he ran his tongue up the side of her cheek. She tried to knee him and connected with his thigh as she managed to shrug him off.

"You'll have to kill me first."

"That can be arranged."

She broke away across the room, but he caught her by the arms and dragged her toward her bedroom, the bedroom her parents had slept in during that warm summer of 1934. She struggled against him, kicking and scratching, drawing blood on his cheek. He forced the door open and threw her down on the bed, the door slamming shut behind them.

"Oh yes, you fight. It's always better that way."

Franka screamed again as he pinned her to the bed and tore her dress, exposing her underwear. She tried to scratch at him again, and he slapped her hard across the face. She lay dazed on the bed before him as he began to undo the notches on his belt. The bedroom door crashed open, and John barged in, a crutch in one hand, the glint of his pistol in the other. Berkel turned around and grabbed at the gun just as John threw a punch with his other hand and connected above his left eye. The crutch fell to the floor. The pistol roared as Berkel lunged for it again, the bullet flying through the back wall. John leaned against the doorframe as Berkel struggled against him. Berkel kicked the casts on John's legs and wrenched John's hand away. John fell back through the open door into the living room. The gun spilled onto the floor as Berkel reached for his own, which was holstered to his waist. Franka jumped onto his back, his body toppling to the floor under her weight. John went for the Gestapo agent's throat and dug his thumbs into his windpipe, but Berkel rolled away. John lunged at him again, but the agent was too fast and rose to his feet, reaching for his gun once more.

"This is your boyfriend, then, is it, Franka?" He laughed as he unbuttoned his holster.

John clawed for his weapon where it lay three feet away, but Berkel already had his gun pointed at him and opened his mouth to say something as his finger tightened on the trigger.

Berkel's chest exploded. The gun fell out of his hand as he turned, a pathetic, perplexed look on his face. Franka was standing behind him, her father's gun smoking in her hand.

"He's not my boyfriend, Daniel. He's an Allied spy, and you were right. I always knew exactly what I was doing."

"You filthy . . ." Franka pulled the trigger before he could finish the last sentence that would ever come from his lips. The bullet struck him in the chest, just below his line of medals. He fell to his knees and then backward onto the floor.

"You bastard," Franka sobbed. "You insufferable bastard."

Berkel's blood was spreading across the floor in an almost-perfect circle of crimson. His eyes were still open, glaring up at the ceiling.

"Franka? Are you okay? Are you hurt?"

John raised himself to his feet, using the wall to get to her. She hadn't moved, still had the gun pointed at where Berkel had been standing. John took the gun from her. He placed it down and took her in his arms.

"The Gestapo is going to come for us," she said as she wrapped her arms around him. "Now they'll know you're here. We'll never get out of Germany alive. You'll never get the film back to the Allies."

"They'll have to catch us first."

She rested her head on him as the tears came again. "You risked the entire mission for me. Why did you do that?"

"No mission is worth standing by and letting that happen," he said. "I'd do it again a thousand times. I could never let anyone hurt you."

Chapter 13

Franka looked down at the blood-spattered corpse in the middle of the living room. The Nazi armband adorning his bicep was saturated red, his uniform stained and torn, his belt still unbuckled. She wanted to shoot him again.

John reached for the crutch on the floor. He put an arm over her shoulders and brought her into the kitchen. She was shaking as he sat her down. He brought his hand up to her face. She leaned into it, putting her hand on his.

"Thank you," she whispered.

"No. You're the one who saved me. Again. I'm just sorry it took me so long to get there." John took a deep breath. "You are right, though. They're going to come looking for him. We have to leave here, tonight."

"We?"

"I'm not leaving you behind. I can't make it without you. I need you. The mission needs you."

"What about your legs?"

"I'm going to need you to break the casts off. They're strong. I didn't feel any pain when I fought with that animal."

"They'll be looking for me now. You're better off going alone. They don't know that you're here."

"I owe you my life. You're coming with me. I'm not leaving without you. I'd rather die trying than leave you behind."

Franka took his hand off her face. "You should take my car. Your papers are good. You can try to slip across the border once you make it down there."

"Stop. Understand this. I'm not leaving here without you. I'll take you over my shoulder kicking and screaming if I have to, but we're leaving together."

"Okay." She nodded. "We'll go together."

"Good, I need you."

"And I need you."

"It's settled, then. The first thing is to get these casts off. Then we're going to pack everything we're going to require for our trip. They'll be looking for us on the roads, so we're going to have to go through the forests. It's our only chance."

"In winter?"

"We have no choice. We do have a head start, however. It's almost nine o'clock. My guess is that it wasn't unusual for our friend on the floor to stay out all night without telling his wife, so he likely won't be missed for another twelve hours or so. But I'm sure he told someone he was coming up here. We have to scrub this place down and hide his body so that by the time they figure out what happened, we'll be long gone. It's about fifty miles to the Swiss border. How far could we get on the back roads if we drive through the night?"

"Halfway perhaps. It's going to be difficult in the dark."

"We've little choice. It's too far to walk. We have to try and get as far as we can. That terrain is going to be rough. We might not make more than ten miles in a day walking." John reached out and took her hands. "This is going to be incredibly hard, Franka, but we can do it together."

"I know somewhere we can make for, where we may be able to stop off."

"Franka, we can't trust anyone . . ."

"My great-uncle, Hermann, lives in a village called Bürchau. It's twenty-five miles or so south of here, between us and Switzerland."

John shook his head.

"Hear me out," Franka said. "He's in his eighties and almost never leaves the house. I haven't seen him in a few years, but he has no love for the Nazis. Both of his sons died in the last war. We're going to need somewhere to lay our heads for a few hours. We can't go through the night and start walking in the morning, not with your legs."

"I'll consider it."

"We'll drive every back road and trekking path big enough to take the car. We can get there by morning and then sleep."

"What will you tell him?"

"That I got lost while hiking and I need somewhere to rest for a few hours. He won't ask questions."

"And if he does?"

"I'll speak to him first. If he suspects anything, we'll pass through."

Franka went to the spare bedroom. The floorboards lay across the hole on the floor where John had jumped out. She brought him his other crutch, and on his way back to the room he shunted past Berkel's dead body. Franka worked in silence, aware of how vital each passing second was. She cut the casts off his legs, using scissors to reveal the wizened, whitened flesh beneath. His legs looked thin in comparison with the rest of his body now, the muscles weakened. He stood up.

"As good as ever," he said, but she wasn't convinced. His legs needed another week, but time had slipped away like water through her fingers.

John felt like a child those first few seconds as he reveled in the freedom of movement that removing the casts had given him. The sight of Berkel's bloodied body lying in the middle of the floor brought him back into the moment.

John went to the bedroom, then reached through the floorboards and grabbed his rucksack. He had blankets, a knife, matches, a compass, and more than enough ammunition. The Luftwaffe uniform lay at the end of the hole, and he folded it into the bottom of the rucksack. A concealed zipper revealed a fold of papers—his alternate German identity as a traveling laborer. John stuffed the papers into his pockets, though he hoped he would never have to use them.

"Papers?" Franka said.

"I won't be using them. It's safer to bring all signs that I was ever here with me."

"What are we going to do about Berkel?"

It seemed strange to refer by name to the grotesque corpse lying in the middle of the floor. It was difficult to imagine it had once been her boyfriend, the virile Hitler Youth leader all the girls had stared at as he strode past.

"We have to hide the body as best we can."

"Outside? Do you want to bury him? The ground is most likely still frozen."

"We don't have time for that. We need to leave as soon as possible. Help me with him."

John led her back out to the living room.

"Let's put him under the floorboards. He'll stink up the place something awful, but we'll be long gone by then." John looked across at Franka and knew he shouldn't have said that. "It's the only place we can hide him easily. If they do a cursory search of the cabin, they might not even find him there. We only need a few days. Hiding his body could buy us some time."

Franka tried not to look into Berkel's open eyes, but they seemed glued to her every movement and followed her around the room.

Berkel's body was still warm as she picked up his feet. John took his arms. She could see John trying to hide his grimace as he bore Berkel's weight. Blood streamed onto the floor, leaving a trail into the bedroom. The hole was waiting. They threw him in. She took Berkel's trench coat and tossed it into the hole on top of him. She felt no sorrow, not even for his wife and children. They would be better off in a world without him. She stopped just short of spitting on his body. She felt relieved that he was dead. It was a comfort to know he'd never hurt anyone again.

John motioned to her to help him, and after replacing the floorboards, they pushed the bed over them once more. Franka went to the kitchen for a bucket of soapy water, and they spent the next twenty minutes cleaning the floor until all the blood was gone, until the murder scene was sanitized. No one would care that she'd acted in self-defense. Franka Gerber was soon to be public enemy number one, and the hounds of the Gestapo would be unleashed. The Swiss border was their only salvation.

They had spoken little as they'd cleaned, but now John took her to the kitchen and sat her down at the table.

"We need to dispose of his car somehow. Is there anywhere we could hide it? Any lane or wood within a short distance we could dump it so it won't be found until we were away?"

"There are places."

John tossed Berkel's keys on the table. "I'll follow behind in his car."

They put on coats and stepped outside. Franka pulled her scarf over her face. Even if they stopped off at her great-uncle's house, they would have to sleep outside for at least one night. It hadn't snowed for a week or more, and the days had warmed, but the nights were still deathly cold. Franka's breath plumed out white in front of her as she looked up at the stars tinseled above their heads.

John searched through Berkel's car. "Thank you, Herr Berkel," he said.

"What's in there?"

"A tent. It's small, but it'll keep the rain off our backs. A medical kit too. We can do this. We're going to do this."

Having stowed the tent and medical kit in the trunk of her car, Franka pulled away from the cabin. White light spiraled out from the headlamps, illuminating little more than the outline of the road and the trees that surrounded it. John had suggested keeping the lights off as they drove but relented; he must have realized that would have been suicidal. It was almost impossible to tell one place from another in the dark of night. The roads were clear but more for the use of sleighs and skiers. She didn't dare go more than twenty miles an hour as she rummaged through her mind for hiding places she'd known as a child.

It took five minutes to reach the spot she remembered, a road that led nowhere, perhaps to a house that was never built. She stopped at the end and directed John to drive down a few hundred yards, then trudged after him to help scatter branches and leaves over the car. It was hard to tell how well they'd hidden Berkel's Mercedes—the night hid almost everything—but they had little time. It would have to do. It was a mile from the cabin, and closer to the village, but no one came here. Not in winter anyway.

They walked back to the car in silence, only just able to make out where it was parked. Franka peered into the black beyond the tree line.

John cursed under his breath, his hand over his face. "We should have hidden him in the car. I wasn't thinking straight in all that panic earlier."

"Can we go back and get the body?"

"It's too late. We'd waste too much time."

"Surely under the floorboards in the house is a better place than stowing him in the back of his own car? The cabin is so remote."

"We'll have to hope so."

It was almost eleven by the time they got back. She held the oil lamp over the floor, searching for traces of blood. John was in the kitchen. The map was already spread across the table when she sat down beside him.

"How well do you know the territory south of here?"

"I know it a little. We used to take hikes down there when I was a teenager, but never at night, and never during winter. It's hilly. Some of it is thick forest."

"All the better to hide out in," John said as he trailed his finger down toward the Swiss border. It was only inches on the paper, about forty-five miles through the forest to the nearest point. "The frontier zone extends out from the border for fifty miles in most directions. The forest is our only realistic chance. There are too many patrols on the roads and railways around the frontier zone. We'd never make it."

"What about the border itself?"

"Making the border would be quite the achievement, but it would only be the beginning of our problems. The Nazis have set up a line of dozens of listening posts within five miles of the border. Guards with dogs patrol between them. The roads and villages down there are swarming with soldiers, and on the Swiss border itself guards are stationed every two hundred yards with orders to challenge everyone they see by day and to shoot without warning at night."

"That's why you were going to take Hahn through the mountains south of Munich."

"Yes, getting there would have been no easy feat, but the mountain passes offer an opportunity that we don't have here."

"And we can't get to them from here because I'll be wanted for murder soon."

"Precisely. We could try to make it before they found his body, but we must assume that he told someone where he was going. You'll be wanted for questioning sometime tomorrow. We'd never make it. The forest is our only chance."

"And once we get to the border?"

"We get lucky. We sneak across, and we're free."

"Luck? That's our plan?"

"It's not our plan, but we're going to need a generous slice of it to get across."

"But we do have somewhere to make for?"

"Yes, near Inzlingen, but let's worry about staying alive long enough to get there."

"No, John," she said, reaching to him. "This would be so much easier for you if we left separately. You could make your way down to the border on the train. With your papers—"

He flicked her hand away. "All right, then. Gather as much food as we can carry. Start with the light stuff—bread and cheese. Pack as much of that as you can. After that, we'll take some cans. Bring water, and the can opener too. I have matches, flints, and I'll take a couple of those kitchen knives. I have a sleeping bag, but I want you to bring at least two blankets also. Wear your warmest coat and hat. Bring any spare ammunition you have for the pistol, and as much money as you can lay your hands on. We just might be able to bribe a guard to let us over the border if we get lucky. How much petrol do we have in the car?"

"Half a tank, perhaps?"

"That should do. We need to get as close to the border as we can without using any main roads. The regular routes will be thick with guards, even at night. We have to avoid being stopped at all costs, particularly once they realize that Berkel is missing. Don't bring toiletries or more than one change of clothes. They'll only weigh us down. Take only what you can carry, starting with food and water." John folded the map and stood. "We can do this." He held a hand out, and she took it. "We've no time to waste. Can we get out of here in fifteen minutes?"

"Yes."

John felt the weakness in his legs. It was something he'd never known before. He wondered if he would be able to run if he needed to, let alone trek through snow-laden forests. He had always been able to rely on his body, whether it was to shoot a basket to win a game or to scale a wall in basic training. He hoped it wouldn't let him down now, not when he needed it most. Not when someone else was relying on him and the mission itself depended on it. He made his way to the bedroom, reveling in the feeling of sitting on the bed, knowing it would be the last time he'd feel comfort like that for a while. He dropped the microfilm into the secret compartment in the backpack and zipped it closed again. His pistols were clean, and he shoved one into his coat pocket, the other down into his backpack. John stood up, ready. He looked around the room one last time, and then down at the floorboards, thinking about the decaying body of the Gestapo officer they'd stowed underneath. The room seemed clean—nothing to signify upon loose inspection what had happened here. He took the oil lamp with him, leaving only darkness behind.

Franka had packed the lighter food into her own bag, leaving the cans and water bottles on the kitchen table. John packed them into his bag, feeling the weight double. It was still nothing like Guadalcanal, or even basic. He could take it.

The sky was clear as he stepped outside. No clouds meant no snow, but also no insulation. He had been in Germany almost six weeks, had only spoken to one person, and had barely left the cabin. It was time for him to complete his mission.

Franka folded her change of clothes and placed it into an old rucksack that had gone untouched for ten years or more. Her hands were still shaking, perhaps from what had happened, or perhaps at the thought of what was to happen. It was hard to tell where one feeling ended and the other began. She worked through the route again in her head. She had skied those back roads as a teenager during winters and hiked them on warm summer days. She had never driven them. They weren't roads as much as mere suggestions of corridors through the forest. She had little idea how far they could get but knew they had no other option. The Gestapo would show no mercy for killing one of their own.

The bag was ready, and she hefted it onto her shoulders. It was heavy, but she'd carried more. With a last look around the room, she realized that she'd likely never see it again. The mundane suddenly became precious. The faded wallpaper was now a wonderful tapestry, each piece of furniture now the keeper of the precious jewel of memory, her old hairbrush on the dresser a family heirloom to be cherished and passed on to the next generation. This was where they'd spent that last summer with her mother.

The living room offered no escape from the feelings bombarding her. She saw her father there sitting in the chair by the fire, her mother laughing at one of his corny jokes. And Fredi. Fredi playing with his trains on the floor, his legs still sturdy enough to walk, and his heart strong, as it had remained until the end. Franka took a step toward the door, feeling the cold breeze on her face. John was standing by the car. She knew she had only seconds now. The dark patches on the wall lingered, and the cuckoo clock went off for the last time. It was eleven o'clock. She paced back to the bookcase. The pictures were in a box on the bottom shelf. She thought to take it but decided otherwise, reaching in to scoop out the dozen or so black-and-white photographs of her family she'd taken off the walls. Franka took one last look around and made for the door.

John took his place in the passenger seat as Franka sat behind the wheel. The car sputtered a couple of times before starting. Franka made her way down the hill, her foot on the brake as they went. The beams of light from the car jutted through the dark, illuminating the way for perhaps twenty yards in front. The tires clawed at the earth for traction, and the car rumbled down the hill.

"Do you know what road to take?"

"For the first few miles, yes, but you're going to have to help me after that."

John took out the map and a tiny flashlight from his pocket. The paper lit up in circles of greenish white as he ran the light across it. Exhaustion was setting in, but Franka dismissed it as a triviality. Sleep was a luxury they couldn't afford.

They proceeded in silence for hours, the car trundling along at less than twenty miles an hour. John stared through the windows in every direction, his gun in hand. The tracks they took ran in general tendencies, sometimes meandering to a halt where the trees had grown back, and they would have to back up, unable to turn around on more than one occasion. The forest seemed determined to retake the roads encroaching into it. Ways that she remembered as a child were impassable now to all but the hardiest of trekkers. The human world seemed to ebb away as they delved farther into the forest. It was a welcome feeling—an escape.

Franka broke the silence as they came to what seemed like another dead end. The blackness of the trees seemed to envelop them. It was almost five in the morning.

"Can we go any farther?" Franka said.

"Perhaps, if we go back. The map's not clear."

"Where are we now?"

"I think Bürchau is dead ahead, down the hill in front of us."

It had been several years since she'd visited her great-uncle here. In years past she would have shouted out greetings to the farmers who lived there as she passed by on her bike. But the National Socialists had eradicated any sense of trust among the people they claimed to be protecting. Trust bred free speech, and that was the thing the Nazis feared most. (WHITE ROSE....)

"It's tiny," John said. "Not more than a few houses thrown together. Do you think there are any guards there? Any military presence?"

"Hard to say. We're deep in the frontier zone. This whole area is crawling with soldiers."

John was just able to open the door. The trees were only inches away on either side. The track they were on had not likely seen a car in years, if ever. He bustled through the tree line until they were overlooking the houses below, pockmarked on the hills. The moon and stars lit the slanted roofs. Nothing was moving, and no lights from the houses pierced the perfect darkness. He turned and made his way back through the snow, six inches thick.

Franka had turned off the car and was sitting in the passenger seat.

John clambered back in. "Nothing's moving down there. No lights, no guards. It seems safe."

The features of her face seemed to blend one into another in the darkness.

"Can we trust your uncle?" he asked. "We can't afford to be complacent."

"Hermann never leaves the house, and I know where he leaves his spare key."

"When was the last time you checked for it?"

"Nineteen thirty-eight, and I guarantee it's still there. I'll speak to him in the morning. You stay hidden. We don't need anyone to know you're with me, even Uncle Hermann."

They got out of the car. They spent a few minutes covering it over with branches and leaves, until it was difficult to make it out in the dark. They were under no illusions—if someone happened down the path, they'd see it. They slipped on their rucksacks and moved in silence past the tree line and into the snow.

Franka led them through and stopped at the top of the hill overlooking the hamlet below. John crouched down beside her. The night was still thick around them, but nothing was moving in Bürchau. It was just as she remembered it, untouched by the National Socialists. It was heartening to see the lack of their flags and posters. It was as if they didn't know about this place. Fifty people lived here back when she had last visited, and she doubted many had left. She motioned for John to follow her as she began to descend the hill. The snow came up to their knees. It took them several minutes to negotiate the two hundred yards or so down.

A dog barked in the distance as they reached the bottom of the hill. John crouched as he moved forward. Mimicking his movements, Franka lead them down the hill to Uncle Hermann's house. Aunt Lotte had died back in the 1920s. Franka's father had said it was from a broken heart, from mourning the deaths of her sons lost in the Great War.

Franka held a finger to her mouth and reached under a flowerpot to the right of the wooden front door. John nodded to her, and she slipped the key into the lock. The door opened with a gentle creak. Franka stopped for a few seconds to listen. The house was exactly as she remembered it, worn down and old. Franka led him up the stairs. A portrait of Aunt Lotte stared down at them. The carpet on the stairs was threadbare, graying in the middle from a thousand footsteps. They kept to the side, but still it creaked. The door to Hermann's bedroom stood at the top of the stairs. They could hear the unmistakable sound of the old man snoring. She led John past the bedroom and down to a door at the end of the hallway. She placed her hand on the doorknob as if it might shatter under her touch and turned it with the same care. The room was dusty but otherwise clean, the bed still made.

"This was my uncle Otto's bedroom," Franka whispered. "We can rest here a few hours."

"What about your great-uncle?"

"I doubt he's been in this room for fifteen years. I'll deal with him. We're safe here."

John took the bag off his back and placed it on a chair in the corner. The curtains were drawn, the light of the morning not yet drifting through. He pushed the curtains back a chink and surveyed the houses below. This wasn't what he'd wanted, but they had to rest. Nowhere would be safer. The long hike to the border was just a few hours away. Weeks of lying in bed had rendered him weakened, and exhaustion was spreading through him. He motioned for Franka to take the bed and got down on the floor.

"Don't be ridiculous," she said.

"It wouldn't be proper. I'm fine on the floor."

"We need sleep. The bed is the best place to get it."

She took off her boots and lay on the bed.

"Come on," she said, turning away. She felt the weight of him shift the mattress, and lay with her eyes open for several seconds before the hushed sound of his breath soothed her to sleep.

Berkel came in her dreams, his fingers coiling around her throat, the weight of him on her, the fury in his eyes as she forced herself awake. John was still sleeping beside her. The day had broken. The sky outside was concrete gray. Franka heard the sound of her great-uncle shuffling around the house downstairs. The clock on the wall told her it was just after noon. They had slept for seven hours—longer than they'd wanted. The light of day would fade in a few hours, and while traveling through the forest at night would be more discreet, it would also be more dangerous. First she needed to see Hermann—not only because it would have been disrespectful not to, but also because he no doubt still had that shotgun he brandished at the first sign of trouble. Intruders in his house would be prime targets.

John was going to need all the sleep he could get. Sheer stubbornness was only going to get him so far. She left him sleeping as she made for the bedroom door. Hermann was at the kitchen table, eating a lunch of soup and bread as she came in. His face was wrinkled and worn like balled paper flattened out. His mustache was white, his full head of hair the same. He dropped his spoon as he saw her.

"Franka? What are you doing here?"

"I'm sorry, Uncle. I was hiking and got lost. I needed somewhere to rest for a few hours, and I knew you wouldn't mind if I laid my head down."

"Of course not," he said, struggling to get out of his seat.

"Please, don't get up for me."

Franka sat down beside him. He offered her food and ignored any attempt she made to refuse it. Two minutes later she was sitting at the table, eating the thin turnip soup that he told her he ate most days of the week.

"I hope you don't mind my resting here a few hours."

"Of course not. It's been too long since I last saw you."

The old man shuffled over to the pot, drained out enough for a full bowl, and sat down at the table once more.

"I was so sorry to hear about your father," Hermann said. "This war gets more and more horrific every day. This Nazi madness has poisoned our nation and led to the deaths of countless innocents. It was said that the insanity thirty years ago was the war to end all wars, but it's happening all over again, except even worse this time."

"It doesn't seem you're too severely affected by the war here."

"Perhaps not."

"Do your neighbors feel the way you do? About the Nazis?"

Hermann shrugged. "Who knows? We wouldn't discuss it. I have nice neighbors, though. The woman next door, Karoline, calls in every day to check up on me. She lost both her sons on the front." He shook his head. "There's no real escape from the war. Not even here." He took a mouthful of soup before speaking again. "What year were you born? Remind me."

"Nineteen seventeen."

"I remember holding you as a baby. You had those same beautiful blond curls back then." He put his spoon down and stared into the space in front of him. "That was the year the great hunger took hold—the great hunger caused by the Allied blockade of Germany."

"I heard about it."

"The British blockaded the North Sea and attempted to starve us out. People wasted away. We had enough food to survive, but were all thin as greyhounds. Your great-grandfather died from dysentery, your great-aunt from tuberculosis, worn down by malnutrition. Every family was touched by the great hunger, by the madness of the kaiser, the French and the British, the ridiculous jingoism that destroyed a generation. And now they're determined to do it all again."

They sat in silence for a few seconds.

"I'll be on my way after lunch, Uncle."

"You won't stay longer? It's been so long."

"I can't. I would love to."

"It was wonderful to see you. I'm so glad you had the chance to visit."

"As am I."

The chair screeched on the stone floor as she got up. Franka knew there was little chance she'd ever see the old man again. She stood hugging him in the middle of the kitchen, letting go only when she recalled John in the room upstairs waiting for her.

He was ready to go, standing by the door as she arrived back at the bedroom.

Franka distracted her uncle by asking to see the view from the backyard as John snuck downstairs and out the front door. Hermann led her back into the house a few minutes later. She took him in her arms, knowing that she'd likely never hold a member of her family again. Cherished family memories would soon be hers alone. She would be the only person able to describe her mother's sense of humor, her father's singing voice, or the love that Fredi shared with everyone he met. Those remnants of her past would fade into oblivion. Hermann bade her goodbye, holding a hand aloft as she shut the door behind her.

She followed John and ducked behind a neighboring house. The tree line beckoned. No other way. They moved in silence up the hill and into the forest. The trees closed in around them. The dull winter sun faded out behind snow-covered branches, and they moved almost in darkness, even in the middle of the day. The cover on the ground was a foot deep. Franka wished she'd brought her snowshoes, as her thick walking boots lumbered through the clinging snow. John found branches to serve as hiking poles, and they trudged on, the cold gnashing at them, the sweat forming on their backs. John had insisted that they maintain absolute silence as they went, so they didn't talk.

John worked through every possible scenario he'd trained in, trying to remember every word his instructors had ever spoken. He searched for the answer to this situation—this problem of getting to Switzerland alive. It had to be there. He remembered the instructions on sneaking through the border. It was possible. There was no barbed wire, no wall—just a line of listening posts. The guards were human. They fell asleep. They read letters from home by candlelight when they were meant to be watching. They talked and joked and ate while they were on duty. There would be holes. The map would tell him where they were. Enough men had already stolen through, and with the strains on the German war machine, perhaps they had cut down on the border guards. They needed all the men they could get to fight the Soviets on the eastern front and to protect against the coming of the Allied forces to the west.

Franka watched John's back as he went. His movements were considered, deliberate. It was hard to say if his legs were affecting him or he was just pacing himself. He put his weight on the walking sticks he'd fashioned as he moved. She tried to picture what lay across the border—that was an irrelevance. The only thing that mattered was getting there. There was no room for hesitation now. Their only chance would be to make it across the border before the Gestapo found Daniel's decaying corpse under the floorboards of her father's cabin. Once they found him, the roadways would be flooded with every available man they could muster, and trying to cross into Switzerland would be almost impossible.

Every frozen step was a step closer. It was less than twenty miles.

John checked his compass. The sky was almost invisible. The forest was all they could see. His legs were sore, but it was hard to know whether it was because of the exertions of today or because they weren't fully recovered yet. Probably both.

John stopped by the stump of a long-dead tree to wait for her. She unfurled her scarf, and he found himself staring at her face as if it were a precious jewel. The mission had to remain his priority, yet the thoughts of bringing her home remained in his mind.

"It's almost five o'clock," he whispered, though all signs of human life had dissipated. "It'll be dark soon. I estimate we've covered about six miles since we started out. How are you feeling?"

"I feel strong," she said.

"I think we should keep going, for another couple of hours at least. Moving at night is dangerous, but we've no choice. For all we know they've discovered Berkel's body and are deploying troops to search for us right now."

"I agree."

"Watch out. Be careful where you step, and we'll try to find a five-star cave to spend the night."

"Sounds fabulous."

"Don't say that I don't bring you to the best places."

"You certainly know how to show a girl a good time."

"If we don't find somewhere, we have Berkel's tent. Are you ready?"

"Yes," she said. They moved off.

Armin Vogel, who had been a policeman for seven years before the National Socialists came to power, had transitioned to the Gestapo with ease. It was a matter of following the law, and the law gave him powers that he couldn't have dreamed of when he'd first joined the force in the 1920s. Such power was persuasive, and the notions he'd held as a young man were swept away in the Nazi mudslide. He was untouchable now, answerable only to direct superiors, who almost never questioned his methods. As long as the putrid stream of information kept flowing, his place as a vital cog in the rule of law was assured. There was no room for pity or remorse. Not in such a crucial role as his. Pity was for the weak, remorse for the defeated. He was neither.

It was just after two in the afternoon when the phone rang. Vogel pushed aside the paperwork threatening to overwhelm his desk and reached for the receiver. It felt cold against his ear. It had taken him some time to grow accustomed to the greeting he used all the time now.

"Heil Hitler."

"Herr Vogel, this is Frau Berkel." It wasn't difficult to detect the anguish in her voice. "Do you know where my husband is? He never came home from work last night, or this morning. I've known him to stay out before, but never this late. I've called and called his desk, but no answer."

Vogel promised to find Berkel and hung up. He had no wish to speak to Berkel's wife, particularly when she was in a mood like this. His own wife was annoyance enough. He stood up for the first time in several hours, his joints cracking as he straightened himself. Berkel's office was next to his. The door was shut. He let himself inside and found it empty. Berkel's desk was in a similar state to his own, but he kept his appointments written in a leather-bound planner. He found it in seconds, leafing through the pages until he found the entry for the day before. Berkel was meticulous in every part of his job, and sure enough, the address of the cabin was scrawled in the space for the previous evening.

"You went to see Franka Gerber, did you?" Vogel said out loud. "Berkel, you old dog." He placed the planner back down among the clutter on the desk, determining to wait an hour before investigating any further.

Berkel's wife called again fifteen minutes later. Vogel didn't have quite the same ease in getting her off his ear this time and had to promise he would look into her husband's disappearance immediately. He didn't inform her that Berkel had gone seeking out his attractive ex-girlfriend from his teenage years. With no phone number in Franka's file and only an address, Vogel had little choice. He made his way out to the car, wondering if Berkel was going to leave his wife. There were ways and means of doing these things, and dragging his partner into his love life wasn't one of them. Despite the niggling thought in the back of his mind about the crutches Franka had acquired, Vogel spent much of the drive up to the mountains cursing his colleague's inability to keep his pants tethered.

It was past four o'clock when Vogel arrived at the cabin. He swore out loud as he got out of the car, knowing that he'd have to drive back in the dark. The cabin seemed deserted, but the footprints and tire tracks in the snow revealed something else. Someone had been here. He kept his eyes trained on the ground and noticed at least two different tracks. Several people had been here, and probably two or more cars. There were no lights on in the cabin, and only silence in the air. No phone calls, no wife nagging, no suspects crying under torture. This peace was something to savor. He'd not felt this alone in years. He rapped on the door once and then again. No answer. It was locked. He moved around to a small window and peered into a bedroom that was almost clean enough to suggest no one had slept there recently, but the bedclothes were creased, and the candle-wax stains on the bedside table were fresh. He went back to the front door and kicked it in. It clattered open on the third try. He was proud that at almost fifty he still had it in him.

The cuckoo clock in the hall greeted him with incessant ticking, and he called out, knowing that no answer would come. He tramped down the hallway into the living room and saw a clean patch on the floor, clearly distinguishable from the rest of the wooden boards. He reached down to touch it with the tips of his fingers and felt the smooth surface.

After getting up from his haunches, Vogel lit an oil lamp in the corner. He ducked his head into the kitchen. It was spotless, but the ashes in the stove were fresh, not more than a day or two old. Vogel emerged from the kitchen into the living room and studied the bare walls. It took him about five minutes of scanning the room before he saw the tiny hole in the back wall. He put a finger over it and felt the hole where a bullet had gone through. This bullet hole was already enough to go back to the Gestapo with, but he knew there was more, and he continued his search. Whoever had been here had left in a hurry. They'd done well in covering their tracks, but there was always something they overlooked, no matter how meticulous they thought they were.

Vogel went into the main bedroom, going through the closets, looking under the bed, finding nothing apart from some old clothes hanging in the wardrobe and some ladies' essentials. He went to the other bedroom. The closet opened with a bang, and he rummaged through old clothes for both sexes, coming up with little. He spent another five minutes rifling through the dresser and bedside table, before sitting on the bed to gather his thoughts. The bedsprings creaked under his considerable weight, and then he felt the breeze, the tiniest lick of cold air on the skin above his socks where the fabric of his pants didn't cover. He peered at the floor and noticed a gap between the floorboards. He stood up and pushed back the bed, revealing the full length of the floorboards. He went to the kitchen for a knife to pry them up, and soon afterward found himself staring into the bloodied, dead eyes of Daniel Berkel.

Karoline Biedermann considered herself a good person, a caring neighbor. At first, it was a sense of duty that brought her to the old man's house, but in time, she developed a genuine affection for Hermann and even looked forward to seeing him on her regular visits. Her husband preferred to sit at home, reading the newspaper or listening to the radio between sips of homemade schnapps. Her sons had given their lives for the Reich, and her daughters had long since gone, one married to a civil servant in Bremen, the other engaged to an army captain in Freiburg, so it felt good to have someone to look after. She visited Hermann most days of the week and made his dinner as he sat recounting stories of better times. His political views were verging on liberal—a dirty word in today's society, but she paid them little mind. Old men were entitled to their ramblings. They had earned that much.

She reached under the flowerpot for the key for Hermann's front door and noticed that it was facing in the opposite direction than she always left it. That jarred her. She picked it up. Hermann was dozing in his armchair, and she went straight to the kitchen to begin preparing vegetable casserole. He awoke to the clacking of her dicing vegetables and called out to her from his chair.

"No need to get up, Herr Gerber. It is only I."

Five minutes later the casserole was ready to cook, and she slipped it into the oven before going to him.

"Karoline, you are so kind."

"I do try, Herr Gerber. That dish will be ready in twenty minutes. Will you need me to come back?"

"No, that's quite all right."

"Did you have a visitor today?"

"I did. My grand-niece Franka was lost hiking. She arrived early this morning and took some rest here. We had lunch together, and she left. It was wonderful to see her. It had been years. I don't know how many."

Karoline felt an itch. "Franka. Wasn't she the one who had the trouble with those awful dissidents in Munich speaking out against the führer?"

"Yes, that was her, but she's served her time and is rehabilitated utterly now."

"Of course," she said. "Everyone deserves a second chance. Well, almost everyone. I should be going now. Let me know if you have need of anything else. Otherwise, I'll see you tomorrow."

She left with the old man's gratitude ringing in her ears, but her thoughts were of something else. It was likely nothing, but with all that was going on these days, it was best to be safe. She was sure that he was correct and that Franka had been led astray. Nevertheless, she was a known enemy of the state—at one time anyway—and the border was close by. What was she doing out hiking in the middle of the night, and why wouldn't she have asked one of her great-uncle's neighbors to bring her back home? The blanket of night was descending, the trees of the forest changing to black. Yes, it was best she called this in. The local police would be most interested.

It pained Vogel to leave his colleague's body beneath the floorboards in that shack in the mountains, but he knew better than to disturb a murder scene. He had never thought of Berkel as a friend when he'd been alive, but he was a good man, a family man, and a loyal servant of the Reich. His murder highlighted the qualities Vogel had never recognized in him while he was alive. Hatred for Berkel's killer surged through him on the drive back to Freiburg, his knuckles bright white on the steering wheel, his teeth almost ground down into his gums. He didn't bother to park his car in his usual space outside the Gestapo headquarters, instead abandoning it at an ungainly angle on the sidewalk. He assembled the agents on duty for an emergency meeting. The men were shocked as he recalled what he'd seen, and each swore vengeance on the murderous bitch who'd dared to perpetrate such a cruel and heinous act. With no picture of Franka on file, a composite artist came in to sketch her face from the memories of several of the agents who'd known her.

"Her car was missing," Vogel said. "Block off all roads for fifty miles in every direction, all the way down to the border. Enlist the local Wehrmacht garrison to help with the search. She's making for Switzerland. I have little doubt of that. She has nowhere else to go. No one can hide from us in the country. Call every local police station and *Blockwart*. Someone knows something. We know she got crutches a couple of weeks ago—which she claimed were for her boyfriend who had been hurt in a skiing accident. She may well have someone with her." The agents muttered among themselves before he began again. "This treacherous bitch cannot be allowed to escape. No one does this to the Gestapo. We are the law, and retribution will be brutal." He slammed his fist against the wall. "Bring her in alive. I want the last miserable hours she spends on this planet to be horrific."

The call from the *Blockwart* in Bürchau came half an hour later, and Vogel called another meeting, with three times more agents in attendance now. The agents were baying for blood like a pack of ravenous dogs. All of their resources would be deployed between Bürchau and the border. That traitorous whore would never see Switzerland alive.

Franka's feet were blocks of ice. If there had ever been a trail here, it was covered, and they had to lift each leg out of the snow as they went. It was past ten o'clock, and her legs ached more with every step. John was two feet in front of her, and every so often she reached out to touch his back with her spare hand to let him know she was still there, to encourage him. Her mind was nearly blank, occupied by little other than the constant need to place one foot in front of the next, and the stifling cold. Her eyes had grown accustomed to the darkness. The moon only appeared when a break in the foliage allowed its silver light to shimmer down. The spread of trees was uneven—sometimes they'd come upon an open field to stride across, or a patch of deciduous trees, stripped of all foliage, their trunks like enormous spikes sticking straight up into the night sky. They passed farmhouses lit warm inside and saw the smoke billowing out of their chimneys, silent as the dead. But they didn't stop.

It was almost midnight when John held his finger in the air and she came to a halt behind him. She put her hands on her thighs and bent at the waist. He motioned for her to stand still and shuffled forward. Franka—with pain, burning, and freezing each fighting for supremacy in various parts of her body—leaned against a tree. Her breaths were heavy, and she was panting as he returned.

"There's a cave among those rocks," he said, pointing a finger. "Do you see it?"

She didn't but said she did nevertheless.

"We need to rest a few hours. Follow me."

John moved forward five or six steps before looking back. She was lagging behind, the energy within her disappearing since they'd stopped. He reached out a gloved hand, and she took it in hers. They went together in silence until the cave emerged as a darker patch against the gray of the rock face in front of them. John took a flashlight from his pack that Franka hadn't known he'd carried. A hedgehog scuttled out as he shone it inside.

"Just wanted to make sure we weren't disturbing momma bear or a couple of wolves."

Franka wanted to acknowledge his thoughts but was too tired to speak. John reached over to take the pack off her back. She felt lightheaded as he took the rucksack off, and he shepherded her inside the cave, sitting her down on the dry leaves that covered the ground. He reached into his backpack and pulled out a half-full bottle of water he offered to her. The cold liquid revitalized her.

John gathered firewood. Within a few minutes a healthy fire burned at the back of the cave.

"Won't they see us?" Franka whispered.

"If they're right behind us, perhaps, but we need this. We can rest here for three hours or so. Then we make for the border."

He took out a map as he sat beside her, their hips touching. Franka took one end of the map, and he took the other.

"I think we're here," he said, "about ten miles from the border. If we walk through the night, we can make it there by morning."

"We're crossing in daylight?"

"No. We need to take a look first. I think we can cross around here." He pointed to an area near the village of Inzlingen. "There's a trail there at the foothills of the forest, which leads to a Swiss customs office across the border. We can follow a stream that should lead us all the way to it. According to this map there are no guards there, no listening posts. It's a blind spot—a narrow sliver that they missed. Have you ever been down there?"

"No, I went to Switzerland when I was a child, but we didn't see the need to steal across in the dead of night on our school field trip."

"That would have livened up your school trip."

"Our teachers didn't share your sense of adventure."

"We'll find that stream and then cross the border after nightfall. We should be safe in Switzerland this time tomorrow."

"You make it sound so simple."

"There's nothing complicated about it."

"And you'll have fulfilled your mission."

He threw a stick into the fire. "Yes, I suppose I will, to some extent." He got up, unable to stand fully in the cave. "Time to eat."

They took the bread and cheese they'd brought and within seconds devoured the amount they'd set aside for dinner. He opened one of the cans of meat. She suffered through hers first and then watched as he finished it. The empty can landed with a soft thud at the back of the cave. He sat beside her as they stared into the heart of the fire.

"So what next, once we cross the border?"

"I expect I'll spend the rest of the war in a Swiss detention center, heaped in with the other refugees and prisoners of war who escaped across the border. What about you?"

"I'll make my way to Bern. We have an office there. I'll report my findings and likely be dispatched home to await my next mission."

"The hero returns, eh?"

"Not quite. But the war won't last forever. What will you do then?"

"I don't know. With everything going on, I was just trying to focus on staying alive. I hadn't thought much past that. I suppose I'll go back to Munich and begin the job of rebuilding. Rebuilding my life, and the country too. My skills will be in demand."

"Germany existed before the Nazis, and it will go on without them."

"Perhaps, but their stain will take a lot to erase."

John coughed, the noise reverberating through the enclosed space of the cave. "I hope we can keep in touch when this all ends, if we're able. I owe you so much."

"I owe you just as much for what you did for me in the cabin, and when I found you."

"When you found me? *You* saved *my* life."

"You gave me purpose when I had none. You were exactly what I needed when I needed it."

"As you were for me."

The fire spat and popped, and John reached down to toss some more dry wood onto it.

"Would you consider coming to America with me? It's different than here, I realize, and it's quite a distance, but you might like it."

"To Philadelphia?"

"Why not?" he said. "Philadelphia's a great town, but you'd be free to go wherever you pleased."

She picked up a stick and took a few seconds to poke the fire before she answered. "Let's just concentrate on surviving the next day or so, shall we? Then we can start thinking about the future."

"Yes," he said. "Perhaps I got a little carried away." He put an arm around her shoulders. "Get some sleep. We hit the trail again in three hours."

Franka took the sleeping bag from her backpack and laid it out on the floor of the cave, which proved to be softer and more comfortable than she'd imagined. John remained seated, staring out the mouth of the cave into the dark of the night beyond. Her last thought before she descended into a deep sleep was when he would lie down too.

Berkel came to her dreams again, but this time with hundreds of soldiers thrusting pikes, swords, and flaming torches into the air as they chanted the songs she'd sung as a member of the League of German Girls as a teenager. Berkel was bloodied and torn, showing the marks of the bullets she'd fired into him. An Alsatian strained against the iron leash he held around its throat. The horde of mad berserkers chased her into the forest, the torches they carried illuminating the night as she trod on her own shadow.

Her heart was thumping as she awoke to the brightness of the fire. John didn't seem to have moved since she'd fallen asleep.

"It's three in the morning," he said. "Time to go."

Chapter 14

Vogel rubbed the tiredness from his eyes as the car pulled up. It had been years since he'd stayed up like this. Responsibilities that would require an agent to work through the night were generally reserved for youth, not for a man of his experience. This was different. The thirst for revenge was fueling him. He greeted the dawn and the chance to question the old man with relish. Sleep could come later. The night had been spent combing the roadways for any sign of Gerber, and it was just after six when her car had been found on an overgrown trail near the hamlet of Bürchau—the same hamlet he was pulling into now with his armed escort. The local Wehrmacht had offered seventy-five men. There was a time when he could have expected hundreds. With little love lost between the local Wehrmacht officers and the Gestapo, he would have to settle for the seventy-five men they'd claimed they were able to spare at the last minute. Together with the hundred or so police and Gestapo men, it would be more than enough to find a little girl wandering in the woods.

Vogel knocked on the door himself, eager to see the look on the old man's face as he answered. The Gestapo officer introduced himself with a salute, ignoring the old man's bewilderment as he invited himself inside along with the five soldiers accompanying him. Vogel took a seat at the kitchen table, opposite where the old man had been sitting drinking his coffee, the mug still steaming. The old man offered Vogel a cup. Vogel refused and gestured for him to sit down. Time was a diminishing asset.

"What can I help you with, Herr Vogel?"

"I heard a report you had a visitor yesterday."

"My neighbor, Karoline, comes to see me most days. She helps me—"

"Don't toy with me, old man," Vogel said, each word an implicit threat. "I'm looking for Franka Gerber. I heard she was here yesterday. She murdered one of my colleagues, a good man with children. Your niece shot him down in cold blood."

"I don't know what you're talking about. I've not seen Franka in years."

"Don't waste my time, Gerber. We know she was here. Your false demeanor doesn't fool me. What did she say? Did she tell you where she was going? Was she alone?" Vogel smacked the coffee cup with an open hand. It hurtled off the table and broke on the tile floor.

"Do you think I'm scared of you?"

"I think you should be. You have no one to turn to here." He looked around the table at the five soldiers in full uniform with their rifles pressed to their chests. "I could take you outside and shoot you in the middle of the street, and no court in this Reich would convict me. I could lock you up in a cell and starve you to death or maybe just torture you for my own amusement. Now, I ask again. Where did that whore of a grand-niece of yours tell you she was going?"

"You watch your language! I remember when this country was great, when we were a bastion of industry and the arts, when bullyboys like you skulked in the shadows where you belonged. But now you wear that armband and that pin, and you think that gives you power over me?"

Vogel took out his pistol and aimed it at Hermann.

The old man didn't flinch or waver.

"I haven't killed a man in many years. Don't make me do that today. Tell me where Franka is. I already told you she murdered my partner. Was she alone, or with someone else?"

"And I already told you I haven't seen her in years."

Vogel cocked the hammer on his gun and pointed it at Hermann's forehead.

"I'm an old man, Vogel. Death comes for us all sooner or later. I'm not afraid of it, and I'm not afraid of you. So go ahead and shoot, because I'll die before I betray my own blood to the likes of some jumped-up Nazi puppet like you."

"Have it your way, then." Vogel pulled the trigger.

The aching was numbed by the sheer cold. Frostbite was now a constant worry in Franka's mind. Hours of wading through snow had left her feet little more than concrete blocks to balance upon. She greeted the stop for breakfast with massive relief. There could be no fire now. They spoke in whispers.

"What do we do if they find us, John?"

"We make sure that doesn't happen."

He laid down a blanket for them to sit on and handed her a bottle of water. Her body longed for a sleep she could not afford.

"We need to be careful not to dehydrate ourselves," John said. "It doesn't seem like a natural concern among all this frozen water."

Franka took the stale bread and cheese he handed her. She chewed three times before swallowing it down. John took out the detailed map of the Swiss frontier. Franka wondered how accurate it was, considering their lives depended on it.

"We're probably only five miles or so from the border. How are you feeling?"

"I feel good. I feel like we're going to be in Switzerland soon. How about you?"

"The same way."

Franka leaned back against a tree and looked up the trunk as it ascended into the sky for thirty feet or more. The smell of morning in the woods—pine mixed with soil and snow—hung heavy in the air. The familiarity of the scent comforted her. This was her place. The Gestapo agents were the ones encroaching. The low-hung clouds looked like sheets of dirtied cotton, and an easy wind from the south was swirling around them, shaking tree branches as it went. John took a knife from his belt, sliced up the last of the cheese, and handed Franka a piece.

"What would you be doing if we weren't at war?" she asked.

"I don't know. I don't think I would have taken over the company, even without the war. I'd have to find some other cause to fight for. Maybe I'd still be married. Who knows? What about you?"

"It's not so simple for me. If this war weren't on, we'd still have the Nazis and the war within my country would still be raging."

"What if the Nazis weren't in power?"

"I don't know. They're all I've known since I was a teenager."

"You'll never be able to live here again, not while they're in power."

"I'm ready. My old life died a long time ago." She brought the piece of cheese to her mouth. "I'm ready," she said again. Neither spoke for a few seconds. "There's nothing left for me here. I have no country now. No family. Only myself."

It would be her decision to make if they made it across the border alive. If. His legs had been aching all night, and he brought his hands down to massage the worst of the pain away. His body yearned for sleep. He knew that if he lay down on this blanket now, it would come, and they would find him, and then they would both die. It was time to leave. He stood up.

"Why did you rescue me from the snow?"

"What?"

"I was in a Luftwaffe uniform. For all you knew I was part of the regime that destroyed your life and your country. Why did you rescue me?"

"Because you're a human being, and I'm a nurse. That's what I do."

"But you risked your life for a stranger, and a Luftwaffe flier at that."

"I needed something."

"We all do," John said, and helped her to her feet. "Now, let's push on. We can make the border in the next hour or two."

Vogel laid out the map on the kitchen table, making sure to avoid staining it with the spattered blood. They weren't going to swim the Rhine. Not in January. They would make for Inzlingen, where the border between Switzerland and Germany jutted away from the freezing waters of the river. He had already dispatched fifty men there to work their way back up through the forest, and a hundred men were sweeping the area from ten miles in. Soon that whore would be caught like a rat in a trap, and slow vengeance would be his. An example needed to be made. Would it be possible to hang her body up in the middle of town like the Gestapo did in the occupied territories? That was an argument he looked forward to having with his superiors. He bundled the map back up and made for the car, his escorts in tow. It was a forty-five-minute drive to the border, and he intended to be there when they found her, to see the look on her face as she realized there was no power greater in her world than his.

Each step was a minor triumph now. The full rigor of the previous day's walk began to bring itself to bear on their battered bodies. John dragged each leg through the snow, using trees for support, leaning all of his weight on the walking stick he'd fashioned for himself.

"This is nearly over," he said. "You'll be free soon, for the first time since you were a teenager."

It was ironic that she would have to spend her days of freedom in a detention center in Switzerland, unable to gain employment, but this war would be over soon. He longed to be the one to free her. The mission had morphed into something different. He imagined delivering the microfilm to Wild Bill Donovan himself, the handshake, the flag, but her essence lingered in every thought. Every glimpse of his future contained her, and he drew comfort and reason from that.

They lumbered on through the snow. He was sure that Berkel had been found by now, and the pursuing forces of the Gestapo were close behind. They weren't more than a mile from the stream that would lead them unmolested across the border—if indeed the map was accurate.

They came to a clearing. A road bisected their path. John motioned for Franka to stop and continued alone to poke his head out of the tree line. He peered both ways down the road. It was quiet, empty for as far as he could see before it curled off. The road was only a few feet from the tree line they were emerging from. The trees on the other side were two hundred yards or more from the roadside. They would be out in the open for several minutes as they crossed, but there was no other way. The stream that would lead them to freedom was half a mile away. There must have been listening posts close by, and this road would not be quiet for long.

She was beside him now.

"The forest is on our side. It's the only reason we're still alive. Outside it, we're dead." He pointed across the road to the clearing and the trees beyond. "The stream we're making for is likely in that clump of forest. We need to make it across, where we'll have cover again. I'm sure they've found Berkel's body and are looking for us now. There's nowhere else to go but where we're headed. They know we're not going to swim the river in winter. If they're not here already, they will be soon, but we're close. We can do this."

"Who do you think left those footprints in the snow?" she said. Several pairs of footprints crisscrossed the field of snow that led to the trees on the other side of the road.

"Hard to say. It doesn't seem to have snowed down here for several days. They look old."

"A farmer and his cows, perhaps?"

"Maybe. I'm sure there's no one over there waiting for us, if that's what you mean."

"It seems quiet."

"Let's stop wasting time," John said as he emerged from the trees, his body low to the ground as he crossed the road. Franka followed a few feet behind, mimicking his movements. John waited for her on the edge of the road as they entered the snow-covered meadow that led to the far tree line. He jogged ahead. She stumbled behind him, her backpack coming off. She reached down to slip the straps over her shoulders. He covered the ground so quickly that she fell thirty yards behind. He was just entering the tree line as the rumble of the truck came around the bend in the road.

Vogel was riding in the front, his eyes scanning both sides of the road as he saw the figure struggling through the snow toward the trees.

"Halt!" he shouted, and the driver jammed his foot down on the brakes. "There she is. Go get her!" He bashed on the tarpaulin hood to wake the troops riding in the back.

Franka turned as the truck stopped, terror flushing through her. She rose to her feet, doing her best to sprint through the sucking snow. John ducked behind a tree, drawing his gun in some kind of false hope that he could outshoot the four heavily armed Wehrmacht soldiers spilling out of the truck. One of the soldiers brought his rifle to his shoulder and began to shoot. Bullets spat around Franka as she ran, John's desperate face willing her toward him, his hand outstretched.

Vogel followed his men into the snow, the truck abandoned as the six men ran after the figure a hundred yards in front of them. He drew his pistol to shoot just as she disappeared into the thick of the forest.

John grasped her hand and pulled her behind him.

"Come on. We've got to outrun them somehow. The border is close. Get rid of your backpack."

She threw it down, remembering the photos of her family she'd stuffed into her pockets. She threw a glance backward at the soldiers and the fat officer lagging behind them as they struggled through the snow. They seemed to be gaining. John dragged her by the hand as they ran, cresting a hill and then running down, trees all around them. The soldiers were invisible behind them, the hill and the trees blocking their line of vision.

"We're not far now," John said as a light formed at the end of her sight. The trees ended two hundred yards in front. A great white light lay beyond them, and Franka saw immediately what the map hadn't shown. The trees ended, and a forty-foot drop onto jagged rocks lay beyond for a mile in both directions.

John cursed. "No. No. We can climb down."

"They're right behind us. They'd pick us off on the way down. There's no escape from this, not for me."

"What?"

"They don't know you're with me. They won't have noticed your footprints among the others in the snow. You were hidden in the trees as they came out of the truck. I couldn't see you, so I know they couldn't either. Go on without me. You can climb down and be across the border before nightfall."

"I won't leave you."

"It's useless, John. We can't make it together. Think of your mission. You have to go now."

"There has to be another way."

"There isn't. I'll go back and draw them off."

"No. I can't leave you. I won't."

"Remember your mission. This is beyond us now. Remember what you were sent here to do. Please. We've only seconds."

She could hear the sound of the soldiers approaching through the trees, perhaps a hundred yards behind.

"Do this for me," she said.

He grasped her against him and kissed her. She drew back after a few seconds and leaned her forehead into his.

"I can't leave you."

"You have to go now," she said.

"I'm so sorry, Franka," he said as he lowered himself over the edge of the cliff. She looked down at him one last time as he peered up at her. She retreated toward her pursuers, her arms in the air. Franka heard the soldiers shouting at her to get on the ground, to put her hands behind her head. She was miles away, years ago, with her parents in the cabin on a warm summer's evening as the sun set over the trees.

The fat officer made a whooping sound as he caught up. "Franka Gerber? I am Kriminalinspektor Vogel of the Gestapo. You're under arrest for the murder of Daniel Berkel, and let me say, you're mine now. You're going to pay for what you did to my friend. I'm enjoying those tears on your face. There will be many more." He replaced the gun in his holster. "Where is your boyfriend?"

"Who?"

"Don't play that way with me," he said, slapping her across the face. "You got crutches for him. Where is he?"

"He left last week. He made his way across the border. He told me the way to come—to follow him."

"Have a look around," the officer said. His men spread out, taking a few minutes to search the area.

Vogel took the time to pat her down, his hands focusing on certain places, withdrawing her wallet and her father's pistol from her pockets.

"Nothing," one of the men said as they came back. "There's no one else. There are footprints all over. It's impossible to tell if there was anyone else with her."

Her thoughts were of John now, and his escape across the border. In his escape victory was hers. She saw John strolling across the border, presenting the microfilm, receiving the acclaim he deserved, and that was enough. The agonies of the next few hours would pass. Their achievement would live on.

John lingered in the trees, knowing he had only to walk away, and the way to the border would be free now. Freedom and the glory of fulfilling his mission beckoned. The microfilm was vital. Perhaps it could even turn the tide of this war. He imagined seeing his family again, and the look of pride on his father's face. He tried to purge Franka from his mind. The rest of his life was an easy trip across the border away.

The soldiers shuffled through the snow as they made their way back to the truck, enjoying the moment. Vogel kept his pistol pointed at Franka's head. And who was going to stop him? This was his world.

Soon this whore would come to realize that. It took fifteen minutes for them to reach the truck. The men celebrated with a smoke as they got there. Vogel forced her to kneel in the snow by the side of the road, her hands on her head as he took out the radio to report his success. He'd experienced many great moments in his career, but this was perhaps the finest. He thought of Berkel as he picked up the radio receiver. The justice his murder demanded was coming. Vogel radioed in the good news, making the announcement several times.

"I'm going to take you back to the local Gestapo headquarters now," he said. "It will be the last place you ever see."

Vogel bundled her into the back of the truck and tied her hands with twine, as he'd forgotten his handcuffs in all the rush. It hardly mattered. She had four soldiers in the back with her. She wasn't going anywhere. The soldiers sat beside her; Vogel, the driver, and another soldier sat in front.

"Congratulations, boys!" Vogel shouted once they were ready to go. "You've got a night out waiting for you when we get back."

The soldiers cheered as the driver started the engine and they began to move off. They had gone no more than a few hundred yards when they saw a figure in front of them, shouting for help. Vogel leaned forward to peer at the sight of a Luftwaffe officer clambering toward them, who was holding up ID papers. His uniform was torn and filthy, covered in snow and dirt. He looked exhausted, maybe even close to death. The driver slowed the truck to a halt.

"Please, help me!" the man screamed.

"What now?" Vogel said under his breath.

The Luftwaffe officer was standing directly in front of the truck, his arms in the air. He was so close that Vogel could see the color of his eyes.

"I've been out here all night. My plane went down on a training mission a few miles into the forest. I thought I was going to die out here. I heard the shots and made my way over."

"We have a prisoner to be transported. We're on important business. There's a town about two miles west."

"I don't think I can make it. My legs. Please, don't leave me out here."

Vogel thought about it for a few seconds. He might get extra praise for rescuing a Luftwaffe officer lost in the woods, perhaps even a medal—those uppity pricks in the Luftwaffe would have to respect him if he delivered one of their officers right to them. He flicked a thumb toward the back of the truck.

"We can take you into town."

The man hobbled around the side of the truck. Vogel called out to the men in the back that they had one more, and one of them reached down to help him inside.

Franka didn't look up at first, but the raising of the tarpaulin at the back of the truck roused her from the state she'd fallen into. She felt the blood drain from her face as John sat beside her in his Luftwaffe uniform, she on his left with another soldier next to her. The other three men sat across from them, their rifles at their sides. The engine started up once more, and the truck rumbled on. John was panting, and he leaned forward, his forearms on his thighs. He put his backpack by his feet.

"Thank you for picking me up. I owe you my life. Who's the girl?"

"A prisoner," one of the soldiers said. "She killed a Gestapo officer."

"And you're arresting her for that?" John laughed. "What's a pretty girl like you doing killing one of our beloved Gestapo officers? You didn't like his black trench coat? You know what they say about Gestapo men, don't you?"

"No, what do they say?" the closest soldier said, a smile forming on his face.

"That the Gestapo are all honest and intelligent, but I have to disagree."

The same man answered. "Why?"

"If a Gestapo man says he's intelligent, he's not honest. If he's honest, he's not intelligent, and if he's honest and intelligent, he's not in the Gestapo."

All four soldiers laughed.

"I know I can get in trouble, but they're only jokes."

"Of course," the soldier replied.

Franka was frozen, incredulous. John hadn't given her any signal. Nothing.

"I have another joke, if you promise not to tell anyone else."

"Of course," the soldier sitting beside him said.

"All right, this is a good one," he said. "What's the difference between Christianity and National Socialism?"

"I don't know," one of the soldiers said.

He paused a few seconds. "In Christianity one man died for everybody. But in National Socialism everybody dies for one man."

The men exploded in laughter.

John rose to his feet and pulled his pistols from his pockets. "Franka! Down!" he shouted as he stitched a line of bullets across the chests of the men sitting across from them. The last soldier rose, reaching for his rifle. John put two rounds into his face. The truck ground to a halt, almost knocking John off his feet. He took a second to regain his balance before emptying his weapons, sending bullets tearing through the tarpaulin and into the cabin. He reached down to her. She had the soldiers' blood all over her face. "Are you shot? Are you hurt?"

"No, I'm fine."

John took one of the dead soldiers' pistols and jumped out of the truck. Franka followed him. The door to the vehicle's cabin opened, and Vogel stumbled onto the road, an ugly wound staining his chest. He got off two shots before John put him down and sent his body collapsing onto the slush in an ungainly heap. John checked him, and the men in the front. All were dead. John was leaning against the side of the truck. Franka went to him.

"You came back. You could be across the border by now."

"I told you I wasn't going to leave you."

She hugged him, but as she drew back she saw a red stain from where she'd pressed against his body.

"Oh no," she said, ice running down her spine. "Show me."

He lifted his arm to reveal a gunshot wound on the right side of his chest, level with his elbow.

"It's not so bad," she lied.

"I can make it, but we need to go now. More soldiers are coming."

"Wait. I need to get something first."

Franka ran to the cabin of the truck and opened the door. The Wehrmacht soldiers were slumped forward like rag dolls, their blood spattered all over the shattered windshield. The driver's body collapsed onto the road in a formless mess. The medical kit was on the floor. John was sitting on the snow as she returned to him. She cut off some gauze and wrapped it around his chest in an attempt to stem the flow of blood. The top of his pants was already soaked red. He took off his Luftwaffe jacket and threw it on the snow.

"Hold this on here." She handed him a thick bandage. "Keep as much pressure on it as you can."

John nodded, but his face was china white. He reached into his rucksack for a civilian coat and just managed to slip his arms into it. It was wet with blood in seconds.

"We have to get out of here right now," she said.

Franka took the map from his pocket. They had traveled several miles from where they'd planned to journey to the border. Once back there the cliff face awaited.

"I can make it," he said. "Get the body out of the truck, and let's drive back to where we were."

Franka moved around to the passenger side of the truck, where she pulled out the other soldier's body. She helped John to his feet, placed his arm over her shoulder, and led him to the truck, where he was able to pull himself up and in. The engine was still humming, the keys untouched in the ignition. She turned the truck around and sped down the road, the cold wind blowing in their faces, the carnage of the dead bodies they'd left on the road far behind now.

"You're going to need a doctor, and soon."

"Get me across the border, and we'll figure the rest out later. You saved my life once. It looks like you're going to have to repeat the trick."

They drove for a few minutes before reaching a point where the cliff face seemed lower, the tree line closer. He put his arm over her shoulder as they abandoned the truck, not bothering to cover their tracks. The border. Freedom. She took his rucksack and dumped out as much as she could before taking its weight on her back. They moved together, him leaning on her, a trail of crimson in the snow behind them.

"I can make it," he repeated.

Trees limped past on either side in the foot-deep snow. They came to the cliff face once more. It was twenty feet high.

"Get the rope. Anchor it around a tree, and lower me down."

Franka reached into his pack for the rope and looped it around a sturdy tree. He wrapped it around his arms and gripped it with both hands as she lowered him inch by inch. John kept his feet on the rocks as he went. She knew how tired he was now but knew also what sleep would bring. Franka climbed down after him. He was sitting against a rock, barely able to keep his body upright, when she reached the bottom. She picked him up again.

"Let's go, marine," she said in English—just as he'd taught her.

She heard the soft rushing of the stream and pushed through the trees to find it. It was frozen at the edges, the flow of water free through the middle.

"This is it," she said. "We can do this."

"I can hack it," he said, but his voice was weak, as if any step could be his last. He stumbled again, and she reached down to pick him up.

"Come on, John. We're nearly there. Just a little farther now." They kept moving along the stream bank, one more step, and then another. His feet began to cross, and he tripped again, bringing her down on top of him. He moaned as she tried to pick him up, but she ignored him, forcing his arm over her shoulder. His grip was slackening, but still they kept walking. Somehow.

"We're so close. Don't give up on me."

Several minutes passed as they trudged forward, until his grip faded and he fell to the ground. The customs building appeared through the trees. It was only thirty yards away.

"We've made it!" she cried. "We're in Switzerland. We're free."

"You're free," he whispered. "Thank you, Franka, for everything. Take the film."

"No!" she shouted. "I won't let you die, not while we're so close. Now get up. Do you hear me? Get up. I'm not leaving you behind."

She reached down, put her arm around him, and took his full weight onto her shoulders.

"We can make it. We are going to make it. I am not letting you die," she said over and over as she lumbered toward the small stone-gray customs building, the trees of the Black Forest so thick above her that she couldn't see the sky.

Chapter 15

The countryside outside the city of Basel, Switzerland, October 1945

The setting sun dabbed the horizon red, orange, and purple. Franka stretched out the muscles in her back while she leaned on the garden hoe in her hand. In the distance the hills and trees of the Black Forest were discernable as dark shapes against the sky. The evenings were cooler now, the heat of summer dispelled by the coming of the autumn air. Neat green rows of potato plants covered the earth for several hundred yards in every direction, their uniformity broken only by the figures of the other farmhands returning from their day's work. Franka bent to pick up the bucket of weeds she'd pulled and began to make her way back toward the barn. Rosa Goldstein was waiting for her by the tree they often had lunch below and greeted her with a smile.

"I didn't think you'd still be here, Franka. I thought you were going home."

"I'm still here," Franka said. "I don't know why, but my trip home was delayed. Today is my last day on the farm. It seems ridiculous, but I'm going to miss this place, and all the wonderful people I've met here."

"The war is over. The Nazis are gone. It's time to get on with our lives, whatever might be left of them."

The two young women walked together. Others joined them as they went, and by the time they reached the barn, the group numbered more than twenty, each wishing her the best as she said goodbye.

Memories of Hans came to her as she washed up before dinner in the bathroom she shared with the ten other women she knew as sisters now. His words had lived beyond the brevity of his own life. Hans, Sophie, Willi, and the others who'd given their lives in the cause of freedom would soon be held up as the heroes she knew them to be. She went back to her room and sat on her bunk bed. The dorm was empty, all the other women outside enjoying a drink in the evening sun. She pulled out from under her bed the case that constituted her belongings. The leaflet was folded in the side pocket. She took it out, as she did often these days, and read its headline:

The Manifesto of the Students of Munich

It was the sixth leaflet of the White Rose, smuggled out of Germany by a lawyer, and duplicated and dropped in the hundreds of thousands over Germany by Allied bombers. Sylvia Stern, a Jewish refugee from Ulm, had carried it across the border with her and given it to Franka as inspiration when Franka first arrived in the camp in winter 1944. Franka never told her, or anyone else, that she'd been there the night Hans, his sister Sophie, and best friend Willi had penned that leaflet. She didn't tell her that she'd helped distribute it, or that she'd spent time in jail for the words on that piece of paper. That memory was theirs now. They deserved that honor alone.

She folded the leaflet, tucked it back into her suitcase, and went to the window at the end of the row of bunk beds. Franka peered out at the Black Forest, miles in the distance. What was she going back to? The Nazis had been destroyed, and their Reich, which was to last a thousand years, had too. But what was there for her now? Everyone she'd loved most was dead. Only their memories remained, bathing her in comfort and sorrow, and immersing her in love. She still spoke to her mother, still felt her father's arms around her, still saw Fredi's smile in her dreams. They would always be with her, as long as she lived.

She still thought of John. She could still feel the weight of him on her shoulders, the warmth of his blood spread over her, and the look on the customs man's face—somewhere between pity and incredulity—as she burst through the door with him on her back. The customs man had tried to convince her to give up, that John was dead, but she'd refused to believe it. She forced him at gunpoint to drive them to the hospital three miles away. She was sure they'd lock her up for that. But they didn't. The US consulate stepped in. The microfilm was smuggled back to the States, and the bombs dropped on Hiroshima and Nagasaki. She'd never know how much she'd contributed to the horror of those days, but the war was over now. The Americans said that those bombs saved hundreds of thousands of lives. It was best to think of it that way, for the alternative hurt too much. Perhaps the role they'd played in ending the war was the legacy that one day she could come to terms with. It was enough to know they'd contributed.

It saved close to 1 million.

She'd been confined to the safety of the camp after he'd entered the hospital, hadn't seen him since that day, and had only been informed by letter of the miracle of his survival. He'd sent letters thanking her for saving his life through the sheer force of her will, asserting over and over his promise to return to her, but somehow she still felt alone. She couldn't bring herself to believe him, and the hope within her faded as the flow of correspondence between them dwindled to a trickle.

Night was drawing in, the light of day little more than a glow above the Black Forest in the distance. She hadn't turned on the lamp in the corner. The room had darkened around her. There seemed no point in lighting a room she was about to leave. It was time. There was no avoiding it now. Her suitcase sat by her bed. She went to it and packed the last of her possessions. It was barely half-full as she closed it. She picked it up and in one hand felt the weight of what was left of her life.

She heard the soft sound of the bedroom door closing. "I told you I'd come back for you," came the voice from behind her—a voice she'd heard only in her dreams these last months. She moved her hand to the lamp in the corner and flicked it on. Golden light enveloped the room, illuminating where John stood at the door, in full military dress, a bright line of medals across his chest. He took off his hat and put it under his arm. "I'll never leave you again."

"I'll never let you," she replied.

He came to her and took her in his arms, all other words lost in their embrace.

ACKNOWLEDGMENTS

I want to thank my wife, Jill, for her belief in me and for being my all-purpose sounding board. I want to thank my beta readers for their work in sifting through the rubble of my early drafts: Jack Layden, Shane Woods, Betsy Frimmer, Carol McDuell, Chris Menier, Jackie Kosbob, Nicola Hogan, Liz Guinan Havens, Morgan Leafe, and of course the beautiful Jill Dempsey. Thanks also to Dr. Liz Slanina and Dr. Derek Donegan for their technical help. Thanks to my fabulous agent, Byrd Leavell, and to my editors, Jenna Free, Erin Anastasia, and Will Champion, who made me laugh out loud many times with his colorful language in the edits. Thanks to Jodi Warshaw and Chris Werner, my fantastic editors at Lake Union, and all the staff there who are so friendly, responsive, and kind.

Thanks to my brother Brian for keeping me honest, and my brother Conor for helping to instill a love of all things historical in me. Thanks to my sister, Orla, for her constant support, and of course to my parents, Robert and Anne Dempsey, for making me this way. And thanks to my beautiful sons, Robbie and Sam. You are the keys to everything now and the main force driving me onward in my journey toward becoming the writer I one day hope to be.

Unfortunately, the portrayal of the 2 main characters are typical. She is of course beautiful, smart, courageous, etc., etc.
And he comes from a rich, well placed family, blah, blah, blah.

This detracts from the accurate protrayal of the history of Germany under Hitler — a monster without equal.